Patrice Gilles was born in 1953 in Cameroon. He is a former manager of a multinational insurance brokerage company, a professional sector where he spent thirty-four years of his life. He now divides his time between Thailand and Italy and his active retirement between writing and growing olives, as well as producing organic oil on his farm in Sabina, about forty kilometres from Rome.

Patrice Gilles

THE TRAP

Original Editing to English
by Dean Finlay
Translated from French to
English by Patrice Gilles

AUSTIN MACAULEY PUBLISHERS™

LONDON * CAMBRIDGE * NEW YORK * SHARJAH

A CIP catalogue record for this title is available from the British Library.

ISBN 9781035830473 (Paperback)
ISBN 9781035832989 (Hardback)
ISBN 9781035830480 (ePub e-book)
ISBN 9781035830466 (Audiobook)

www.austinmacauley.co.uk

First Published 2024
Austin Macauley Publishers Ltd®
1 Canada Square
Canary Wharf
London
E14 5AA

Saturday, 27 November 2010

It was a balmy Bangkok evening on the terrace of Vertigo, a rooftop restaurant on the 61st floor of the Banyan Tree Hotel. It was a warm and sophisticated atmosphere of like-minded people at an event organised by More Life, a British charity. Mike Robertson occupied a table with a breath-taking view of the city. He was accompanied by Lila Antonova. He was American; she was Russian.

They'd been married for fifteen years and had taken a bit of a back seat to the other guests after greeting each other and engaging in the usual: "How are you doing? How have you been?" and all that sort of trivial stuff. It was a very lively cocktail party. The music was loud; the waitresses were all smiles as they tried to give the best of the establishment. Their discussion was about their next holiday in two months' time.

They had planned a week in St Petersburg with Lila's family and then two weeks in Sausalito, California, where they had a house in the hills above the city. She loved this house, which had always been synonymous with holidays and maintenance. She liked to take care of it and planned the improvements they made to it each time they stay. This time she had decided to change the kitchen. They bought the house ten years ago and had been gradually renovating it to their taste and ideas.

Lila was the one who took care of it. She used to say that she would have liked to be a decorator. A great lover of architecture, she had acquired over the years an impressive collection of books on interior design by various renowned architects from different countries, both Asian and European, American and Oceanic. This had been a source of inspiration for her in designing her Californian interior. And, although she enjoyed a very pleasant life in Thailand, she would prefer to return to the United States to live in this house and enjoy it to the fullest.

She was looking forward to her husband's transfer to San Francisco, which was expected in two years. She liked to talk to Mike about this and to imagine with him their future life in this idyllic setting: a beautiful house, the gentle way of life in Sausalito and its many galleries of painters and artists, her husband's successful professional situation, meeting their relations and friends, sailing in the bay…. A dream life awaited them. For her, it will be wonderful. She knows that they have everything to be happy.

They were already happy, and complete happiness was getting closer and closer. After a few glasses of an excellent New Zealand cabernet sauvignon and two hours later, they decided to take their leave and returned to their vast villa.

They took the lift. She exited at the lobby level and went to wait for him outside the entrance of the Banyan Tree where many people were waiting for a taxi from the reception staff in traditional nineteenth-century Thai costumes. Mike continued down to the second basement to collect his Mercedes S-Class 350.

Lila moved away from the crowd of people rushing to the taxi booking desk when a man in his fifties in a dinner jacket approached her with a big smile. She didn't seem to know him and thought it was a relation of her husband's, so she was not too surprised and smiled in response. He came very close to her and whispered in her ear, "You won't be here much longer. It's over for you."

With these enigmatic words, the stranger slipped away and returned to the hotel. She was taken aback and felt uncomfortable with a sense of dread. Mike arrived at the hotel entrance and waved to her. The bellman in the Thai suit rushed to open the car door for her. Mike immediately realised that something was wrong, as his wife's face appeared dishevelled.

"What's the matter, darling? Are you not feeling well?"

"Mike, a man came up to me and said that we're not going to be around much longer and that we're finished. Those were his exact words. He really scared me."

"Was he an American or Thai?"

"An American, I think. About fifty, quite tall, maybe six feet. In a dinner jacket. Could that mean anything to you?"

"I know a lot of people who fit that description. It's hard to tell. You don't think he was drunk, do you?"

"No, I don't think so. Anyway, I found it very disturbing."

"It's a bit odd. But don't worry. It's probably a bad joke."

"If it is, it's a really bad one. That guy seemed really strange."

"Yes, he probably is. Let's not think about it. It won't spoil the evening."

"Yeah, I hope you're right."

Mike entered the mooban, which was a small development of luxury villas in the Onut district, a little way from the heart of the city. He parked his car in the driveway of their villa. Entering the house, Lila first went to see her ten-year-old son, Marat, who was fast asleep. Reassured, she went to the bathroom and undressed before going to bed. A few minutes later, Mike joined her. She shivered.

"Did you lock up?"

"Yes, I did."

She snuggled up to him. They made rough love as if to forget and get out of a bad dream.

Monday, 29 November 2010

The family was sitting on the terrace for breakfast by the pool. The maid, a Burmese woman in her forties, had prepared everything and served tea for Lila, coffee for Mike and chocolate for Marat. Lila was still worried about the man who threatened her on Saturday night.

"Don't worry, darling. It's just a bad joke."

"What's a bad joke?" Marat asked.

"Nothing," replied his mother. "Hurry up, the school bus will be here soon, and you'll be late."

"Well, I have to go too," said Mike.

He signalled to Thanit, his driver and occasional bodyguard, who was also an expert in karate. He understood and already opened the back door for his boss, who got into the car.

"Thanit, please take me to the office and then come back here to transport madam if she wishes."

"Yes, sir."

The school bus chartered by the American School of Bangkok arrived at the same time. The attendant got off and welcomed Marat who joined the other children on their way to class.

"Hey, Marat, how are you?" one of the children called out to him.

"Hi, Peter. Look, I brought a book about dinosaurs."

"Come and see… But you can't read… What's this writing?"

"It's Russian. Mum bought it for me last time we were in Russia."

"Oh, yes, she did. It's true that you're Russian."

"Yes, and American too, from my dad."

"Yeah. Let me see the T. Rex. Yeah, great."

"I brought my marbles too. We'll play at recess."

"Oh, great. I brought mine too."

Mike was the manager of the U.S. branch of Golden Star Bank in Thailand, with its head office in San Francisco. The thirty-eight-year-old Yale graduate started his career at the bank's head office and was soon offered a position as managing director of the Bangkok branch where he had now worked for five years. He had been managing mainly local U.S. corporate interests, and since he arrived, the branch had seen growth every year. The head office was very happy with his performance and was considering bringing him back to California to manage the U.S. private banking business within a year or two although a final decision has not yet been made.

However, Mike had already been approached by his superiors who had asked him how he felt about the promotion. He was enthusiastic and had told San Francisco so. The move back to San Francisco had been agreed with only the date of appointment to be finalised. He also knew that his wife was eager to return to find the American way of life that she loved so much.

Mike entered the tower of the Golden Star headquarters. Once in his office, he summoned his deputy, John Finmore, to give him his instructions.

"Right, John, we need to get on with the Barton property deal. Did you contact their manager this morning to present our financing offer?"

"Yes, Mike. He's coming in at 3:00 pm today with his staff."

"Great. We'll meet them in the boardroom. It's the nicest place in the world for a hundred-million-dollar deal. Make sure the reception is absolutely perfect."

"You can count on me. It is obvious that we will carry out this project. The competition is not up to scratch anyway. We don't have much to fear."

"That's fine. But let's not underestimate them. You can't be too careful."

"Yes, of course, Mike."

Later that afternoon, Mike's secretary informed him that the Barton Group team had arrived. There were four of them, and they had been ushered into the boardroom where they awaited him.

Mike was joined by John Finmore in the corridor.

"Mike, did you see that yesterday, a whole bunch of state documents were leaked on the Internet via Wikileaks… *The New York Times* website released them. It could be a real shit storm. We're talking about some 250,000 American diplomatic documents. Can you imagine that?"

"Yes, it's incredible. The repercussions this is going to have… I don't even want to think about it. Well, we have to get to our meeting."

They were going into the boardroom. Their clients were there. Tea, coffee and cold drinks were available, along with biscuits. The meeting was very cordial, and agreements were made for the financing of the real estate project of a new hotel to be built on Sukhumvit, the biggest avenue in Bangkok. All the participants were satisfied and left each other with warm congratulations.

Mike went home, happy with his day. He was confident that the Barton case would speed up his return to the US. He couldn't wait to see his wife and share the day's success.

"Hello, darling, how was your day today?"

"Hello, quiet. I stayed at home today, had a swim in the pool, read, did Marat's homework, well, supervised it, and made us some dinner. How was your day? Everything went well? No bad encounters like me the other night?"

"No, everything's fine. We signed a huge deal that should move my appointment to San Francisco forward."

"Oh, really? Mm-hmm. That's great. So when do we leave?"

"I don't know yet, but I'm thinking no later than the next twelve months."

"Oh, that's so great!"

"Yes. Shall we celebrate? Do we have any more of that amazing champagne?"

"Crystal Roederer? Yes, we have a bottle left."

"Go get it. I'll open it. We'll celebrate by the pool."

"Yes, that's a good idea. I'll get it, my love. And I'd like us to spend Christmas in Sausalito. Will you think about it, darling?"

"Yes, I'd love to. I'll make the flight reservations tomorrow."

"Wonderful. Can't wait for Christmas! And Marat will be delighted too!"

Settled by the pool, in comfortable armchairs, they contemplated their future world, their life in Sausalito and their future happiness and finally emptied the bottle of Crystal. The evening was sweet. They were happy.

Tuesday, 30 November 2010

Everyone was back to work. Lila was doing her chores; Marat had gone to school, and Mike had returned to his office. The morning passed quickly, handling the Barton file. At noon, he decided to go and have lunch at the Sheraton buffet, which for him was the best value for money in the neighbourhood, the bank building being only a ten-minute walk away.

Suddenly, a heavyset man passed him and stumbled. He held on to him to avoid falling. He was sweaty and out of breath.

"Help me, they want to kill me," he said.

He fell down and slipped a marble into Mike's pocket, but Mike didn't realise it. Mike then saw a huge bloodstain on his back. He called for help, and immediately two policemen who were regulating the traffic came running. They immediately saw that the stranger is dead. They asked in bad English if the man is a friend of Mike. They saw the stranger has been shot. They also noticed that he had been stabbed. The policemen called for reinforcements and informed Mike that he had to follow them to the police station.

Once at the station, he was taken to an officer who asked him various questions to make sure that he did not really know the victim.

Finally, convinced that Mike did not know the victim, they let him go.

Mike left the police station and hailed a taxi to the Sheraton where he went for a late lunch. After looking around the buffet and choosing some dishes, he sat down at a table. As soon as he sat down, a man came over and sat opposite him.

"Good afternoon, Mr Robertson. I hope you are enjoying your meal."

"Good afternoon. Do we know each other?"

"I know you. You probably don't."

"Are you a client of the bank?"

"No, I'm not."

Mike noticed a strong Russian accent from the person he was talking to.

"What do you want? And who are you exactly?"

"My name is Aïdar Klotz. But we're not going to play that little game of introductions, Mr Robertson. It's a bit too formal, don't you think?"

"I don't understand…"

"Listen to me carefully. I'm not going to beat around the bush. You give me the chip. Better yet, I'll buy it from you. Our department doesn't need to know about our arrangement. I'm offering $500,000. That's a fair offer."

Mike was stumped.

"What are you talking about? What services?"

"Fine. $1 million. Paid where you want. That's my final price."

"I don't know what you're talking about. You're obviously making a mistake about me. I'll have to ask you to leave my table and leave me alone."

"Robertson, we know perfectly well that you are a CIA agent. We've known it for a long time. Your job in this bank is a nice cover. Financially, I mean. But one million dollars can't leave anyone indifferent. Besides, your contact clung to you before he died earlier. You can't deny that. And he gave you the chip, obviously. You see, I know everything."

"I think I'm starting to understand."

"That's the least of it, Agent Robertson. So we have a deal?"

"Very well. Listen to me carefully, whoever you are. I'm a banker, and I don't work for the CIA. The poor man who died, I don't know him; I've never seen him before. He died saying only to me: 'They will kill me'. That's all. And, obviously, I know absolutely nothing about your chip story. Now you leave my table, and I never want to see you again."

"You're crazy. We'll do anything to get back what's ours."

"Get out of here, or I'll call security."

"I'm leaving. You're making a big mistake. And you're being watched so closely, didn't your lovely wife tell you? I'll see you soon."

"What's the matter? Did you threaten her?"

"See you soon, Agent Robertson."

After quickly paying the lunch bill, Mike decided to go home. He called his secretary to ask her to cancel the afternoon's appointments and rearranged his schedule accordingly.

When he arrived at his villa, he went to change and discovered that his wife is not there. He asked the maid.

"Nok, do you know where madam is?"

"She left with Thanit to go shopping with Mr Mike. Central or Siam Paragon, I think."

"OK. Thanks, Nok. How long ago?"

"Yes, this morning around ten o'clock."

"So she must have had lunch there. OK."

Mike was in a state of worry, not knowing what to do. He was well aware that his family was in real danger although he knew nothing of the stories told by the man called Klotz. *And who exactly was Klotz? Probably a Russian spy, since he confessed to being part of an organisation that was watching him. And this story about the chip that the man gave him when he died...*

But then the car entered the courtyard. Lila got out smiling.

"You're here already? That's great. Have you decided that we should spend the afternoon together? Thanit, Nok, take the shopping home!"

With these words, she rushed to kiss her husband.

She realised that something was wrong, and Mike looked anxious.

"Mike, what's wrong? Is something wrong?"

"I met the guy who threatened you on Saturday night."

"No, you didn't?"

"Yes, I did. I'll tell you what happened to me this morning. Come on, let's sit down."

Lila was upset and now thought that their safety was no longer assured in Thailand. She thought they had to leave. They couldn't stay here with such a threat to the whole family.

"Mike, we have to go back to America. It's too dangerous."

"You and Marat are going back to San Francisco. I'll join you later. I can't leave my job like this."

"No, you're taking an unwise risk. You must come back with us. Imagine if something happened to you. You can't stay here."

"But, darling, I absolutely must complete my mission. Especially since I can apply for a quicker return. I'm sure it will only take three or four months at most."

"Anything can happen in three months. I don't want you to take any risks. Just resign, and we'll all go home together next week."

"Resign..."

"You have valuable experience. You can easily find another job. Why don't you explain the situation to the management tomorrow? You negotiate with them to go back right away. After all, they care about you, and probably don't want to lose you."

"Yes, you're right. Tomorrow morning, I'll call head office and make the proposal… this ultimatum I should say."

"We don't have a choice, Mike. This is a matter of life and death. And, with this whole CIA/Russian spy milieu or whatever it is, we can't play games."

"Yes, you're right."

Meanwhile, the school bus brought Marat back from school.

"Mum, dad, look, I won twenty marbles today!"

"Hi, champ," said his father. "I left my jacket on the bed, and I thought of you. I bought you a bag of very nice, multicoloured marbles."

"Yeah, great!"

"Good," said his mother. "Go and change now. By the way, Mike, we're invited to the Safronovs for dinner tonight."

"We are? I must admit that I would have preferred to stay home."

"I've already confirmed our agreement. And it will be good for me to see Olga and Andrei, to talk about the country. Don't forget we're all from St Petersburg. And the news from Petersburg is always something important for us, you know. It's the cultural hub of our country," she said with a smile.

"Yes, I know. Lermontov, Pushkin and so on."

"You're a romantic."

"By the way, did you tell them about our situation?"

"I mentioned it to Olga, but I was rather vague about it."

"They will probably ask us questions…."

"Yes, it's possible. But didn't you tell me that the guy who approached you in the restaurant had a Russian accent? You never know he might work at the embassy. Andrei has an important job there. We could talk to him about it. He might know who it is if you give him a description?"

"You know, Russian officials at the embassy don't usually say anything. Especially since the intelligence services have always been part of their diplomatic delegations all over the world, it's well known. It's in their DNA."

"Yes, I know that the FSB and its ancestors KGB and NKVD have always been very active, both in our country and abroad. Do you think Andrei is part of it?"

"Of the FSB? Most likely."

"So, if he asks questions, what will your attitude be?"

"I'll talk about it because I want to see his reaction, and how much he knows."

Marat went to change in his room, which was next to his parents' room. He went into his parents' room to look for the bag of marbles. He rummaged through Mike's jacket pockets and pulled out the small packet. Reaching into the opposite pocket, he felt something round and pulled it out.

"Wow, a ball, that's worth at least three marbles in the triangle game. I'm going to play with Ivan tonight and win easily."

Marat joined his parents.

"Thanks, dad, for the marbles. And the ball is beautiful."

"The ball?"

"Yes, it's a marble that's bigger than the others and worth more when you play."

"Oh, well…"

"I'll play with Ivan tonight and pluck it."

"All right, then. You have to win; you're an American."

"Don't forget he's Russian too," added Lila.

Mike winked at her.

"American first!"

"That's it!"

Mike asked Thanit to get ready to take them away.

"What destination, Mr Mike?"

"Sathorn, at the Safronovs. Do you remember where they live?"

"No problem, sir."

When they arrived at the building where Andrei Sergueïevitch Safronov, his wife Olga and their son Ivan were living, they got out of the Mercedes and introduced themselves to the receptionist who hurried in front of them to open the vast automatic glass door leading to an impressive reception room. There, a hostess greeted them and called the lift.

"What floor are you going to, and who are you visiting?"

"Andrei Safronov."

"Oh, this is the fiftieth floor. One moment please, I'll announce you."

The hostess called the Safronov flat and immediately accompanied them into a wide marble corridor that housed eight lifts. She engaged a magnetised card in one of the readers at the entrance to each portal. The door opened, revealing a lift decorated with brass and beautiful bronze mirrors.

"Please enter."

The hostess pressed the button for the fiftieth floor and withdrew with a broad smile.

On the landing, Olga and Ivan were waiting for them in the doorway.

"How happy I am to see you! Lila, Marat! Hello, Mike!"

"We're delighted to be here too!"

"Marat, you're coming to play. Ivan is looking forward to seeing you."

"Yes, I'm coming. I brought my marbles with me."

"Oh, great! Come on, let's go!"

The two children ran to their play area, leaving the parents to their reunion.

"Come in, come in, please."

"Hello, Andrei! How are you?"

"Hello, Lila. Hello, Mike. You're welcome. I'm fine. Come into the living room. Olga has prepared the zakouskis."

"Just like in St Petersburg!"

"Yes, absolutely, and I would even say as usual! You have to keep in touch with our dear country, at least in terms of taste."

"Yes, you're absolutely right, Andrei."

"And, with vodka, isn't it?" added Mike.

"Of course, with vodka. Do you know the meaning of this word, Mike? Vodka means little water. So, you see, it can't hurt! But, originally, in the fifteenth century, the Russians wanted to make alcohol from wheat. It was then called bread water."

"You know that in America, we say brandy. But our Indians say firewater. Only the French, I think, say *eau de vie*, water of life. In fact, you have a philosophy quite close to them on this subject. I have always heard that the French drink a lot. The same goes for the Russians."

"You mustn't fall into old clichés that date from before the revolution. Now, for the French, I don't really know, they are not a people I know very well. However, they had a beautiful revolution, and at the beginning of the takeover by the people, our patriotic song was the *Marseillaise* from 1917 to 1922. We wrote a Russian text to this music. It called the tsar a vampire. And, in 1922, we opted for the Internationale. Then Stalin decided that the Soviet Union should have its own patriotic song. That was in 1944. The composition of the text was entrusted to Serguei Mikhalkov and Gabriel El-Registan, and the music to Alexander Alexandrov."

"El-Registan, you say? He wasn't a Russian. Where was he from, Spain?"

"No. In fact, El-Registan was a pseudonym. His name was Gabriel Arkadievich Oureklian. His parents were Armenian although he was born in Uzbekistan in Samarkand. He had chosen this pseudonym after the central square of Samarkand, which is called Registan."

"Interesting. But today, it's still the same hymn, I think?"

"Not exactly. El-Registan, in his memoirs, revealed that Stalin had asked him to add a belligerent verse in honour of the Red Army, especially about how they were fighting the fascists and warning that they would continue this struggle forever. So a new verset was added. From memory, it said: 'We have raised our army in battle/we will sweep the vile invaders from the road'. But, in 1977, the text was corrected by our authorities. In a more peaceful way. And Stalin's name was also erased. When the tragedy of the disappearance of the Soviet Union occurred in 1991, a new anthem was introduced, the *Patriotic Song*, music by Glinka. There were no words. Wasn't that strange, an anthem without words? If you want to know, the government even organised a competition to find the words, but unfortunately, or I would say personally, fortunately, nobody was selected because, in 2000, shortly after his accession to the supreme power, our President Vladimir Putin decided to take Alexandrov's music and add new lyrics glorifying Russia. Of course, there are always fools who oppose ideas no matter how ingenious, and this was the case. Putin has been accused of wanting to revive Soviet symbolism. Ridiculous, isn't it? The Soviet Union was gone, and the Russian empire was a shadow of its former self, with all the republics gaining independence and the economy in tatters. Fortunately, all that has changed."

"You have a great understanding of this subject, Andrei."

"I am Russian, and I love my country deeply, Mike. Everything Russian delights me. I would even say that for me, to be Russian is to live Russian, to think Russian. In a word, to be in perfect osmosis with the mother country. I live like that. And it's a joy."

"A fine patriotic statement."

"And you'll see. Let's go to the table. The Russian enchantment, you'll experience it with vodka and zakouskis prepared by Olga."

"With pleasure."

On the table were a plethora of dishes offering halved Malossol gherkins, cucumbers with dill, cheese dips, smoked trout rillettes, mushrooms marinated in garlic and dill, buckwheat blinis, caviar, crème fraiche, the inevitable Olivier salad, salmon egg canapés, salmon canapés, pirojkis, syrnikis. And also bottles of Baltika beer and three bottles of Tsarskaya Vodka in a large ice bucket.

"We're in for a treat," said Lila.

"Yes, I was lucky to find everything. And, after that I prepared golubtsy and pielmenis with lamb. And, for dessert, we will have chak-chak and vatruchka."

"You're going to kill us, Olga. In any case, it's really nice to be back in our country."

"You see, Mike, your wife is like me," said Andrei.

"Yes, I see. It must be said that resisting is neither more nor less inhuman in the face of so much beautiful food."

"You are being won over by the Russian spirit, Mike. You see, it starts with either food or women. You certainly started with both!"

Everyone burst out laughing.

Meanwhile, Marat and Ivan, who had ended up in Ivan's room, had started a game of marbles. They drew a triangle on the floor and put a marble at each end, plus one in the middle. After a few games, Marat had already gained three marbles on his opponent.

"Look Ivan, I have a multicoloured ball."

"Oh, yes, it's beautiful. Put it in the middle of the triangle."

"No, I don't want to risk losing it. It's too beautiful."

"Put it on. You play better than me anyway."

"No, I don't want to. I tell you."

"Look, let's make a rule for this: If I win it, OK, that's fine. But, if you win, then I'll give you three more marbles to choose from."

"Three extra marbles if I win my ball?"

"Yes, you will."

"All right, but first, we'll play a practice game that doesn't count for anything."

"If you want."

And Marat wins the game again.

"You're really good, Marat. Now let's play for real, OK?"

"OK."

They rearranged their triangle by putting the three balls at on the corners and the ball in the middle. As Marat is the last winner, he shot first. As he shot, Nawarat, the maid of the house, opened the door to ask them to come and join the parents for dinner. His interruption suddenly distracted Marat, who missed his first shot.

"Yes, we're finishing our game," replied Ivan. "We'll be right there."

Marat was very annoyed. It was the first time all evening that he missed his target, one of the marbles that was at one end of the triangle. And he knew that Ivan had every chance of winning the game if he managed to hit one of the marbles with each shot.

"Now it was my turn."

Ivan applied himself and took his time to aim. He shot. His ball hit one of the balls in the triangle and came out. This one was acquired and allowed him to continue shooting. The second shot was successful. And the third one too. Marat was upset. He realised that he was going to lose the game and especially his ball, which he held so dear. And that's what happened, Ivan adjusting the ball that came out of the triangle with a very precise shot.

"You win!"

"Did you play well, or were you lucky, Ivan?"

"Maybe both, don't you think?"

"Yeah, I think so."

"Come on, let's go eat. And, you know, you'll probably find another ball although I've never seen one like that before."

They went to the table where their parents had already started to help themselves.

"Come on, children. Settle down."

"Mum, we can have a tray and eat in the room. We'd like to continue playing."

"OK, I'll prepare it for you, and Nawarat will bring it to you."

"OK. Come on, Marat, let's go back."

The maid took the tray to the children.

"This is excellent, Olga. You've really worked wonders. And your vodka is excellent, Andrei. Did you bring it back from St Petersburg?"

"Yes, Mike, in the diplomatic bag."

"It's got to be good for something once in a while."

"As a vodka lover, did your wife take you to the vodka museum in St Petersburg?"

"No, never. Do you know this museum, Lila?"

"Yes, but I've never been there. It's not far from St Isaac's Cathedral, is it, Andrei?"

"Yes, it is. You should go there. It's very interesting, and there's a brasserie that serves very good food."

"I think it's a good idea. Lila, you'll have to organise it for us when we come back to see your family."

"No problem, darling."

The golubtsy and pielmenis were served. Olga filled the plates.

"By the way, Andrei, I want to tell you about something that happened to me this week."

"Yes?"

"I was contacted by a man with a strong Russian accent who told me his name was Klotz. Aïdar Klotz. Do you know him?"

"Aïdar Klotz? No, it doesn't ring a bell. Aïdar is a name that is more common in the Muslim republics. I would say Chechnya, for example. Or Kazakhstan, or Uzbekistan, Turkmenistan. And all these people speak Russian in addition to their local languages."

"And this name, Klotz, doesn't sound very Russian. What do you think?"

"I would say that it reminds me curiously of a Jewish name. Curiously because it has a Muslim family name. So maybe a Ukrainian or a Georgian. Here's a riddle."

"It would be nice to solve it."

"Yes, of course, it would. Now maybe he gave you a fake name."

"I don't think so. He sounded sincere when he said his name."

"And what did he want from you?"

Mike told of his meeting with Klotz, following the death of the stranger in his arms.

"And the person who was killed, was he identified?"

"I confess I don't know. *The Bangkok Post* in its edition the day after the attack did not mention the name. It spoke of an American tourist, but nothing more."

"This is very strange. In general, Thai criminal cases give information to the press."

"What do you think?"

"It is most likely a case in which powerful states have an interest. So espionage or something like that. In any case, you have to be careful and protect your family. Because from what you tell me, they are looking for a chip, which must contain sensitive data."

"What can I do? I called the U.S. embassy this afternoon to make an appointment. I'm going there tomorrow morning. The person I spoke to was rather vague, which I think is normal. I told him that I was taken for a CIA agent, which is obviously not the case. But there was no reaction, obviously."

"Was there?"

"Of course, there wasn't! Stop pulling my leg, it's not really funny."

"Yes, I understand."

"Darling, didn't you tell me that you had contacted the embassy?"

"Yes, I'm sorry. It slipped my mind. I had a very busy day today, you know."

"Yes, of course, you have."

"What would you advise me to do, Andrei?"

"The first thing, as I said, is your protection. You should hire a security company to look after your house and then go armed."

"I don't have a gun, and I wouldn't know where to go to get one."

"I'll give you a gun and some ammunition. I'll get it for you. And we'll do a little training session in the building's garden later, OK?"

"Is it possible here?"

"Yes, you just have to give the caretaker a thousand baht."

"OK then."

Andrei slipped away from the table and came back with a box, which he opened and presented to Mike.

"Look at Mike. It's a Makarov. Do you know it?"

"I know Colt, Winchester and other American guns, but not that."

"This is the official weapon of Russian officers and NCOs. We have had this weapon since the fifties. I think we'll soon have a new, more modern outfit, but these pistols work well. They have proved themselves."

"Yes, I suppose so."

"This is nine millimetre. And, you see, it's fed by an eight-round box magazine. It's an extremely reliable weapon. Come on, let's try it. The two friends take the lift down to the reception of the building."

Andrei gave the concierge a thousand baht and showed him the gun. He answered with a smile and went ahead of him to open the door to a nice garden. No one was there.

"Come on, Mike, I'll show you how this thing works."

And he began a series of four shots aimed at a tree a hundred yards ahead.

"Did you see that? Now it's your turn."

Mike grabbed the gun and aimed at the tree as well. He shot twice and hit the target too.

"Hey, not bad. You never told me you could shoot that well."

"Yes, these are the remains of the Wild West. Somewhere in the DNA of us Americans."

"I can see that."

They practised for another twenty minutes or so, then headed back to the apartment.

"At least you can ensure your own immediate safety with this weapon."

"Thank you, Andrei."

"It's only fair. I would be sorry if anything happened to you. But you should also see a security company. That's important."

"Yes, I'll find out."

They went into the flat.

"So, Olga, what about the dessert? Is it not served yet?"

"There you are! We just put it on the table, Andrei. We've been waiting for you."

"Well, here we are. I congratulated your husband, Lila. He's a good shot."

"Mike is a very resourceful man, Andrei. That's why I married him."

"I don't doubt it, Lila. I don't doubt it."

"Mike and I talked about these threats that we received. And we think it would be best for us to leave Thailand and go back to the States."

"Oh, yeah? That's a return you'd schedule for the end of the year I guess?"

"Actually, we'd like to leave next week."

"That soon? But Mike and your position at the bank, have you negotiated a transfer yet?"

"I want to talk to my management tomorrow. I need to hear back from them soon so I can decide what to do. I'm going to put pressure on them."

"That's a new one. And you're sure that pressure as you say will work with them? Are they capable of such quick decisions, I would say a bit of a cookie cutter?"

"I think so. I have an important position here, and I know they were thinking of me for a management position in the United States, at the headquarters in San Francisco."

"Or somewhere else in the world maybe?"

"No, in the U.S."

"Then you're definitely an important part of the game."

"If you can call it a game…"

Andrei's face darkened a little.

"Oh, but this is sad news. I'm going to lose my best friend in Bangkok."

"Don't worry, Olga, we'll keep in touch anyway, and we'll make arrangements to see each other again in St Petersburg when we're staying with our families."

"Yes, Lila. Are you going alone with Marat, Mike will join you afterwards, or are you waiting for the bank's reply?"

"I hope we can all go together, don't you, darling?"

"Yes, I hope so."

The evening came to an end, and the friends take their leave. Lila called Marat. They went downstairs and called their driver to come back.

"It was a beautiful evening. A little sad at the end when we announced we might be leaving earlier than planned."

"Yes, Lila. It's true. They are good friends."

"Olga is my best friend. We've known each other for so long. When you think that we were next-door neighbours in St Petersburg. Her parents had moved in across the street from mine, in our building, I was six and she was seven. We went to school together from primary to university. And we never had any friction, never a bad word. A true and rare friendship. And we ended up here in Bangkok. It's really extraordinary when I think about it."

"Yes, it is. And, Andrei, did you know him for a long time? I never asked you."

"Andrei is also from St Petersburg. She knew him through his cousin who was a student at the Frunze military academy in Moscow like him."

"Yes, he used to be a soldier. Do you know what he did exactly?"

"He stayed in the army for about ten years. He served in the Caucasus at the time of the terrorist unrest linked to Chechen activists. I think he ended up with the rank of Colonel. It was a hard time for Olga, who had followed him to Grozny, because of the insecurity and violence. Then he was appointed to Moscow where he held a position in the Ministry of Defence. And, finally, he was appointed here to the embassy in Bangkok."

"He has an important position here, doesn't he?"

"He is number two in the embassy."

"It's a big job indeed, and I'm sure that at that level he's FSB."

"Yes, it's very likely."

"Do you think we can trust him?"

"Mike, these are our friends. Olga is my best friend. And I've known Andrei for as long as she has. These are people who have always helped me. Look at the way we were received tonight. And did you see how Andrei behaved? He lent you his gun, which is no small thing. And he advised you to protect yourself. They are certainly true friends because I can tell you that it is hardly customary in our country for an officer to help and entrust his weapon to someone else and especially to a foreigner who is moreover American."

"Yes, you are certainly right. Andrei is indeed trying to help us. There's no doubt about it."

"Mum, I lost my ball playing with Ivan. But I won more marbles than he did. Dad, can you buy me a ball?"

"A ball?"

"You know, the one you bought me with the bag of marbles…"

"Oh, yes. I'll see. But, you know, in the bags of marbles they sell, it's not always easy to know exactly what's inside. It's a bit of a luck factor."

"Well, all right."

They arrived in Onut's neighbourhood and went home. With a loaded gun in hand, Mike went around the villa, checking that everything was in order, and went out onto the street to have a look around and saw if they had been followed or watched in any way. Reassured, he returned to the house and inspected each room, looking closely for signs of intrusion, even if the maid had stayed behind during their short absence, and for hidden microphones in the lamps and light fittings. Finally, he joined his wife in the bedroom. Marat was already in bed and tired, falling asleep straight away.

"You know, Mike, since we are planning to leave next week, whatever happens, I don't want to send Marat to school tomorrow. I'm going to call the school secretary in the morning to let them know that we're moving and that we're withdrawing Marat. I think it's much safer to do that. Do you agree?"

"Yes, it's a good decision. He'll be back in school in Sausalito in a couple of weeks, so it's not a problem."

"I'm nervous, Mike."

"I know you are. I am, too. It's traumatic, this kind of situation. I'm looking forward to California, too."

"We'll be fine there."

"Yes, we will."

Mike moved closer to Lila, and they abandoned themselves to each other, making love with more tenderness than usual.

Wednesday, 1 December 2010

Mike had gone to the bank very early. It was 7:00 in the morning when he got back to his office. This was so he could talk to his supervisor in San Francisco, Gordon Hoffman. It's five o'clock there. Gordon never left his office before nine o'clock.

"Hello, Gordon. This is Mike Robertson."

"Hi, Mike. You're up very early, aren't you?"

"Yes, it's the only way I could get in touch with you, given the time difference."

"Yes, it is. To what do I owe this pleasure? Nothing broken, I hope?"

"No, business is good. I'm the one with the problem."

And Mike's gave an update on the situation.

"Gordon, we can't stay in this country anymore. I want to go back to the States."

"You're catching me off guard. It takes a little time. And it's odd that an organisation identified you as CIA. You're not holding out on me, are you?"

"Of course not. And I don't have time, Gordon. You have to understand me."

"Yeah, I do. Look, give me a day or two. I'll talk to the Big Chief and see what I can do."

"Gordon, I'm sorry to rush you, but we're planning to go back to San Francisco next week. If the bank won't accept a transfer, then I'll resign. I have no choice. I have to protect my family."

"OK, I understand. I'll call you this time in two days. I'm going to be as supportive of your transfer to headquarters as I can be. For the job, I'll have to talk to the board."

"Thanks, Gordon."

Mike was a little more reassured. He had always had a good relationship with Gordon Hoffman who was the number three man in the Group globally. He had the ear of the Chairman and thought he should easily get a new job.

He decided to inform his deputy, John Finmore, as he knew that he would be leaving his post at the end of the week. He called him as soon as he arrived, at about nine o'clock. Once Finmore was informed, he classified his files and passed them on to him. At around 1:00 pm, Mike left the bank and asked his driver to take him home. Since the beginning of the week, he had preferred to have lunch in the secure comfort of his villa. But, as soon as he finishes his conversation with his driver, three men, probably Thai, surrounded him and seized him. They shouted at him in broken English.

"You're coming with us. We have some questions for you."

"Let me go! Let me go!"

One of the men shoved him violently and punched him in the stomach.

"Hurry up. We are expected."

At that moment, Mike's Mercedes appeared. Thanit, the driver, immediately understood the situation and got out of the car. He launched himself at the three men and put them to flight with his martial arts skills.

Mike was stunned and suddenly realised that his wife was right when she insisted on leaving in the next few days.

"Thank you, Thanit. We won't go home just yet. We're going to Wireless Road, to the U.S. embassy."

"Very well, Mr Mike."

Arriving at the embassy, Mike made his appointment and asked to see an official in charge of the security of American citizens. He was ushered into an office after half an hour's wait and was received by a young woman in her thirties.

"Hello, my name is Diana Garwin. What can I do for you?"

"Hi, I'm Mike Robertson, the CEO of the Golden Star Bank in Bangkok."

"Nice to meet you. I'm listening."

"I'd like to know if there is a file on me, particularly in relation to the CIA."

"This is a bit of a curious question. Can you tell me a little more about it?"

Mike then recounted the latest events he had experienced during the week.

"This is my situation. Do you understand my question now?"

"Yes, of course, I do. However, as you know, we have no authority or delegation from the CIA. It is impossible for me to answer as I have no contact with the agency."

"You must be joking. Everyone knows that embassies have contact with the CIA."

"Yes, the embassy does have contact with the agency. But we don't handle their business. They run their business. Do you understand?"

"Who is in contact with the agency at the embassy?"

"It is a diplomatic attaché, but he is not there at the moment."

"Where can I contact him?"

"I'm not qualified to answer that question."

"But don't you understand that my family and I are under threat? You can't leave me in this situation! I'm an American, and you owe me your protection. And I want to know why they think I'm a CIA agent!"

"Calm down. There's no point in getting carried away. Look, I'll defer our conversation to the appropriate person, and the person in charge of your case will contact you. It may be someone from the CIA who contacts you, given what you say."

"How long will it take?"

"I can't tell you."

"And when does the diplomatic attaché return?"

"He should be here tomorrow."

"Then I can come back here tomorrow morning and meet him?"

"No, Mr Robertson. You will be contacted for an appointment. That's how it's done."

At that moment, the office door opened.

"Oh, sorry, Diana, I didn't know you were busy."

"Please, Harry. This is Mike Robertson who is the CEO of the Golden Star Bank in Bangkok. Harry Douglas is the First Consul."

"Nice to meet you, Mike. I've heard a lot about you. It seems that your establishment is doing good business in the country."

"News travels fast. Yes, business is good. Actually, I came here because I have a personal problem involving the safety of my family."

"Here in Bangkok? Well, it's a pretty quiet country here. What's so bad about it?"

And Mike again related the facts.

"I see. It's a strange thing. Have you never been in contact, at least once in your life, with the CIA or one of its agents?"

"No, I have not. Mrs Garwin told me that there was a person here who was their contact but that he is away."

"Yes. He'll be back at the embassy tomorrow. Diana, get that information to him as soon as he arrives. Do you have a mobile where we can reach you?"

"Yes, I'll give you my card, you've got everything on it. And what's this person's name?"

"He'll contact you directly."

"No name?"

"He'll introduce himself. That's the custom."

"OK then. I hope nothing happens to us until then."

"It's good that you came to meet us. We'll take care of your file."

Mike left and asked Thanit to return to the bank. When he arrived in his office, he asked to see his deputy, John Finmore.

"He's been away, Mike. He should be back around four o'clock. He had a meeting outside with BEACT INDUSTRIES."

"OK. Thanks."

Mike logged on to his computer and entered his assistant's domain. He went to the diary to review his latest appointments.

Finmore. Let's see… Meetings over the last week. What do we have here?

On the screen appeared a series of names and addresses including a number of probably Russian citizens, which made Mike wonder:

Aleksandr Khoudovekov Union Thai Trade, 2 November 2010, 10:00 am

Dmitri Akhremenko National Building Corp, 3 November 2010, 3:00 pm

Igor Gounine Grand Construction Thailand, 5 November 2010, 10:00 am

Sergueï Ierkoulaïev Ural Thai Corp, 12 November 2010, 10:00 am

Artiome Siantchouk Klioutchevskoï Summit Invest, 16 November 2010, 10:00 am

Mike realised that these meetings had been taking place every month for over a year. He went to look at the positions in each account and discovered regular bank transfers to accounts of offshore companies located in Belize. All had the same bank destination: Central Bank Pacific.

This is not normal. Every month at least one million dollars of funds are transferred. Let's see the purpose of the transfer: interim dividends. That is strange. There's an agreement between those two for sure. Finmore is involved in this for sure. What if all this is connected with what's happening to me? And how come the bank's general control at headquarters hasn't reacted during the time this business has been going on? Could there be complicity in the U.S.?

The situation seemed complicated, and Mike understood the extent of the danger, given the amounts involved. All these people would defend their business, and he knew that the Russian mafias didn't hesitate to use extreme means to protect their business. But what did this have to do with the chip that Klotz came to ask him for? It all seemed so confusing.

He called his secretary.

"Mary, can you tell me if John is back from his appointment?"

"No, he's not there, Mike. He left a message that he won't be coming back to the bank. He'll go straight home to avoid the traffic."

"OK. Thanks, Mary."

Mike took his mobile and looked up Finmore's number. He called him. After about thirty seconds, John Finmore picked up.

"Hello, Mike, how are you?"

"John, I want to see you. It's important."

"Is this about you leaving? We can talk about it in the morning if you like. I'm going home. I don't want to get stuck in traffic. I'm having a romantic dinner tonight with my wife Helen. It's our wedding anniversary."

"John, you get back here right away. Or I'll come over to your house, tonight and I guarantee you'll remember this wedding anniversary."

"What's the matter with you, Mike? Something wrong?"

"Do you know anything about monthly capital transfers sent to a bank in Belize by a Russian group?"

"An association of Russians? No, these are companies properly registered in Thailand. These are important companies that have various activities such as construction or finance. It's all very clear; don't worry, Mike."

"I am worried. I demand an explanation. You come here right now. I'll wait for you. If you don't come, I'll report you to Internal Control at headquarters."

"You're worrying about nothing. Well, I'm coming. I'll be at the bank in an hour."

"I'll be waiting for you."

John Finmore entered Mike's office. He immediately realised that there was extensive documentation on the five Russian-run companies spread out with Mike's pencil notes.

"This story is clear, Mike. There is nothing extraordinary about it."

"What do you mean by that? Millions of dollars flying to a tax haven, and you think it's nothing? Did you see that? Just numbered accounts. And you know, I suppose, and this is really a minimum, that Belize openly claims to be the best tax haven in the world? International pressure has had no effect on this country; the names of the account owners are not even known by the authorities of the country with these numbered accounts. Obviously, no accounting is required, and even trusts are not mandatory. What the hell are you doing with these people? What are you into, John? Explain yourself, or I promise you that there will be trouble."

"These companies, as I said, are transparent in our market in Thailand. They are respected and known. Moreover, they are excellent clients for us. And, after all, what would prevent them from remitting their dividends to their holding companies, regardless of the host country? Because that's what it's all about and nothing else."

"No. They are not dividends. They are advance payments on future dividends, which is what you yourself have indicated on the objects of the transfers."

"It is legal here."

"On such amounts, it is not clear, I am sorry."

"And what was to be done then? These are important clients. Their assets, as you must have checked, total eight hundred million dollars. And, yet, during the previous year, we made a total of twenty million dollars in transfers. And I think we should reach more or less the same amount this year. In view of the assets, there's nothing to worry about."

"You broke the banking code by dumping this money in a tax haven. What is your relationship with these Russians?"

"Professional banking relationships only."

"I'll have to report this. I think your career's about to end, John. You sure you don't want to tell me more? How are these five guys connected? Well, since they're transferring money to the same bank, it's obvious they're working together."

"Yes, they know each other. I know they work together. I understand that they are former members of the FSB, which they left during the Yeltsin era in 1991."

"When the Soviet Union collapsed..."

"Yes, that's right. They took advantage of the system, I think, and were able to acquire quite large shares in state conglomerates for very little money, as was done in those days."

"I see."

"I don't know much more. The accounts of their companies in Thailand are clear. They are audited by one of the big four. There is no problem."

"In any case, I don't like all this. I find your answers unsatisfactory. I will not keep you. Go home. I want you to know that I am revoking your credentials, and you will no longer have access to the bank. I will call San Francisco and report back to them. There is a possibility that this case will have criminal consequences in the United States. Goodbye."

John Finmore got up and left without a word.

Mike grabbed the phone on his desk and called Andrei Safronov.

"Hey there, Mike. How have you been since yesterday? I hope you've had a good night's sleep."

"Hello, Andrei. Yes, your wife is great for arranging such a nice invitation. I'm calling you because I'd like some information."

"Information? It's a taboo word, you know?"

"Yes, I know it is. But I really need your help. And I'm also going to give you some information that might be useful to you."

"Go on, then."

"I've discovered in the bank's books five fairly important companies run by Russians, and I'd like to know if you know them."

"They have accounts with you… Tell me more, please."

"OK, these are big accounts worth hundreds of millions of dollars, and they're making transfers to a bank in a tax haven."

"Where?"

"Belize. I'll give you the names:

    Aleksandr Khoudovekov, President of Union Thai Trade

    Dmitri Akhremenko, Chairman of National Building Corp

    Igor Gounine, President of Grand Construction Thailand

    Sergei Yerkulayev, President of Ural Thai Corp

    Artiome Siantchouk, President of Klioutchevskoï Summit Invest

Here it is. Do you know it?"

"I have noted it. I've heard of Khudovekov. Very rich, I think. Yerkulayev is a former director of the Ufa oil group in Bashkortostan. I know that he left in early 1992 after he bought a diamond mine for almost nothing with the support of the local political leaders. That's what allowed him to go on to build buildings in Russia and Thailand. And Siantchouk comes from Kamchatka, from Yelizovo

I think. He has a reputation as a mafioso. These three we are watching because we suspect them of various trafficking. The others I don't know."

"Do you think they're dangerous?"

"As soon as there are big financial interests, everyone becomes dangerous, don't you think, Mike?"

"Yes, I do."

"What are you going to do about it?"

"Refer to my superiors in San Francisco."

"Yes, that's the right thing to do."

"What about you? Can you use this information?"

"I don't know. I have to do some checking."

"Will you keep me informed about the outcome?"

"No. This is Russian business."

"I understand that."

"And, your departure, where is that?"

"I'm due to have contact tomorrow or the day after for the response to my enquiries."

"All right, then. Let us know, so we can say goodbye."

"Yes, it will be a pleasure, my friend. Give our love to the family."

"Thanks as well. Good night, Mike."

Thursday, 2 December 2010

At the Russian embassy, Andrei Safronov summoned an officer, Lieutenant-Colonel Nikita Vladimirovitch Chelaguine.

"Nikita Vladimirovich, I want the people on this list to be bugged. They are dangerous traffickers, and they dishonour our country. I want to know everything. Give me a thorough investigation. I am convinced that they are traitors to the country. Give me a report within ten days. Decisions will be made based on what you find out."

"Yes, sir!"

"In addition, have all our embassy personnel, without exception, screened for the past ten years."

"Yes, Colonel, I'll give instructions to that effect immediately."

"I want to know if anyone has had contact with Americans in the past."

"Understood."

"Get me the results as soon as possible."

At the same time, Mike received a call from the U.S. embassy.

"Hello?"

"Mike Robertson?"

"Yes, this is Mike Robertson."

"My name is Tony Rogers. I want to meet you at the U.S. Embassy. Is an hour possible for you?"

"I understand. Yes, I will be at your office in one hour."

"See you then."

Mike was ushered into a meeting room at the embassy. The secretary who welcomed him offered him coffee, which he accepted. After a few minutes of waiting, Tony Rogers appeared.

"Hello, I'm Tony Rogers."

"Nice to meet you."

"So tell me everything."

"Didn't anybody brief you?"

"Yes, but I'd like you to tell me everything."

So Mike took the story from the beginning.

"Now you know everything. What I'd like to know is why the man called Klotz thinks I'm in the CIA. Do you have any idea about that?"

"It's hard to say. I know that you are not CIA."

"Good thing too!"

"Tell me, has no one ever contacted you or offered you any services?"

"You mean our country's spy service?"

"Yes, or from elsewhere…"

"For that matter? You're joking, right?"

"No, not that much. It is not uncommon for people in important positions in financial institutions to be contacted by foreigners. And you, Mr Robertson, are the head of a powerful American bank in a fairly economically active Asian country. So you could attract that kind of contact."

"No, I have never been approached by anyone."

"You know your client portfolio well, I think?"

"Yes, I do."

"Could you have been in contact with people or companies that seemed suspicious… of financial malpractice, for example, or other crimes punishable by our laws?"

Mike paused at this question and seemed lost in thought. This question made him uncomfortable, and he hesitated to talk about what he discovered the day before.

"Mr Robertson, is something wrong?"

"No, it's nothing."

"Is there something you want to tell me? I'm here to help you, so speak up if you can think of anything even remotely trivial. It can always be a lead that we can dig up. Don't forget that you need protection. You know you can count on us."

"OK. I recently found out that my senior associate has relationships with Russian companies here who are clients of the bank."

"Russian companies? It's not a crime in itself to be Russian, but if I understand correctly, you are suspicious. Can you tell me?"

"I think there's a massive money-laundering operation going on."

"And your bank is involved?"

"Yes, I'm afraid so. Yesterday, I called in John Finmore, my deputy, and told him what I'd found, implicating him firmly in these operations. I took away his credentials so he wouldn't set foot in the bank again, and I'm officially firing him today."

"This is interesting. Can you give me the names of the suspected Russians?"

"Yes, I can."

Mike pulled from his pocket the paper on which he had written the names of the Russians and their companies for Andrei Safronov and handed it to him.

"Here are their names and companies."

"Thank you, sir. We will proceed with an investigation."

"Today, I will send a report of Finmore's actions to the Group's headquarters in San Francisco. You think the threats against me may have originated in these cases?"

"Anything is possible."

"Do the names I gave you mean anything to you?"

"No, I don't know them. But I would like to come back to this man who was murdered."

"Yes, I didn't know him."

"I want to believe you. I'll be honest with you. This man was a CIA agent. He worked for me. We were able to steal an extremely important document from the Russians. This is about national security, do you understand me?"

"Yes, but I have nothing to do with it. I don't even know what you are talking about."

"Yes, and with good reason, since these are secret documents. However, when our agent rushed to you, you must have had something that encouraged him to come to you. Tell me, that Star-Spangled Banner pin, do you still have it on you, on that jacket?"

"Yes, I do."

"And you were wearing that jacket when it happened?"

"Yes, that's right."

"So he knew you were a fellow countryman that explains his movement towards you. Did he hand you anything?"

"No, he just grabbed onto me when he fell, that's all."

"Are you really sure he didn't hand you anything?"

"No, I'm not."

"Tell me something else… Your wife is Russian, isn't she?"

"Yes, she is."

"Does she have any Russian connections in the country?"

"She has friends, yes."

"At the Russian embassy?"

"She is friends with the wife of an embassy official, yes. But she is a childhood friend. They were neighbours when they were children and went to school together in Russia. This is not a recent relationship that was initiated in Bangkok."

"You have to admit that it is suspicious."

"They are childhood friends. There is nothing suspicious about it."

"What exactly does her husband do?"

"He's an officer."

"What's his name?"

"Andrei Safronov."

"Safronov, you say? He's the number two man at the embassy! And you're seeing him?"

"Excuse me, but they are old friends. I've known them personally for fifteen years. He was witness at my wedding, and his wife was my wife's witness."

"And I insist, you are seeing them?"

"We don't see each other often. We invite each other three or four times a year. My wife sees her friend Olga regularly, though."

"And when was the last time you met?"

"Last night. We were invited to dinner."

"Last night? And what did you talk about?"

"Look, my wife and I don't get involved in espionage stories. We have a friendly relationship with them and nothing more."

"Please answer my question. It is very important. Moreover, if you do not cooperate with me, I can have you arrested for intelligence with a third country to the detriment of the interests of the United States. In a word, for espionage and high treason. And you can trust me to take care of you."

"Wait, but I didn't do anything wrong."

"Prove it…"

"But do you really believe that? You're completely insane."

"I only believe what I see or hear. And what I hear doesn't satisfy me. So I'll ask you again. What did you tell Safronov at your party last night? And mind you, if your answers don't satisfy me, I'll keep you here. Let's hear it."

Mike reviewed the exchanges from his evening at Safronov's.

"So at no point did he bounce back to you about your history with our agent?"

"No, he did not."

"I find that very curious since it was one of his agents that gave us the document we're looking for."

"You mean he is directly and personally involved?"

"Yes, because he is the local FSB boss. Didn't you know that? It seems unlikely to me."

"We never spoke about this together. I thought he was part of the FSB because of his previous military career, but I didn't know what level he was operating at."

"Your friend has the rank of Colonel, and it is very likely that he will be appointed General Major in the very near future... and especially if he recovers... or if he has... the document we are looking for..."

"If he has?"

"Did you give it to him?"

"You are crazy! I'm telling you I never had any document."

"We are talking about a chip, Mr Robertson. You know that because the man called Klotz came to ask you for it."

"I gave him the same answer as I gave you."

"Yes, you told me. And this Klotz probably works for the FSB. Didn't he have a Russian accent, you said?"

"Yes, he did."

"And, when it comes to recognising a Russian accent, we can trust you. By the way, how is it that your son has dual nationality, Russian and American?"

"This seems normal to me since he has parents of both nationalities."

"For me, it is not patriotic. In any case, morally, it's not clear."

"There are plenty of bi-nationals in the US and nobody has ever had a problem with that."

"Really? What about September 11? There was certainly complicity with dual nationals."

"Are you comparing my family with Islamic terrorists?"

"Only extrapolations."

"I don't accept it. My family is American and we love America."

"Then prove it! Give me the chip!"

"I never had the chip in my hands. How many times do I have to say it?"

"OK, fine. We're gonna polygraph you."

"A what?"

"Polygraph. Follow me."

"And if I refuse?"

"I'll keep you here on ice for two months and give you a polygraph anyway. And if it turns out you lied to me, you're off to prison in our fair country. Satisfied?"

Mike followed Rogers and entered a room that appeared to be an infirmary. And it was indeed a nurse who entered and invited him to sit in a chair.

"OK, sir, we're going to take a polygraph. Agent Rogers will ask you a number of questions that you must answer. Failure to answer is a negative factor that can be used against you, so you need to know that. We will measure your heart rate, skin conductance, respiratory rate, body temperature, blood pressure and pupil diameter, all simultaneously as you answer. Do you understand me?"

"Nice program. Yes, I got it. And I've always told the truth anyway."

"Well, that's what we'll be able to check."

After an hour of various questions on simple topics and then on Mike's specific situation, the experiment ended.

"Very well, Mr Robertson. I see that you have not lied to me."

"And this is a discovery for you I suppose?"

"I'm sorry, but this type of verification was necessary. It is essential that I can trust you, do you agree?"

"Yes, I understand that."

"I understand. Now, the problem is your wife. I would like you to bring her here so I can ask her some questions."

"And give her a polygraph?"

"Sorry, but it's necessary. Come tomorrow morning."

"And, by the way, she can't refuse?"

"Refusing would be bad form. And it would raise legitimate suspicions of Russian embassy intelligence. This of course to be avoided."

"OK then. I'll be there with her tomorrow at 9:00."

"Good, you're being reasonable."

"What about the safety of my family?"

"We'll keep a discreet watch on your house. If there's any danger, we'll be there."

Mike went back to the bank. After two hours of document searching, he sent a detailed report of the situation to Gordon Hoffman. Fifteen minutes later, his mobile rang.

"Hello, Mike."

"Hey, Gordon, are you still working? It's 11pm in California!"

"I'm at home, I wasn't sleeping. I got your message. What the hell is this?"

"Finmore exceeded his authority levels, he has put the bank in danger."

"You fired him?"

"Yes, I had no choice after what I discovered."

"You realise you can't get a transfer after that? You'll have to wait at least six months."

"Gordon, I can't stay here. I'm gonna quit."

"This is a very big problem, Mike. We don't have anyone to replace you at a moment's notice, especially as Finmore is no longer there. I can tell you the board is not going to like it."

"I can't do anything else, Gordon. My god, we're in danger here. I was mugged by three guys again yesterday."

"You got mugged again?"

"Yeah, I got away with it thanks to my driver who also doubles as my bodyguard."

"I'm sorry about that. But I want you to stay at your post for at least one month. You can't just leave everything and walk away."

"Lila will never agree to that."

"Send her back to San Francisco with your son and you can join her later."

"No, that won't work. And once again I'm threatened."

"Mike, you're the head of our Thailand branch. Since you arrived there the bank has been operating under your responsibility. So you're directly responsible for what Finmore did. You failed in the control operations, it's no more complicated than that. You'll have a commission of enquiry on your hands. And even if the bank gets a mega fine, you're going to face criminal proceedings that could well land you in jail. So think carefully."

"Think about what?"

"Think hard. On the other hand, it's still strange that you're threatened as a CIA agent. It is, isn't it? Word of advice, Mike, do what I tell you if you don't want things to get complicated. Do you understand me?"

Mike hung up the phone and remained dejected. He thought he could count on Hoffman's support. He saw no immediate solution, unable to gamble with the lives of his family and finding himself at the centre of a deadly spider's web.

Some BMW 740s arrived at the Shangri-La Hotel. The doors were opened by uniformed staff. Each man who got out and went to one of the lounges for an expected meeting, refreshments and a waitress giving them a warm welcome. The five men greeted each other and asked the waitress to leave them alone. They were Aleksandr Khoudovekov, Dmitri Akhremenko, Igor Gounine, Sergueï Ierkoulaïev and Artiome Siantchouk. It was the latter who started to talk.

"Comrades, as you know, we have a big problem. That idiot Klotz has failed in his mission. He couldn't get the Seumkwang chip. The dying American may have passed it on to another agent. We know who he is. His name is Mike Robertson, he's a bank officer undercover. And guess where? Golden Star Bank. He's the CEO. Where we handle our financial operations! Which means this guy can trace our business history with complete ease.

"Plus I found out that he is married to a Russian woman who is a friend of an oil woman from the Russian embassy. Finally, to top it all off, I'm contacted every day by Cheong, one of Division 39's executives and close to the Great Leader. It is obvious that North Korea holds us responsible for the loss of the chip.

"We must absolutely find it before the Russians and the Americans do. This is not only for the sake of our business but also for our power and influence in the South American and Asian markets. North Korea is a fantastic partner that can accompany us wherever it can assert a predominant political role. We have a great opportunity and we cannot pass it up. Yes, Sergei?"

"We have to get the chip back but then, we have to eliminate Robertson and his family."

"I agree. We have to make the American talk first. Then you will be in charge of making them all disappear."

"We have another problem, it's the bank's number two, John Finmore. Robertson fired him. He called me and asked me to help him."

"Help him how? Does he want money?"

"Yes, he asked me for a hundred thousand dollars. He reiterated his dedication to our interests, the idiot."

"You're not going to pay that, I hope, Artiome?"

"No, of course not. We'll eliminate him. Klotz must see him tonight to settle the matter."

"That's fine."

"Good. We'll keep each other informed of developments."

The five men left the lounge and returned to their cars.

Mike had returned to his office and informed the bank's management that John Finmore had left. Orders were given to have no contact with him in view of the operations he covered up with the Russians.

"Well, I'd like to have a chat with Steve Marsham, our local compliance officer."

"I'll call him, Mike."

"Thank you, Mary."

Steve Marsham arrived and was escorted by a young Indian associate, Arjun Gotra.

"Mike I took the liberty of bringing Arjun. Following this morning's meeting I asked him to trace all the movements of the companies run by the Russians whose names you gave us."

"All right, Steve. Hello, Arjun."

"Hi, Mike. Here's what I found out. Each company over the last three years has over a thousand movements of money. The vast majority of these are what I would call normal movements, which are trade within the country."

"In Thailand you mean?"

"Yes, that's right. A minority are international movements which are all to Belize. These are large and regular transfers. In three years, this represents $327 million $854,000 dollars, to be exact. And all this from one hundred and eighty transfers over the last three years."

"How come nobody reacted? Steve, is that your job?"

"Yes, it is. It was John Finmore who initiated all the transfers. But it was you, Mike, who approved them."

"What?"

"Yes, by signing the code to your digital key. And as CEO, you're the only one who has it. Which means that I am exempt from any written report to you, as you are my sole point of contact."

"So I can only think of one explanation: Finmore managed to recover my code. But how? It's not written anywhere."

"Yes," said Arjun. "You inevitably wrote your code in the digital operations you approved, and for a high-level computer scientist, the trail can be traced and revealed."

"Apart from you, Arjun, there is no one in this bank who would be capable of doing that. So what am I to conclude?"

"It's obviously not me. On the other hand, since we are here, it is only Finmore who could have done this… or organised it."

"Are you implying that he could have brought someone in here competent enough to retrieve my code?"

"Yes, I do. I don't see any other way."

"These Russians are a global organisation, that's clear. And they're the ones who provided the manpower for this job."

"Yes, Mike," said Steve. "That's for sure how it happened. You need to lodge a complaint immediately and request an audit of the bank's services. And especially since your signature implicates you directly, it's imperative that you can prove that the systems were breached with Finmore's complicity."

"Yes, you are right."

The same evening Aïdar Klotz met John Finmore at the Patpong night market. Their relationship seemed friendly and very relaxed. They walked quietly along the stalls displaying fake watches, fake Hermes scarves, fake Gucci bags, and glanced at the bars where gogo girls were trying to get them in. They continued on their way.

"Shall we go for a drink?"

"No John, not here. You know me, I prefer the neighbourhood next door."

"You mean the Jaruwan soi? The gay place?"

"Yes, let's have a drink there."

"OK then."

They entered the street known as Bangkok's gay hot spot. They were soon approached by the doormen of the gogos who bragged to them about their goods. Eventually, they were guided into one of the clubs and sat down to enjoy the show. There were about fifteen naked boys swaying to 80s disco music, waving unequivocally at the customers sitting in the gloom of the tables. They stayed there for about an hour and then left.

"John, we need to talk."

"Yes, of course, we do. We need to settle our business, the hundred thousand dollars your bosses owe me."

"Yeah, we'll talk about it. Let's go somewhere quiet."

They walked to a narrow alley where three men were sitting, who rushed towards them as soon as they saw them.

"Cheap sex video. Men, girls, very young. Interested? Good price! Lots of choice. Watch it! Watch it!"

Klotz then pulled out a gun and threatened the three men.

"Get the hell out of here, get out! Take your shit and get out or I'll shoot you like dogs!"

The three video salesmen picked up their stuff and ran away without asking for help. Finmore burst out laughing.

"Ah. Ah. Ah, you really scared the shit out of them!"

Klotz, with a crazed look in his eyes, came up to him and pressed the barrel of the gun to his forehead.

"Hey, what are you doing? What's wrong?"

"Yes, I'm fine, asshole. On your knees!"

"Kneel down?"

"On your knees I said. You're gonna suck my dick."

"Are you crazy?"

Klotz hit him in the nose with his pistol butt, which instantly caused a stream of blood to gush out.

"Ah, you broke my nose!"

"Suck it! Otherwise, I'll kill you."

Finmore did so in disgust.

"I got a kick out of all those pussies jerking off earlier, didn't you? Keep sucking, it will come. And I'm warning you, swallow it all or I'll punch the shit out of you, understand?"

"Hm."

He hit him on the head with the barrel of the gun.

"Did I say that right?"

"Hmmm hum."

"Well, go on then, you bastard. Faster! Faster, faster! Aah. You're a real little bitch, you bastard. Oh, that's good."

Finmore pulled away in disgust, bending down to vomit.

"Hey, asshole, don't act so disgusted. And I forbid you to throw up, you hear?"

But Finmore didn't listen and in a series of hiccups started to vomit. At that moment, Klotz pointed his gun at his head and fired. Finmore collapsed dead on the spot.

"Mission accomplished, the good with the bad is always better."

Mike returned to his villa and was greeted by his son.

"Dad, I didn't go to school today."

"Yes, I know. Didn't you get bored?"

"No, I was at the pool all the time."

"That's nice. Is mum there?"

"Yes, she's in the kitchen."

"OK."

Mike passed the maid coming out onto the terrace with some zakouski dishes and a bottle of wine. He managed to see the label which indicated that it was a Shiraz from Australia, one of his favourite wines.

"My darling, there you are. I have prepared a light meal tonight with a wine you like."

"Hello, my love. Yes, I saw what Nok was wearing."

"I wanted to surprise you."

"Actually, I'm going to surprise you, and I don't think you're going to like it."

Mike told Lila about his day and ruined the evening. Lila was very unhappy and refused to go to the American embassy for what she considered to be an aggressive interrogation. He insisted on going with her the next day to meet the head of the CIA.

Friday, 3 December 2010

Andrei Safronov was in his office at the Russian embassy. He was due to receive a visit from Polkovnik General (Colonel-General, the third highest rank in the Russian military hierarchy) Lèv Ilitch Droski, who had arrived specially from Moscow and was a member of the FSB Directorate.

"Very happy to see you again, General!"

"Hello, Andrei Sergeyevich. We have a serious problem, I am not telling you anything new. In the higher echelons, as you can imagine, there is a lot of anger. The chip has been stolen from the embassy premises, and this is absolutely unacceptable. I don't understand how anyone could get in here."

"General, I'm convinced that no one has broken into our premises. I'm thinking treason. An embassy employee."

"Do you have any idea?"

"I've been researching the background of everyone who works here, and I found out that a staffer who is attached to the cypher, Natalia Kovalenko, had a love affair with Paul Stockwell about ten years ago, when he was stationed in Moscow, at the American embassy from 1999 to 2007. I had her flat inspected and we found an envelope containing five hundred thousand dollars. So I had her arrested last night, and I've scheduled an interview for this morning."

"Interesting. I want to attend the interview."

"I was going to suggest that, General. Stockwell was murdered by a man called Aïdar Klotz, an Azerbaijani national, the son of a Ukrainian Jewish father who died an alcoholic twenty years ago and a Lezgin mother, a practising Sunni Muslim, now ninety-two years old, from a village near the border with Dagestan. He was made aware of the radicalisation speeches of the terrorists who were active in Dagestan, in particular the Lezgin independence fighters, the political-terrorist group SADVAL."

"In Derbent? We cracked down on those bastards. They are terrorists who hide behind a political image. The worst."

"Yes, General. It is very likely that he was part of the SADVAL commando group that intervened to free Kassoum Makhmoudov in July 1999."

"Makhmoudov? The man who masterminded the 1994 Baku metro bombings?"

"Yes, General."

"Do you think he could be involved in this?"

"No, I don't think so. According to our investigation, Klotz is today more attracted by money than by ideology. He has turned into a sort of mercenary and hitman. He hires out his services to the highest bidder."

"Who is his sponsor?"

"It was discovered that he works for a Russian consortium."

"A Russian consortium? What is that, a mafia? Who is it?"

"It's a group of five businessmen who control a group of local companies that are quite powerful financially. Their names are Aleksandr Khoudovekov, President of Union Thai Trade, Dmitri Akhremenko, President of National Building Corp, Igor Gounine, President of Grand Construction Thailand, Sergueï Ierkoulaïev, President of Ural Thai Corp, Artiome Siantchouk, President of Klioutchevskoï Summit Invest. All are former KGB officers who left the services when Yeltsin came to power. They helped themselves handsomely to some former state companies that they appropriated after a series of murders and bribes as part of the widespread corruption that was rampant at the time."

"Of course. Go on."

"These men are laundering huge sums of money in Belize from a local US bank. We found their henchman in this bank, who is none other than the number two man, a certain John Finmore. What is surprising is that there has been no reaction from headquarters to these financial movements. We have our doubts about the CEO of their local branch, Mike Robertson, who could be identified as a CIA agent, his position as director being his cover. But we have no formal proof of this. We have him under close surveillance."

"Right. What's next?"

"The Russians are in touch with the North Korean embassy. The man who appears to be their leader, Artiome Siantchuk, has his headquarters on the same street, Pattanakarn Road, which makes it easy for him to make contact. In the last three years, he has made seven trips to Pyongyang."

"We are in business with the North Koreans. What are they doing with them?"

"After analysis and reflection, I deduced that the North Koreans have certainly instructed their friends to get the chip back with the sole aim of ousting us. And that would be why Klotz killed Stockwell. Now I know he didn't get the chip back because he threatened Mike Robertson to give it back."

"Would this Mike Robertson have the chip? If so he would have handed it over to his handlers at the US embassy. In that case, it's war!"

"Actually, I know Mike Robertson very well. He is married to a Russian woman, a childhood friend of my wife. I don't think he has the chip."

"Did you interview him?"

"Yes, in a discreet way. He told me what happened to him and it doesn't seem that he is compromised in this case."

"But you still don't know if he's CIA?"

"We have nothing on that."

"You should investigate further and if necessary have him removed for questioning. We need to know everything, no matter what the cost. Get him to talk. With our methods! We need to get that chip back. Maybe he still has it, you never know, if he's as rotten as those Russians who betray themselves by selling out to the North Koreans. As for the North Koreans' double-dealing, I'm not really surprised. But they made a mistake: they underestimated our effectiveness. And that will pay off in due course. We have already lost a lot of time, and the Kremlin is getting impatient. I want results! Bring me that chip! You have until next week. Don't forget that your promotion to the rank of general depends on it. As well as your future position at the Lubyanka! I won't insult you by drawing you a picture if you fail. Would you like to go to Dagestan? Or would you prefer a post in Ussuriysk, in the Primorsky Krai? Take your pick, Colonel. A word of advice: don't let me down."

"You can count on me, General. I'll get the chip back to you one way or another."

"All right, then. Let's go interrogate Kovalenko."

They left the office and took a lift to the fifth basement. There, they were met by a guard who escorted them to a cell. On Safronov's orders, the guard opened the door, and the two men entered the room. Natalia Kovalenko was handcuffed, arms behind her back, sitting on a chair. Her face was tense, and she looked as if she had not slept much.

"Hello, Natalia. How are you?"

"Good morning, Colonel."

"This is General Droski. You're lucky to be visited by someone so important in our hierarchy. You must be flattered, you are someone who counts."

"So I warn you, I have no time to lose. Tell us what you did and what you know. Quick!" barked Droski.

Natalia began to shake and cry. Droski slapped her in the face with a masterly blow that knocked her off her chair. The guard rushed to sit her down again.

"You're going to talk, bitch! yells Droski."

"Natalia, did you give Stockwell the chip from the Seumkwang programme that we are developing with North Korea? Safronov asked in a soft voice."

"Yes," she replies, crying.

"Did you get money for it?"

"Yes, I did."

"How much did you get?"

"Five hundred thousand dollars."

"You betrayed your country, you know that?"

"Yes, I know that."

"Why did you do it?"

"My parents are sick and can't afford to pay for their care."

"And you betrayed for that?"

"Yes, I needed that money to pay for the care they need."

"Where do your parents live?"

"In Irkutsk."

"There's a state hospital there. And it's free."

"They went there, the doctors don't do anything. They don't care. You have to go to private clinics you know, if you want to be treated."

"That's ridiculous. Your mind is corrupted, poor Natalia. I can't help you."

Droski pulled out his pistol and shot Natalia twice in the heart, she died instantly.

"Safronov, now we must move on with this case."

"Yes, General."

Safronov took Drosky home. He then called Chelagin.

"Have you made any progress?"

"Yes, Colonel. We've just learned that the number two man at Golden Star Bank was murdered last night. John Finmore, remember?"

"The one who was in league with the traitors?"

"Yes, he was. Shot in the head. We had him under surveillance since yesterday. It was Klotz who dealt with him. He was with him all evening".

"Either they got rid of him because he was blackmailing them, since he'd been fired from the bank the day before, or he had the chip and gave it back. Did you witness his execution?"

"No, I arrived too late. I think about ten minutes later. There was a crowd and police but it was him, I saw him."

"I want Klotz removed as soon as possible. Don't waste time, I want him interrogated and I want him to spill his guts. There's no time to lose, start hunting immediately."

"Yes, sir."

Mike and Lila arrived at the American embassy. They were greeted by a smiling Tony Rogers.

"Hello, Mike. Do you mind if I call you Mike?"

"Yes, good. This is my wife, Lila."

"Nice to meet you, Lila. Tony Rogers. I'm delighted to meet you. We talked about you a lot yesterday. It's good you're here."

"I'm not as pleased as you to be here."

"Now, now, don't worry. If you're not to blame, you're in the clear. You see, Mike, we're in complete confidence now, and everything is fine."

"That's putting it mildly."

"Come, follow me. Mike, you can come with us of course. But you'll have to wait for us in the small meeting room next to our technical room."

"I wish to have my husband with me."

"Unfortunately, that's not possible. It's a question of technique and psychology. I'm sorry. But you will see him as soon as we have finished, I promise you that."

Lila entered the room after Rogers. The nurse, or woman who looked like a nurse, was already there and was busy with the equipment.

"Are these your instruments of torture?"

"Hello, Mrs Robertson. Yes, as you say. But don't worry, it's all perfectly painless. We are going to ask you some questions that you must answer. An unanswered question would put you in a delicate situation and would be interpreted as a refusal to collaborate."

"Yes, I understand."

"Very good."

The technician gave Lila a further explanation of how the lie detector works and installed it. Tony Rogers also took a seat opposite her.

"What is your name?"

"Lila Robertson."

Simple questions about her and her husband's situation and problems followed.

"Very good, Lila, it's a no-brainer."

"I'm glad."

"Oh, one more question: do you like the United States?"

"Yes, I do."

"Do you like Russia?"

"Yes, I do."

"Good."

"Are you done?"

"Yes, we are."

"What do you think?"

"Too bad you like Russia."

"I'm Russian."

"I know you are."

"Is that a problem?"

"It's always a problem to have two countries."

"I don't see it as a problem. It is rather a cultural enrichment."

"Everyone has their own point of view."

After releasing Lila from her seat, Rogers walked her back to the meeting room where Mike was waiting.

"Everything went well. Your wife is clean."

"Good. So we can count on your protection for the rest of our time here?"

"I told you, yes. Are you planning to leave the country soon?"

"A month, I think."

"Mike, we said faster than that, remember?"

"Lila, I still have some things to put in order. I told you that."

They left the embassy. Mike called his driver and asked him to take Lila back to the villa. He took a taxi to the bank.

When he arrived at the bank, he took the lift to the executive floor. Just outside, his secretary beckoned him to join her. She pointed out two Thai men who were sitting in the meeting room.

"Mike, these two gentlemen from the Bangkok Crime Squad."

"Crime Squad? What do they want?"

"They wouldn't tell me anything except that they would wait as long as it takes to meet you."

"What's all this about? As if I didn't have enough problems."

Mike went into his office and asked his secretary to bring him the two policemen.

"Good morning, gentlemen."

"Good morning, sir. Are you the managing director of the bank, Mr Mike Robertson?"

"Yes, I am."

"I am Major Khun Buncha Yoobamroong of the Criminal Investigation Department, and this is my deputy, Lieutenant Khun Sutichai Larpthawornkiet."

"And to what do I owe your visit?"

"Can you confirm that Mr John Finmore is employed here?"

"Yes, he was. He's been dismissed. Are you looking for him?"

"Should we?"

"I don't know, but since he lost his job, maybe he did something wrong?"

"Actually, he's dead."

"Is that not possible?"

"He was murdered by a bullet in the head at close range."

"Murdered? That's terrible."

"Yeah, it is. You knew him well, I take it?"

"I knew him in our professional capacity. We didn't socialise outside the bank. I knew almost nothing about his private life."

"You knew nothing about his relationships, his friends?"

"No, I didn't."

"Did you know he was gay?"

"No. He was married. His wife's name is Helen."

"Yes, we've already informed her. It seems she also knew nothing about her husband's sexual proclivities. Poor woman. We investigated and were able to trace his schedule for the last few hours. He spent about an hour in a gay gogo in Patpong with another man, a European from what we were told, possibly his boyfriend."

"Do you have any idea what happened?"

"The body was found in an alley about hundred metres from the club they were in. Maybe a jealousy drama, who knows, maybe it was his lover. We had an autopsy done at the forensic institute at Siriraj Hospital. He was vomiting when he was killed. Whisky and semen were found in his stomach."

"What?"

"Yes, he most likely performed oral sex on his boyfriend before he died. That's why we think there was a domestic scene between them. And so this is the man who killed him, according to the witnesses who saw him leave, his description matches the description given to us by the gay club employees."

"It's unbelievable. I could never have imagined that about him."

"But tell me, Mr Mike, we saw that you gave a statement in a police station as a witness to a murder a few days ago."

"Yes, I did."

"There's a lot going on around you."

"It's beyond my control, believe me."

"It's a bit strange, don't you think?"

"I have nothing to do with these events. I'm just unlucky, that's all."

"Well, that's that. Yes. Do you have any statements to make? Have you noticed anything?"

"No, I told you, the relationship I had with John Finmore was limited to the professional world."

"All right, fine. I'll leave you my card, in case something comes up, you never know."

"OK, fine. Thank you."

"Oh, yes, one other thing, I forgot. Are you planning to travel?"

"You mean outside Thailand?"

"Yes... That won't be possible for the moment... at least until the investigation file is closed. We need you to remain at our disposal... you understand... it's routine..."

"I have to go to the US next week."

"I'm afraid you'll have to postpone... unless we find out more about this murder than I think we will... we never know..."

"But this trip is scheduled..."

"I'm sorry. Don't try to run away, you'll get arrested at the border. And you'll be in serious trouble with the law..."

In Langley, Virginia, at CIA headquarters, Charly Williams, Director of the East Asia Division, summoned his top aides Ron Parson and Bob Rimino for a videophone meeting with the head of Thailand, Tony Rogers.

"Good, everyone's here. Tony, can you hear us well?"

"Yes, sir."

"OK, let's have an update on the situation. Ron?"

"Yes, sir. So we have a problem with the Wikileaks leak. Classified documents have been released relating to CR87. That is, the agreements that we uncovered between North Korea and Russia. There are about thirty documents on the net. You might as well say everything that has been produced in this department. Today the press has not picked up on this. I would say... not yet. But it's a safe bet that it won't be long."

"Fucking hell, if I had the bastard who did this!"

"I know, sir. But we have no choice but to adapt and find solutions very quickly."

"Bob?"

"Yes, sir. We had already made a point with Tony. It's not brilliant. We have nothing."

"This can't be right! What are you being paid for, Tony? To screw the little Thai girls? You've got to be kidding me! You'd better get your fingers out of your asses and get back to us as soon as possible, got it?"

"Yes, sir."

"Bob, you told me about an American who's a director of the Golden Star Bank?"

"Yes, sir. Tony polygraphed him and his wife, there's nothing there. They're not involved."

"But finally, are we sure that Stockwell got that chip back? Tony, did you inspect his body or not?"

"I did, sir. I was able to bribe the morgue attendant and I searched him, he had nothing on him."

"So I ask again, did he really have that chip with him?"

"As you know, he had managed to make contact with a Russian at the embassy..."

"Hell yes, I know that. I especially know that we had to throw five hundred thousand dollars at the son of a bitch to get the chip back. Uncle Sam is tired of paying for things, guys!"

"Yes, sir. We all know that here."

"Yes, Bob, here, yes without a doubt. But over there in Bangkok we're taking it easy and that's not acceptable. Right, Tony? It's a party every night, isn't it?"

"Excuse me, sir, but I can assure you that we are doing our job."

"Yes, Tony, we have the proof, the fruits and the consequences… which are bound to happen if it continues on the same track. Get the fuck moving! I demand results! We have a sword of Damocles hanging over our heads with these asshole journalists, not to mention the Oval Office which is waking up to the subject! I don't suppose you want me to come and do the investigation for you?"

"No, sir, I don't. You can count on me, we're going to work twice as hard. To complete what I started to say, it seems that the contact we had at the Russian embassy has disappeared."

"Of course, he left with the money."

"It's not certain, sir. In fact, it looks like she was murdered. A few days ago, a corpse was fished out of the Chao Praya River in Bangkok."

"She? A woman?"

"Yes, sir."

"And Stockwell told you that the chip had been handed over to him, can you confirm that?"

"Yes, sir. The day he was killed we had contact."

"It's probably an FSB hit. I'm waiting for the results of your research Tony. And quickly."

"Very good, sir."

Tony Rogers called Doris, his secretary, and asked to be joined in his office by Captain Frank Sheldon, also of the CIA, and in charge of sensitive missions. Sheldon arrives and sits down opposite Rogers, as the secretary entered the office and handed Rogers a paper.

"A message?"

"Yes, Tony, it just came through. It's from the police in Bangkok, informing us of the death of an American citizen. I think you'll find it interesting."

"Let's see…Oh, John Finmore…murdered…."

"That's the number two guy at Golden Star Bank?"

"Yes, Frank. He was suspected of colluding with a local Russian mafia. He was probably executed by them. I'll call Mike Robertson, I'm curious to get his reaction."

"Did the Thai police send photos of the body?"

"I think so. Doris, go and see if we've received any since…"

"OK."

"I'll call Robertson… Hello, Mike? It's Tony Rogers. Did you hear what happened to John Finmore?"

"Hi. Yes. The Thai police are on their way out of my office and get this, they've just told me I can't leave the country while the investigation is ongoing. Can you believe it? I was planning to return to the US in the next fortnight while I put my successor in place. Could you intervene with them to free me from this problem?"

"No, that's not possible. Do you have any idea who might have eliminated him?"

"Maybe the Russians for whom he made the bank transfers?"

"I think the same thing. Have the police given you their view?"

"No, they didn't tell me anything. They just informed me what had happened."

"I see. Well, cheer up, Mike. And have a good day."

"Thank you too."

Tony Rogers hung up and turned to Frank Sheldon.

"Did you hear that, Frank?"

"Yes. We're going to follow up on that."

"Did you read the report on Robertson? Remember: he mentioned a guy who approached him in a restaurant. He said he had a Russian accent and that his name was Klotz. Well, I'll give you this: I'm convinced that's where we have to look for the chip and Finmore's murderer. It's all very convoluted. And that brings us back to the Russian mobsters who will probably want to sell this chip they must now have. Unless they're working undercover for North Korea, which is also a reasonable assumption."

"Yes, well-reasoned. I share that belief."

"Let's get to work, Frank. We need to untangle this web and get to the chip before the FSB does. At Langley, Williams is like a madman. He had a fit earlier on, calling us incompetent and lazy. He couldn't stop. He's put me under a lot of pressure, we need to get results as soon as possible. Take a team of three technicians with you. I want you to visit the offices of the Russian Five."

"OK, Tony. I've got it."

Night of Friday to Saturday, 3-4 December 2010

Around midnight, a car drove towards the Ramkhamhaeng district. The driver was Sam Chenney, and the passengers were Frank Sheldon, Peter Keldrick and Jack Wang, all CIA agents, on a mission to penetrate the secrets of the Russian companies owned by the five oligarchs suspected by Tony Rogers of collusion with the North Korean embassy. They arrived at a small four-storey building on Rom Klao Road and park opposite. They got out of the car, armed with their revolvers and each carrying a briefcase containing their working tools, which should enable them to bypass the security systems and enter unhindered for a systematic search. On the roof, in red letters, UNION THAI TRADE was proudly displayed.

Peter Keldrick went ahead of his colleagues, and within a minute, he used his computer to identify the security system and turn off the alarms. They entered the reception area and began a systematic tour of the rooms, inspecting desks, cupboards, and any storage space they came across on their way. After an hour, Frank Sheldon, who was in Aleksandr Khoudovekov's office, discovered a file in a drawer with PODNIMATSYA STAL written on it in Russian. He opened it and found some building plans. One in particular caught his eye, which he identified as the plans for the American embassy.

He took photos of each plan and sent them digitally to Tony Rogers. Jack Wang broke into the company's computer system. He went into various folders and found a file called PS. He displayed the file and found exchanges between the Russian Five. There was a lot of correspondence about money transfers to Belize but also about the famous CR87 file.

Wang inserted a USB stick and downloaded all the files. It was 1:30 in the morning. They left the Union Thai Trade headquarters and got back into their car. They headed for the Phahonyothin district, this time to visit the headquarters of the National Building Corp.

It was not too far, and they quickly arrived at their destination and parked on Ram Intra Road. They entered in the same way as in the previous building and started searching for any suspicious documents that would allow them to deepen their knowledge. They found various documents, including a folder in which writings relating to Podnimatsya Stal were filed. This name appeared to be an association of the five oligarchs, making it an evil group. Photographs were taken.

Wang also easily penetrated the computer's hard drive and downloaded the documents that seemed worthy of interest onto the USB stick. In less than an hour, they emerged and returned to their vehicle. It was twenty past two, and they set off again for their third objective, Grand Construction Thailand which was located on Ratchadaphisek Road. They positioned their car just in front of the building. However, they noticed that unlike the previous buildings, this one was guarded.

There were two men at the reception who seemed to be sleeping in armchairs. They were carrying revolvers on their belts. The four Americans slowly approached the large glass door. It was a sliding door that should open automatically when approached, but here it was closed. It was decided that Sam Chenney should go and knock on the door pretending to be ill to encourage the two guards to open it.

He arrived with one hand on his heart and the other drumming on the door. The guards immediately woke up and approached the closed door. At that moment, Sam collapsed face down on the door and started to vomit. The guards immediately opened the door, insulting Sam copiously, and one of them wanted to kick him to prevent him from continuing to soil the door, which they would have to clean. But, surreptitiously, the American agent reached into his back trouser pocket with his right hand and pulled out his Beretta M9, directly threatening the two men, who were stunned by the surprise.

His three companions came running in, disarmed the guards, bound and gagged them and locked them in a broom wardrobe after knocking them out with a rifle butt to the back of the neck. And, again, the same ballet took place with the visit to the premises, the search for compromising documents and digital downloads on USB sticks. They also found links to what they think was a mafia-type association, the now-famous Podnimatsya Stal. At 3:00 in the morning, they were in their car for the Ural Thai Corp, which was in the centre of the city, on Sukhumvit Road, at the junction of Ekkamai Road. It was a very large building in which a large number of companies had their commercial offices and headquarters.

There were also cafes and restaurants. There was also a corridor that led to the Sky Train, Bangkok's aerial metro. There was no parking on the street, but they saw access to an overhead car park next to the building. They walked down the corridor and reached a barrier where a security guard gave them a ticket and opened the barrier. They went up from floor to floor and finally reached the ninth floor of the car park where they parked their car.

They then took a lift and went to the reception where a guard was slumped behind a marble counter. They asked where they could find the Ural Thai Corp. But the guard explained that it has his first night, he had just been hired, and he did not know the companies in the building. But, at this time of night, they wouldn't find anyone anyway, and it would be better to come back in the morning so they could get the information they wanted. Frank Sheldon kindly thanked the guard and took his team to wander around the huge complex.

After ten minutes or so, they finally arrived at a vast lobby and froze in front of a wall some fifty metres high where brass plaques were displayed with the name of each tenant or co-owner company in the building. And, among them, they found that of Ural Thai Corp. on the ninth floor. In fact, on the same floor as their parking space, but opposite. So they went up to this level and realised that they would have only had to go through the door of the car park to find themselves where they were now.

They found themselves in front of a wooden door, and they soon realise that it is armoured. Sam Cheney is the expert for this kind of job. He gets out his tools and manages to open the door, while Jack Wang disables the alarm system with his computer. They then entered the offices, which, to their surprise, only had a reception area and four other rooms of about twenty square metres each. The furnishings, however, were much more luxurious than those of the other companies they visited.

On a small platform in the reception area was a motorbike of the URAL brand, with a small sign: model M72, 1944, Irbitski Mototsikletny Zavod. It was as good as new despite its age and was much admired by the small group. The same scenario was then repeated, and the information was again downloaded, photographed and recorded. Again, information was found about Podnimatsya Stal. They set off again and returned to their car.

They stopped at the security guard's post, Chenney handed him the ticket and paid the hundred baht he was asked to pay. It was four in the morning. They left for the financial company, as it was called, Klioutchevskoï Summit Invest, located on Pattanakarn Road in the Suan Luang district. Sam Chenney was driving fast because it would soon be daylight. Time was of the essence.

The address he had been given was in a small street probably adjacent to the main avenue, soi (small street in Thai) number 28, the minor streets leading to the main avenues often having the same name as the main avenues but with a number, which was the case here. He finally spotted soi twenty-eight and goes in. When they reached the building, they realised that it was a private house and that the immediate neighbour was none other than the North Korean diplomatic mission. Moreover, the place was well guarded, with Thai policemen in front of the Korean building and private guards in front of the company's headquarters. They counted a good dozen of them.

They decided to continue without stopping and headed back to the US embassy. The traffic was getting a little heavier. They arrived at their destination; it was five o'clock in the morning. Frank Sheldon separated from his colleagues who were returning to their respective homes and went straight to his office to prepare for the meeting that would take place in three hours with his superior, Tony Rogers.

Saturday, 4 December 2010

It was eight o'clock in the morning, and Tony Rogers entered Sheldon's office.

"Hello, Frank, how did you sleep?"

"Did you make up this joke yourself?"

"We were able to visit all the companies except Klioutchevskoï Summit Invest. It was already early, the day was about to break, and on top of that, there was a very high level of security with armed guards. And it's right next to the North Korean embassy, which is guarded by the police. To go there you'd need a squadron."

"And the harvest?"

"It's good. Everything's downloaded."

"OK, I'll get our analysts on it, get a summary. The last company, we're going to try and infiltrate from the inside. I think Jack, who is of Chinese descent, would be a perfect fit. We'll work on that scenario. That's good, you can congratulate the team. Get some rest. I'll see you Monday morning."

"All right. I'll see you Monday morning. Bye, Tony."

"Bye, Frank."

In the morning, Aïdar Klotz came out of Chatuchak Market, the big market in Bangkok that took place every weekend. He liked to stroll through the aisles and enjoyed a typical Thai lunch with a local beer in one of the many bars where a colourful melting pot of tourists and locals gathered. He arrived on the street bordering the market, always jammed with marauding taxis and tuk-tuk drivers looking for customers, trying to negotiate fares that were often twice as high as the metres they were legally supposed to use.

Klotz knew all about them, having lived in Bangkok for a decade. He had stopped on the pavement and scanned the waving pack, looking for the person he was going to speak to. He had received a message from Siantchouk asking him to identify a vehicle. Suddenly, a van slowly arrived and pulled up to him.

The side door opened, and two men grabbed him by the shoulders and pulled him into the van.

Everything happened very quickly, and nobody noticed anything. It seemed as if Klotz had climbed into the vehicle of his own free will, so much so that he was not even aware that he was there, the coordination of the manoeuvre was so precise and fast. Immediately, Klotz received a shock from a stun gun, which made him lose consciousness. The van drove for an hour, during which time two more electric shocks were administered to keep him unconscious and finally to a riverside shed in the Phra Khanong district.

The vehicle entered the shed, and the two men carried him down a flight of stairs into an underground passage. They followed a corridor and entered a small cell-like room. There they left Klotz lying on the floor. Another man arrived, the driver of the van. He stripped Klotz of all his clothes and, with the help of the other two, stood him up and tied his hands with handcuffs to iron bars running across the room.

He was thus left hanging by his hands, with the tips of his feet touching the floor and completely naked. One of the men attached each foot to a ring on the floor, giving the view of a man being torn apart. The driver then grabbed a bucket of water and threw it over the prisoner, which had the effect of reviving him. Klotz looked around and suddenly understood the situation.

"What do you want from me? Who are you?"

The three men paid no attention to him. They left the room and lock the door, leaving him in total darkness. After two hours, the door opened, and five men entered. They turned on the light. Klotz recognised the two men who kidnapped him and the driver. He did not know the other two. One of them, who appeared to be their leader, addressed him in Russian.

"Hello, Aïdar Klotz."

"Are you Russian?"

"Yes, Aïdar. I am Russian. And what are you? A scumbag! That's your nationality. Scumbag. I'm sure you agree with me, don't you Aïdar?"

"Who are you working for? You're risking a lot. When they find out I'm missing, they'll look for me... and they'll find you. You can already consider yourself dead. Do you hear? You are dead!"

"You've got a big mouth on you, haven't you, boys?"

The four men burst out laughing.

"Let's get down to business. I want you to tell me where you put the chip, you know what I mean?"

"No, I don't."

"Do you like playing the fool? I wouldn't advise it. Now, it's very simple: either you answer me intelligently, or my executioner will take care of you. And don't worry, he's a real professional. Do you know us Russians?"

"I don't have a chip."

"Boris, it's your turn."

One of the men designated as the executioner approached Klotz. He held a briefcase and stopped in front of him. He crouched down and opened his briefcase. He pulled out a hammer and, with one swift, impressively forceful blew, struck the two smallest toes of the prisoner's right foot, who screamed in pain.

"Where did you put the chip?"

"I don't have it. That's right. I don't have it."

The man waved his eyes at the executioner who brought the hammer down on the two smallest toes of the left foot. Klotz screamed again.

"Where did you put the chip?"

"I swear, I don't have it. I never had it."

"Did you kill the American agent?"

"Yes, I did."

"Did you also kill the man in the bank?"

"Yes, I did."

"Who do you work for?"

"A Russian conglomerate. We're on the same side, you and I. Believe me."

"Is Siantchuk in charge?"

Klotz was astonished for a moment. The man looked at the executioner and nodded. And the hammer fell with the same violence as on the previous occasions on Klotz's knee. Klotz's face turned up in fear as he understood the man's sign to the executioner, and he shrieked with an inhuman cry of pain.

"Is Siantchuk in charge? A word of advice: answer me quickly and without any attempt at a lie. I can't stand not being answered, it's very impolite. And I don't like rudeness, it makes me worse. Answer my question."

"Yes, Siantchuk is the boss."

"And so it's him I should be afraid of?"

"Yes, it is."

"I'm going to reassure you, Aïdar: I'm not scared of him. It's him who should be afraid. You know why Aïdar, don't you? You know now why you should be afraid of me too?"

"Yes, I do."

"Tell me something else. Who does Siantchuk work for?"

"He works with the North Korean government."

"OK, good answer."

"Who's his contact?"

"I don't know. All I know is he's in regular contact with them. He's been to North Korea a lot. And he is in contact with their embassy."

"Who is his contact at the embassy?"

"I don't know. I swear I don't know."

"Why did you go after the manager of the Golden Star Bank?"

"I think he's the one with the chip. He's a CIA agent."

"You have proof he's a CIA agent?"

"I do. I'm sure he is."

"You didn't answer my question."

"I don't have proof. But we all do."

"Who's us?"

"Siantchuk and the North Koreans."

"Who else are you working for?"

"I'm not working for anyone."

"I don't believe you. Boris to you!"

"No, please!"

With a gesture of the head, the man stopped the hand of the executioner.

"Then speak."

"But I swear, I don't work for anyone else. Please!"

"I know everything about you, Aïdar. Even if you particularly enjoy having your cock sucked by guys; does that bring back memories? And I imagine that a big faggot like you likes to be fucked? So you see, now that you have nothing more to teach me, I'm going to give you a nice present. I know that plastic surgery is not for everyone. Go ahead, Boris."

The executioner took out a butcher's knife and approached Klotz. Klotz had a horrified face and was screaming in panic. He swung his body with all his might but could do nothing to escape his fate.

The executioner took a firm grip on his penis and slashed it lengthwise, gently up to the pubic bone. The penis was cut in two, blood spurting profusely. The executioner stepped aside so that everyone could enjoy the spectacle. The men laughed.

"Look, it looks like he has two cocks now!"

"Hey, Boris, cut them off and put them in his mouth. Let him eat his cocks!"

And the executioner went back to work, cutting off the two halves of the penis, cutting the scrotum and pulling out the two testicles, emasculating Klotz for good, and he screamed even more. He picked up one half of the penis and forced it into Klotz's mouth, forcing him to swallow it. The other men gloated and congratulated the executioner on the spectacle he had put on.

Finally, the executioner took a percussion hammer drill out of his suitcase.

"Put the drill in his ass, he likes to be fucked!" shouted one of the men.

The executioner went behind Klotz and shoved the drill bit into his anus, the drill running at full speed. Klotz screamed. After ten seconds, the executioner stopped. There was blood everywhere.

"Listen to me carefully, Klotz. Before you die, I want you to know who I am. My name is Andrei Safronov, a colonel of the FSB. What you have been through is nothing compared to what I have in store for your mafia friends. Too bad you won't be able to tell them. Give my regards to the devil!"

Safronov pulled out his pistol and put a bullet through his head.

"I never had the soul of a torturer, that's why I put him out of his misery."

"You're still too good a colonel."

"You can't do it again, Boris. You can't do it over again."

And the two men left laughing.

Sunday, 5 December 2010

Mike and his family were having lunch on their terrace. Nok, the maid was serving.

"Mike, you know we should have left today if everything had gone well. I can't take another week of living here."

"But I told you, you and Marat can leave, and I'll join you as soon as possible."

"What does that mean, Mike, as soon as possible? That's not an answer."

"Lila, you understand that I can't give up my job now. The bank's management has threatened me with criminal proceedings by making me take the rap for John Finmore's wrongdoing. And now that he's dead, it's even worse. They can pretend they don't know what he did. And you know how much lawyers cost in our country. We'd give up everything we have for a result that couldn't be more random. And I have no desire to lose what we have already acquired with great effort."

"So there is no solution. I don't want to leave you alone. I won't leave without you. You know that."

"Yes, I know that. I need to assemble enough evidence of mafia collusion between Finmore and the heads of these Russian companies. So I can't be sued by the bank. Especially, since if I resign, they won't hesitate to charge me with anything they can find."

"And you think you can do it?"

"I'm working on it with my compliance officer. We should be able to update a number of things. The problem is, I need time to gather this information."

"You mean we'll need more time?"

"Yes, darling. Again, I have no choice. Unless the bank were to fire me, but then that would mean they'd be engaging in hostilities with heavy ammunition against me."

"And how much longer do you think?"

"A month at the most. Not much longer."

"A month? That's terrible."

"I'm sorry. Besides, the Thai police asked me to stay at their disposal while they finish their investigation into Finmore's murder."

"God, how much longer do we have to put up with these horrors? Mike, we're gonna have to put Marat back in school."

"He could be home-schooled. Can you follow him?"

"You know, he speaks better English than I do, and I don't know the American curriculum."

"Yeah, of course, you do."

"We'll put him back in school. But I don't want him to take the school bus. It's too dangerous, it makes too many stops, and anything can happen. I want Thanit to take him and pick him up. I will go with them. And I will wait for him at the school gate. Thanit will come with me for our protection. What do you think?"

"Yes, I agree. Let's do it that way. I'll take a taxi to get around. You keep the car with you."

"That's fine."

"Marat, do you want to come for a swim in the pool?"

"Yes, dad, I'll take the ball!"

Artiome Siantchouk had gathered his co-religionists in his house, which also served as his office and activity centre on Pattanakarn Road. He had a bad day face and appeared very angry.

"Igor, you have something important to tell us."

"Yes, Artiome. There were four men who broke into my office on Saturday night. They neutralised my two guards and went around I think. My computer was hacked. According to the guards they are British or American."

"Igor, they are certainly Americans. They are looking for the chip, it's obvious."

"Yes, Aleksandr, I think so."

"All right, listen up. You must check if you have not been robbed too. I'm telling you this because on Saturday at about four in the morning, my guards spotted a car with four guys driving slowly, I would say too slowly, past my house. I asked Cheong to provide me with the tape of the images at that time of the day because they obviously passed in front of the embassy. And these images are there. I had them loaded and look, it's a Toyota Camry and you can see quite clearly the driver: Caucasian. And look, we're lucky, we can read the registration: you see? I asked Klotz to go to the Department of Land Transport to see who owns this car. He was going to go there on Saturday, he knows one of the officials who works there. It's next to Chatuchak Market. I was waiting for him to call, but the jerk hasn't called me back yet. I tried to call him several times but he doesn't answer. He must have gone to get drunk in the market's bars. Anyway, tomorrow morning he has to be here at 8:00. But I asked a guard what was written on the plate, it's Bangkok. We'll soon know who came to your place, Igor. And you, Serguei, you didn't notice anything? Dmitri, you either?"

"No, Artiome, but I'll have my computers checked."

"Yes, I will do the same."

"I think it's urgent to do it. I'll bet they went to your place. I'll call Klotz again, you never know… He doesn't fucking answer."

"Artiome, I think our friend Klotz is in trouble. Look, he's never there when we need him, he screws up on every mission. Well, he did take out that bastard Finmore. But still, the results are not up to scratch. And we're paying dearly for it… too dearly considering what we're getting."

"You're right, Aleksandr. We'll give him another chance. I want him to take out the director of the Golden Star Bank, this Robertson. I want to get him to talk. I'm sure he has the chip."

"All right, I'll do it. If he fucks up this mission, we'll have to get rid of him."

Around midnight, a car passed on Pattanakarn Road and slowed down at the Klioutchevskoi Summit Invest building. At that moment, the left rear door opened, and a naked corpse was thrown at an approaching guard. It was Aïdar Klotz. The car accelerated suddenly and disappeared into the night.

Artiome Siantchouk looked at the corpse of Aïdar Klotz lying on the pavement. He saw the torture he had suffered. He remained very puzzled. Not wanting the police to interfere in his affairs, he ordered his guards to make the body disappear. Two men lifted the body and laid it on a tarpaulin. They covered it up and carried it to the back of a van. They load a bag of quicklime and drive off.

Mike Robertson arrived at his office. His phone rang. It was Steve Marsham asking to see him.

"Hello, Mike."

"Hello, Steve. Have you got any news?"

"Yes. We've traced all the transfers from the five companies. They all have John Finmore's signature on them, without exception. And, obviously, there's your control signature all over them."

"Unfortunately, that was to be expected."

"But we have discovered something interesting. Your signatures were introduced into the system afterwards."

"What do you mean?"

"The first transfer took place on Thursday, 8 February 2007. Your signature was inserted on Sunday, 25 February. The second transfer was executed on Friday, 9 March. And your confirmation signature was inserted on Sunday, March 11. The third transfer was executed on Wednesday, 18 April. And your signature is dated Sunday, 22 April. And so on. The last transfer was made on Tuesday, 16 November 2010. And your signature is dated 21 November."

"That means Finmore was here every Sunday with a specialist."

"Yes, it's obvious. We have taken all the videos over the past twelve months, that's the farthest we can go. It is clear that the Sundays in question have a time span of about twenty minutes that has been deleted. There is a break in each case."

"All of this can already be recorded in a report."

"Here is the report."

"Excellent."

"The problem, Mike, is that even if your signature was forged, you should have known about these transfers."

"Yeah, I know. I know. But Finmore kept me in the dark."

"I pulled up the monthly reporting slips that go to headquarters. The amounts of the transfers appear normal. You were never questioned?"

"You mean by the head office? No. I mean, they could have responded."

"They should have reacted, Mike. That's a point for you in your defence if they ever come after you."

"You're right, Steve. They should have alerted me and they didn't. That's a fault on their part, legally speaking."

"Now if we could just get some information on Finmore's accomplice…"

"Right now we have nothing. But Finmore's wife, maybe she knows something. You should contact her, you never know."

"Yes, that's a good idea. The funeral is scheduled for this afternoon at two o'clock. I wasn't planning on going, but I'll go. That way I can try and talk to Helen."

"She might not take it very well, an interrogation after her husband's funeral…"

"We mustn't forget that we're dealing with an assassination. Questions are warranted."

"Good luck then, Mike."

"I hope I have some of it to get the information we need."

"By the way, did you know he was a Buddhist?"

"No, I didn't. I saw that the ceremony was on the Ekkamai side, but I thought it was a Catholic church or a Protestant temple?"

"No, it's not. It's in a Buddhist temple, Wat Tha Thong."

"I had no idea. What about his wife? Is she a Buddhist too?"

"Yes, absolutely. But they were already converted to this cult in the United States. That was when they were young, and I understand they met through that. Did you know that they were both native Hawaiians?"

"I knew he was born in Honolulu, it's in his file. But I didn't know about Helen."

"There's the explanation. And you may know that the highest concentration of Buddhists in the United States is in Hawaii?"

"No, I didn't know that. Thanks for the information, though. I'll look less stupid when I approach Helen."

Mike arrived at the temple. The taxi pulled into the car park and stopped in front of the large gate. He paid his fare and went to look for a room among the many places used for ceremonies. He finally found it. The room was festively decorated and heavily air-conditioned.

He walked over to Helen to offer his condolences. She thanked him with an appropriate smile. There were about fifty people present. Bank employees Mike greeted, a few Thai couples, probably religious relations. Mike stared at the people he did not know, imagining that it was possible that the accomplice who accompanied John was among these people who had come to pay their last respects.

Suddenly, Mike heard his name being called behind him. He turned around and recognised Major Buncha Yoobamroong and his colleague Sutichai. They greeted each other in silence. Mike then approached the coffin which was placed on a platform covered with flowers. A white thread emerged from the coffin, which was a symbol of the last moments that the relatives had with the deceased.

Mike bowed down, lighted a stick of incense, meditated for a few moments, and went to a table where a basket held the gifts of the guests. He placed an envelope in the basket like everyone else. He then approached a buffet where a waiter offered him various fruit juices or mineral water. There was a strange good mood. He took a glass of pineapple juice.

The door opened, and four monks entered. They sat behind the podium carrying the coffin and began to recite sutras in chorus. Twenty minutes later, the monks left; the ceremony was over. Porters entered and took the coffin away for cremation. Most people took their leave of the widow. Helen remained alone, waiting for her husband's urn to be brought to her. Mike approached her.

"I am so sorry Helen. What happened to John was really awful."

"Yes, Mike, but you know, he's on his way to another life now. And I hope he lives happily. Because I know that his karma hasn't been reached yet."

"You believe in reincarnation, don't you?"

"Yes, of course, Mike. That's why even though I'm obviously sad that he's gone, I know he'll soon be reborn."

"Tell me, Helen, I know this is not the time, but I have a question. You know I think Mike had a friend that he sometimes went out with on Sundays?"

"Do you know anything about that?"

"I had a friendly relationship with John, and sometimes we would talk about our weekends together. And I remember that he liked to spend time with this friend from time to time. But I can't remember his name."

"But he was there. You didn't see him?"

"Actually, John had told me a lot about him but he hadn't introduced me to him."

"His name is Payom."

"Payom? Payom what?"

"Payom. That's it."

"You don't know his last name?"

"No, I don't know his last name. You know, Thai last names are complicated."

"He's Thai?"

"He is. Didn't John tell you that? That's surprising."

"Yes… Yes, he did. Maybe, as we talk…"

"Yes, there's no way he didn't tell you."

"I would have loved to talk to him. Do you know how I can contact him?"

"I can give you his mobile number. Wait… Here, are you writing this down?"

"Yes, thank you."

"Well, I see the cremation is over. I'll leave you to it, I have to go and get the urn and pay for the ceremony."

"Thanks again, Helen. And cheer up."

"Thanks, Mike. Goodbye, Mike."

Mike went to the avenue and hailed a taxi. He headed back to the bank. He was amazed at the information he was able to get so easily.

He locked himself in his office and dialled the number Helen gave him.

"Hello?"

"Hello, who is this?"

"I'm a friend of John's."

"Oh… Poor John is dead."

"Yes, I know. I wanted to see you."

"To see me? Why would you want to see me?"

"To exchange memories."

"Oh… But who gave you my number?"

"It was John. He's told me a lot about you."

"About me?"

"Yes, he would have liked us to know each other. Unfortunately, he's no longer here. But in his memory, we can meet and get to know each other better. Would you agree to that?"

"Why not?"

"Would you be willing to meet today?"

"Today? I don't know."

"How about in an hour?"

"Where are you?"

"Do you know the Landmark Hotel on Sukhumvit?"

"Yes, I know it."

"Let's meet on the terrace, OK?"

"How will I recognise you?"

"I'll be wearing a blue jacket and a red tie."

"All right, then. I'm wearing a white shirt."

Mike arrived twenty minutes early and sat on the terrace of the Landmark. The position was strategic, as the terrace was higher than the pavement, and made it easy to see the customers arrive. He ordered a beer. He didn't have long to wait. He recognised Payom, having seen him in the funeral hall. He had fine features, well-dressed and a bit effeminate. As for Payom, he also recognised him immediately as he too had noticed him. Mike discreetly turned on the camera on his mobile phone.

"Hi, I'm Bob. My name is Bob."

"Nice to meet you. I'm Payom. We met at the funeral this afternoon, didn't we?"

"Yes, we did. I wish I'd met you under slightly less sad circumstances."

"Yes, poor John."

"Can I get you something to drink?"

"A whisky. A double, please. I need it after this."

"OK. Waiter! A double whisky."

"I really liked John, you know. I knew him for six years. And Helen, a very nice woman too. They're very nice people."

"How did you meet him?"

"At the temple."

"At the Buddhist temple? Where we were?"

"No, that one's only for funerals. No, at the temple near his house. You know they're both Buddhists. Very religious. I knew them there. I was twenty-five at the time. I was finishing my studies."

"You were a student?"

"Yes, I graduated as a doctor of computer engineering. I was top of my class."

"Well done. That's a very high level of competence."

"Yes, I worked hard to achieve that."

"I can believe that. And where do you work now?"

"I am an IT project manager at Mitsubishi Bank here in Bangkok."

"That's a nice job."

"Yes, I am very happy with my job."

"And you Bob, how long have you known John?"

"About three years."

"It's strange, he never mentioned you."

"Yes, that is strange. He was a bit secretive too, wasn't he?"

"Maybe he was after all. You never know people very well, even your friends, in fact."

"Yes, that's true."

"And do you have an important job, the way you're dressed, or was it just for the funeral ceremony?"

"Actually I dressed like this for the ceremony. I don't have a big job. I'm an editor at an insurance company, National Prakanphay Corporation."

"Oh, in a Thai company? You speak Thai well then?"

"No, I don't. I deal with English-speaking clients."

"Oh, very well."

The waiter interrupted them by bringing them two drinks.

"Happy hour! A round of drinks is on you. Beer and a double whisky."

"Oh, Bob, you chose the right place, it's very nice."

Payom drank his glass straight down.

"Well, you were thirsty, weren't you?"

"A little bit. And it relaxes me."

A waitress asked Payom if he would like another drink. He accepts.

"Bob you'll think I am a drunk."

"Don't worry Payom. I understand. It's the situation that warrants a little drink. It's only natural. You know, so do I."

"You drink slower than I do. It's true that half a beer is more in quantity than my whisky."

"And what were you doing with John?"

The waitress came back with a beer and a double whisky.

"Happy hour! Chokdee! Chokdee!"

"Thank you, sir. Here's to you too."

"You understand a little Thai Bob."

"Yes, for simple things, but I am very limited."

"That's not bad. Thai is difficult for Westerners. They don't know how to use tones. They say everything the same, it makes you laugh a lot."

Mike realised that the alcohol was starting to take its toll on Payom.

"John had a good job, he was a banker."

"Oh, yes, he had an important job."

"I remember him telling me he was having trouble with computers in his bank."

"Oh, that was peculiar. But you mustn't say that."

"Don't say it?"

"Not say anything, ah, ah, ah."

"I don't get it, do I?"

"John wasn't a computer genius, that's all."

"But he wasn't a computer scientist, he had another job, didn't he?"

"Yes, he was a bank manager."

"He was the CEO of that bank?"

"Yes, you didn't know that? I went there, I saw."

"I didn't know he was the boss. I thought he was a department head or something."

"No, no, he was the big boss."

"But what's that got to do with computers?"

"I can't say. I swore. To John."

"You know, now he's dead, you can say what it's about, he can't blame you. I don't suppose he'd want anyone to know he wasn't up to speed on his own bank's software, would he?"

"Yes, that's what it comes down to."

"If I understand correctly, you helped him? It's not a big deal, although I can understand that his self-esteem would have suffered if it had been known."

"Yes, it's true, I helped him. He didn't know certain technical procedures. But it's not his fault. He needed a signature to confirm operations."

"Did he?"

"Yes, he had an assistant manager who was not doing his job. Who should have signed with him for operations, but he never did. He was someone who always just shrugged and said that his signature was not necessary. So you know John and his kindness. In order not to have relationship problems he didn't insist and let it go. And in order to comply with the rules, he asked me to put in the electronic signature of his colleague. You see, it's not a big deal. We did this on Sundays. It avoided having to give explanations."

"Oh, yes, I understand. It was indeed the right solution."

"Yes, it was. And you Bob, do you like computers?"

"I'm not a champion. And in my job, I only have to type up contracts in English. It's not like you, an engineer's job. I'm not even close."

"I have to go, Bob. Shall we split the bill?"

"Yeah, I got it. By the way, I'm going to enter your details into my mobile. Can I ask your last name?"

"Yes, of course, you can. Be careful, it's complicated: Narkhirunkanok."

"Yes, it is. Can I have your address too?"

"Yes. Thonburi, Khlong San, Thanon Itsaraphap 245. Can we stay in touch, Bob?"

"Yes, of course, we will. See you soon."

Mike watched Payom leave. He stumbled a bit and waved to a taxi. He saw him lean towards the driver, then got into the back of the vehicle. He turned around and gave him a friendly wave to which he responded. Once the taxi had gone, he got up, walked to the pavement and walked back to the bank, which was about hundred metres away.

At his desk, Mike called Steve Marsham and told him in detail about his afternoon, from Finmore's funeral to Payom's departure. As far as Payom was concerned, Steve was flabbergasted that a computer scientist of this level could have been tricked in this way.

"Mike, do you think he told you everything?"

"Given what he drank, I'm sure of it."

"In vino veritas."

"That's right. What is clear is that we are not dealing with a gangster. He's an honest kid who wanted to help a friend who's completely smoked him out."

"Yes, Mike. You're going to have to turn him in, though. That's evidence you're going to need to take to headquarters. And having him filmed and recorded was a great idea."

"I know, Steve. Tomorrow I'm going to a police station to lodge a complaint in my name and in the name of the bank. I will ask our law firm to assist me."

"You're right, especially as they are Thai. They will be able to support you effectively."

Aleksandr Khoudovekov received his colleagues in the boardroom of his company. The meeting was held at the request of Artiome Siantchouk. The latter took the floor.

"Good. You know what happened to Klotz. I've been thinking about it. It wasn't the Americans who did it. Torture, emasculation, and all those refinements, it's not their style. The fact that they dumped his corpse in front of my house is an explicit message. It's a declaration of war. I can only think of Russians who would do that."

"Can you explain what you mean?"

"Igor, I think it was the FSB that did this."

"The ones from the embassy?"

"Yes, and perhaps others from Moscow. I've made some enquiries. The FSB boss in Bangkok is called Andrei Safronov. I'm sure he's at the head of this action. They probably think we have or are looking for the Seumkwang."

"Taking on the FSB is risky."

"Dmitri, we are not the ones attacking. It's them."

"Doesn't that make it the same? We'll have to face them…"

"Yes, Aleksandr, you see very clearly. Serguei, can you bring your shock troops?"

"I've got about twenty guys I can get from Ekaterinburg. No problem with that. All well-trained… former spetsnaz."

"That's what we need."

"Good. They'll be here in three days."

"Good. Another subject: did you carry out the checks I asked you to do after the introduction of these Americans to Igor?"

"Yes, Artiome. We have all been visited. Our computers were all hacked. Documents related to Podnimatsya Stal have disappeared."

"We have to find these guys. This morning I sent one of my Thai secretaries to the registration office. She managed to get the name and address of the car's owner. It is a rental car company based in Chonburi. So I asked her to go there to get the name of the client. It is a woman called Malee Paowsong who lives on Sukhumvit, in soi thirty-nine, Phirom Garden Residence. Tonight we will pay a courtesy call to this lady. It's a luxurious residence, another one of those whores that gets maintained I think."

"Who are you sending there now that Klotz is dead?"

"One of the guards."

"They're Thai. It's hard to trust them for this type of mission."

"Do you have another solution to propose?"

"Aleksandr, you do have a Chechen working for you?"

"Yes, Serguei Bohdan. He's a good man. He trained in Kadyrov's militia. Fully trained for this job."

"Good, then it's agreed. Send him to me for a briefing."

"OK, Artiome. I tell him to meet us here."

A few moments later, a giant of almost two metres, with a scarred face, hard features, steel-blue eyes, a square chin and impressive bulging muscles, appeared in the doorway.

"Come in, Bohdan. We're going to give you a job tonight. Artiome will brief you."

"Your orders, sir."

At about 10:00 pm, a car pulled into the car park of a French restaurant in soi thirty-nine, not far from the residence designated by Siantchuk. Bohdan got out and headed for the entrance. He entered a park where there were games for children. He walked around the building, and after climbing a few steps, he found himself in a large, luxurious lobby. The guard sitting at a reception desk asked who he was looking for, having immediately realised that he was not an occupant of the residence. Bohdan gave the name Malee Paowsong.

"Oh… thirtieth floor, flat three hundred and one. Take the lift to the right."

Bohdan thanked him with a nod and went to the lift. In the corridor, he spotted the door of the flat and rang the bell. A man opened it for him.

"Good evening…"

Bohdan didn't answer but pushed the door so hard that the man was hit in the face. His now broken nose was bleeding profusely. A woman appeared and screamed when she saw the man on the floor. She rushed to him and lifted his head in panic. The Chechen man grabbed her by the hair and forced her to get up. With his right foot, he immobilised the man still on the ground.

"Your name?"

"Malee," answered in tears.

"You, your name?"

"Fuck you!"

His giant hand then clutched the poor girl's neck and like a vice, slowly and firmly closes, making her choke.

"What's his name? Speak or die."

"Peter. It's Peter."

"Peter what?"

"Keldrik."

"Is he American, Peter?"

"Yes, he is."

"And where does he work?"

"At the American embassy."

"That's good, you're talkative, I like that. And I like you too. I find you very agreeable. You, Peter, are going to come with me. But first I'm going to take care of you, my darling."

"Let her go, you bastard!"

The Chechen dropped Malee and punched Keldrik in the face with an oxblade. He then jumped on the girl and ripped off her clothes, bra and panties. He knocked her to the ground and penetrated her with unprecedented brutality. In addition to the pain, she struggled to breathe, crushed by the enormous mass of her rapist's body, she was very thin, forty-three kilos dressed and measuring one metre sixty, under the thrust of her two metres and one hundred and thirty kilos aggressor.

"You're good, baby. Too bad I have to kill you."

He grabbed her head and turned her one hundred and eighty degrees. She died instantly. He approached Keldrik, punched him again and took him with him. He left the flat, took the lift again and passed the guard.

"Peter can't hold his liquor and he wants to drink again. So we're going to drink!"

"Oh, alcohol is not good, drink too much," the guard replied laughing.

He opened the trunk of the car and threw Keldrik into it, but not without picking up his pocket and taking his mobile phone. He quietly set off for the Union Thai Trade and arrived safely at his destination where Podnimatsya Stal's five accomplices were waiting for him. Khudovekov welcomed him.

"Good work, Bohdan."

"Thank you, Bohdan."

"We'll cook the gentleman properly."

Peter Keldrik was forced to sit on a chair in what looked like a cellar. He was chained there, hands and feet.

The five oligarchs entered. Bohdan was waiting for them. He was the executor of Aleksandr Khoudovekov's dirty work.

"So Mr Peter Keldrik. You are American, and you work at the embassy. You like Thai women. And you like to violate the private property of honest citizens who enrich their host country and offer work to its inhabitants. You recognise these places I suppose?"

"Screw you."

"And besides, I don't think you're very polite. Believe me, Mr Keldrik, this is a luxury you won't be able to afford very much longer. We'll give you a taste of it. Bohdan, break our guest's finger. Wait, we'll let our friends choose. So comrades, which finger shall we sacrifice?"

"The middle finger of the right hand!"

"Awarded to Dmitri! Execute Bohdan!"

"The Chechen grabs Keldrik's finger and slowly lifts it up to a cracking sound and pushes it until it sticks upside down against the top of the American's hand, who lets out a howl."

The five Russians enjoyed the spectacle. Siantchouk spoke up.

"You see, Keldrik, it is in your interest to cooperate. You have come to see us, it is normal that we return the invitation. We Russians have the education and manners that you cowboys never had. You are comfortable with your herds of cows, I readily admit. But apart from that, we outdo you in everything. So let's move on to something more interesting. You are CIA, aren't you? A word of advice, answer me."

"You stupid bastard."

"Well, I see you're as stubborn as a mule. It's your choice if you want to suffer. Bohdan starts peeling."

The Chechen took a large mechanical razor of the cabbage cutter type and prepared to begin a flaying in the purest tradition of oriental torture, removing the epidermis, the dermis and the hypodermis, right down to the envelope of the muscles. He was obviously an expert and certainly had a record, given the precision of his skills. Peter Keldrik screamed after the first four passes on his right arm, exposing the muscle. Bohdan continued his work for another thirty minutes. The whole right arm was raw. The pain was intense and acute, unbearable.

"You want to talk, Peter?" asked Goumine.

"Enough, tell him to stop!"

"I repeat Igor's question: do you agree to answer our questions, yes or no?"

Siantchuk continues: "Yes or no?"

"Yes."

"Do you belong to the CIA?"

"Yes, I do."

"How many people were there when you broke into our respective offices?"

"Four."

"All from the CIA?"

"Yes."

"I want the names of the other three."

"Frank Sheldon, Sam Chenney, Jack Wang."

"What were you looking for?"

"The chip from the Russian-North Korean program."

"So you don't have it… Interesting information."

"Do you know Mike Robertson?"

"No, I don't know Mike Robertson."

"How could you not? He's CIA like you."

"No, I don't know him."

"Careful Peter. I'll tell Bohdan to keep peeling you back a bit more, it'll loosen your tongue."

"I swear I don't know that name."

"Bohdan continues."

"No, please! I don't know him. I don't know who he is!"

"As he shaved his head before coming to us, and this is a delicate attention Peter, peel off his head and go down his neck to his shoulders so as to join his right arm."

And the razor in Bohdan's expert hand gently peeled away the layers of skin. The face dripped with blood under the cries of the victim. After an hour, the skull, neck and shoulders were raw.

"Good Peter. Are you willing to talk?"

"Yes, I am."

"Let's talk about Mike Robertson."

"I've heard of him but I don't know him."

"He's CIA, isn't he?"

"I swear I don't know."

"Well, considering the way you've been treated, I think you're telling the truth. This man works at the Golden Star Bank. That's an American bank, right?"

"Yes, it is."

"And you don't know him?"

"No, I don't know him."

"Do you think a CIA agent could have such a cover as he is the manager of this bank?"

"Anything is possible."

"Who is the CIA boss here in Bangkok?"

"Tony Rogers."

"When you came to our offices, how did you breach our programs?"

"Our expert, Jack Wang, took care of that."

"You transferred our data?"

"Yes, we did."

"To where?"

"To the embassy and Langley."

"What happens now?"

"It'll be sifted and analysed."

"That means the CIA will soon know everything about our activities, right?"

"That's right."

"How long will it take to summarise?"

"A week, maybe two."

"What should we fear after that?"

"An arrest warrant for you will be sent to the Thai authorities. A probable seizure of your businesses and personal assets."

"I see. One other thing, did you kill Aïdar Klotz?"

"No, I did not. I don't know who he is."

"OK, I believe you."

"What contacts do you have with the Russian embassy, especially with their FSB agents?"

"None."

"Good. I have to tell you, Peter, that I'm not happy about the news you've given us. We're going to have a lot to do and a lot to pay to buy off the police and the judiciary in this country. Your outing the other night is going to cost us dearly. Do you understand me?"

"Yes, I understand."

"Then you also understand that there is a price to pay for that. That you will pay. You're going to pay for your friends because you're the only one we have on hand. That's normal and I think all CIA agents are prepared for that, it's part of your training of course. Bohdan, finish your work."

The Chechen picked up his instrument and continued to flay Keldrik. He shouted and insulted the mobsters. He knew he was lost. After two hours, his whole body was raw. The pain was horrible.

"Nice work, Bohdan. Nice show. You have received a just and deserved punishment Peter Keldrik. All that remains is for you to die in pain. Farewell."

Everyone left the torture chamber. Bohdan, the last, locked the door. He would return three hours later to find the victim dead. He would take charge of the body and bury it in a pit hastily dug behind the building after having sprinkled it with quicklime.

Tuesday, 7 December 2010

Mike Robertson went to the police office on Thonglor Road. There, he met his lawyer, Wichian Cheenchamras of the American firm Blain & Finlay, which had a large unit in Bangkok, not far from the U.S. embassy. The day before, he had explained the problem to him. Wichian welcomed him and called the policeman with whom he had already arranged a meeting. An elegant woman in her forties in an officer's uniform arrived and ushered them into a small meeting room at the back of the building.

"Hello. I am Senior Colonel Apsara Amornchantanakorn of the CSD, Crime Suppression Division. We are attached to the Central Investigation Bureau."

"Hello, Senior Colonel. This is my client, Mr Mike Robertson. He represents the interests of Golden Star Bank in Bangkok in his capacity as Executive General Manager. And as I told you, he is also acting on his own behalf, as the fraud we are here for penalises both the financial institution and himself, right Mike?"

"Yes. Hello, Senior Colonel. Indeed what Wichian has told you is the consequence of the actions of this man, Payom Narkhirunkanok."

"Yes, Mr Mike, your lawyer has already explained everything to us. I will have your statement taken for your complaint file. Wichian, have you prepared the Thai text?"

"Yes, here it is. Mike, this is the one I gave you in English by email last night. Have you read it?"

"Yes, I have. It's what I told you."

"Well, I'll have it typed up and you can sign it."

"Alright, Senior Colonel."

"Mr Mike, did you make a copy of the recording?"

"Yes, here it is."

"Thank you. We'll attach it to your file and forward it to the Attorney General's office. Are you familiar with our judicial system?"

"No, not really."

"You should know that you will be heard as a witness, on the one hand as a legal representative of your bank and on the other hand in your personal capacity."

"Only as a witness? I don't understand…"

"In Thailand, when one is prosecuted for a crime, it is not the victim who prosecutes, but the state which prosecutes the alleged perpetrator. Here, crimes are considered an offence against the peace and order of the kingdom. The victim then becomes a witness for the state."

"I know nothing about the penal system in your country, although I have been here for some years now."

"It is no worse. That means that you have never been confronted with the underworld."

"Yes, I have. But what are you going to do now?"

"We will arrest this person. We will question him and certainly detain him until he is brought before a judge."

"How long do you think that will take?"

"Are you talking about the investigation or the trial?"

"Actually both."

"The investigation will go quickly, it depends on my authority. The trial will have to wait. There are many criminal cases and delays are noticeable. Now, Wichian, you know that you can file the case directly in a court of law. Although this applies to delays in investigations and prosecutions, which is not the case here."

"We know each other well and we trust you Apsara. So we will stay with you for the rest of this case."

"That's fine. Mr Mike, would you come with me to sign your statement?"

"Yes, of course."

Mike followed the senior colonel into an adjacent office. Taking the pen she handed him, he casually touched her hand. He began to sign the documents. Their eyes met, and he sensed a confusion between them. She smiled at him. But everyone smiled like that in Thailand, he knew. It only meant politeness and courtesy.

He continued with the signatures. He looked at her again. She was a beautiful woman, very attractive; her voice was soft.

"I thank you very much for what you are doing for me."

"I am just doing my job."

"I feel you are involved, and I am very touched."

"It's quite normal, believe me."

"I would love to meet you. Would you like to have a drink with me after work?"

"Today it is not possible."

"So tomorrow?"

"Yes, OK."

"Can I call you?"

"Yes, I'll leave you my mobile number. Here you go."

She handed him a card. He gave her his.

"I'll call you tomorrow, Apsara?"

"Yes, Mike."

They went back to the office where the lawyer was waiting. The lawyer took a copy of the complaint.

"Very well, that's a done deal. Mike, are you satisfied?"

"Yes, thank you Wichian."

They took their leave of each other, each going back to their own business.

At the American embassy, Frank Sheldon asked for an urgent meeting with Tony Rogers. He tried all day to reach Peter Keldrik without success. In desperation, he went to his home and discovered Malee's body lifeless. He could see that she had probably been raped. Blood stains are scattered all over the place, which suggested a fight with the assailant. And there was no trace of Peter, who had disappeared. He then questioned the guard, who could not give him any information, as it was another guard who worked the night shift. He decided to go back to the address that evening to question the night watchman.

"Hello, Frank."

"Hi, Tony. We have a problem. Peter has disappeared. I'm sure he's been kidnapped."

"Did you go to his house?"

"Yes, I went to his apartment."

And Frank was telling what he knew.

"Poor Malee. She was a nice girl."

"Yeah, it's sad. But we have to find Peter."

"Do you think this is a hit from the people you visited?"

"Yes, I think so."

"To go to them we need the support of the Thai police. Otherwise, it will be a sure failure."

"Can you get it?"

"I'll try."

"We have to move fast if we want to have any chance of getting him back alive."

"I'm aware of that, Frank."

Tony went to the ambassador, Richard Howard, and explained the situation. He immediately called the Home Office and asked to speak to the Deputy Minister, whom he knew well. After a ten-minute conversation, he got the agreement to support the police force with a visit to the site.

"Good, Frank, we have the agreement to visit the premises escorted by the police. The officer in charge of the escort will have a search warrant with him and a document confirming that our presence is required."

"All right, then. When do we go?"

"Now. The police are already on their way to the scene."

"OK."

"Frank, you're not coming with me. You never know. You might have been photographed or videotaped, you never know."

"I understand. I understand. You're going to search the area around the North Korean embassy?"

"Yes, we are. From the information we're getting from the downloads during your surprise visits, we have every reason to believe that's where the command post is. And if Peter has dealt with them, I'm sure he's there."

"I'll wait for you here. Come back with Peter!"

"I hope so."

The embassy's Lincoln pulled up in front of the house housing the Kliutchevskoy Summit Invest offices. Tony Rogers got out and went to meet the officer who was waiting for him accompanied by about twenty policemen.

"Hello, I'm Tony Rogers from the US embassy."

"Captain Supan Kongpaisarn of the Royal Police."

"Very well, Captain. Do you have the search order?"

"Yes, we do."

"Then let's go."

Rogers and Supan followed by their police escort arrive at the door, where a guard stopped them.

"Search order. Let us through."

The bewildered guard moved aside and let the group through. Supan went first, search order in hand, and entered the house. A young Thai woman stood up and asked what was going on.

"Search order. A team searches the whole house. Five men in the garden. Turn everything over!"

The policemen spread out and entered all the rooms, turning over everything without mercy. That's when Artyome Sianchuk appeared.

"What's going on? What do you want?"

"A search warrant!"

"What is it? Who signed that order?"

"Minister of the Interior and the Judge of the Criminal Court!"

"And what is this mess all about?"

"I think you're Artyome Sianchuk?"

"Yes, that's me. And you are?"

"Tony Rogers from the American embassy."

"From the American embassy? And what are you doing here with the Thai police?"

"We are looking for one of our people."

"And you think you'll find him here?"

Siantchuk burst out laughing.

"You won't be laughing for long, trust me on that, Sianchuk."

"There are no Americans in this house. We don't like Americans here."

After two hours of searching, nothing was found. Not a trace, not a single clue. The police team withdrew. Tony Rogers returned to his car and went back to his office at the embassy. He called Frank to share his disappointment.

"Tony, if he wasn't there, he's in one of the other Ruskies' buildings. We need to search every building until we find him."

"Frank, we got a search warrant for nothing. That other bastard Siantchuk is bound to react and you can imagine he must have connections given his financial clout. You have to look at things differently. We'll talk about it later."

"OK, Tony."

At the embassy, Tony Rogers reported to Richard Howard on the events of the search. The ambassador was upset at the outcome, with Peter Keldrik now missing, and it was now difficult to request more support from the Thai ministry.

"Richard, can we bring Frank in?"

"Yes, of course."

Sheldon entered Howard's office.

"Frank, we've talked about the problem we're facing."

"I'm ready to go to the other Russians tonight."

"They're certainly expecting a visit. I'm sorry, but I don't think that's wise."

"I agree with Richard, Frank. If you go tonight, you won't get away with it. They're on guard and they're waiting for us. And given what they did to Malee, there's a good chance Peter's been killed."

"We can't let this go unpunished, can we?"

"No, but we mustn't act in haste. We need to think of a plan. I'm relying heavily on the results of our analysts at Langley of the downloads we sent. From there we can work out a strategy for elimination with the support of the Thai police if the files are strong enough and everything suggests that they are."

Andrei Safronov received Lieutenant-Colonel Chelagin who gave him his report on the surveillance of the oligarchs.

"Your report is very interesting. Especially from an economic point of view. Their activities seem to work well by taking advantage of a high level of corruption. This explains their development and the results. Also, their links with this Belizean bank are not helping. You say that they are involved in drug trafficking and that they have connections with narcos in Peru? How did you find this out?"

"I made enquiries to our various diplomatic missions in Central and South America. Our correspondents in our embassy in Peru were particularly interested. They had observed that a terrorist group from the Shining Path, a group that wreaked havoc in that country in the 1970s and 1990s, was very active in cocaine trafficking and seemed to have greatly increased its business.

"Finally, they had identified funds from Belize. They had also intercepted messages they received from Asia in Russia. By comparing our information we were able to deduce with certainty that this was coming from an organisation calling itself Podnimatsya Stal. After local investigation, it turns out that this is the association of five oligarchs who act in concert."

"Podnimatsya Stal… Future Steel… a whole programme…"

"Yes, exactly."

"And to top it all off, they kidnapped an American agent from the US embassy and almost certainly tortured and killed him."

"Yes, we're pretty sure of that, given that we know that a CIA team penetrated their premises except for Siantchouk's."

"All this is excellent. The Americans will not stop there. They will do everything to destroy them. Keep watching them. Things will happen in the near future, that's for sure."

"Your orders, sir!"

Mike Robertson returned home. He felt energised, galvanised by the complaints he had made, which he was able to report in writing to his management in the United States, and his meeting with the beautiful Apsara.

"You seem to be in good shape tonight."

"Yes, my darling, and with good reason. I managed to identify the guy who had Finmore go to the bank to forge my electronic signature. I managed to contact him and meet him. I posed as a close friend of Finmore's and he fell into the trap. I went with the bank's lawyer to file two complaints against him, on my behalf and the bank's. He is now going to be arrested. I made a full report and sent it to San Francisco. This should clear me and if I manoeuvre well, exonerate me from any responsibility in this matter."

"That's great news, darling. Do you think it will speed up our departure?"

"I don't know yet. I need to talk to Gordon Hoffman. I'm hoping with this news, I can get a transfer."

"You think you can trust him? You told me the other day that he was very upset with you."

"He's the boss of all the foreign branches. Which means he'd be liable if we had a problem with the US Treasury Department's oversight. But if we can prove that John Finmore is solely responsible, and he is, then everything should be fine, especially as he is dead."

"But you think a Treasury Department audit is possible, despite the evidence of Finmore's guilt?"

"It's obviously still possible."

"But won't all those millions you told me about being transferred to Belize get you into trouble?"

"It all depends on what the bank does. Either they don't say anything and it goes away, or they come forward and ask for an audit to prove their bona fides and expose the people that are to blame."

"And what do you think it will do?"

"In my opinion, coming forward is not the best solution because, whatever happens, the state will be liable and will make her pay a huge fine. That's why I remain optimistic."

"I hope you are right. In the space of a few days, an avalanche of worries has fallen upon us. We've had years of peace and quiet and now it's all falling apart. You can't imagine how stressed I am. I'm tired, Mike. Tired. I don't feel like anything anymore. I'm scared all the time. And I wonder what else is going to happen to us."

"Lila, it's OK, calm down."

"But when are we going to get out of here Mike? You said we could stay for another month, but who's to say we won't be here until next year? Especially if you're planning to stay at the bank. You know that your transfer was only a possibility for them in two years?"

"Yes, but when I spoke to Gordon about it, he said that by the end of the year, it would probably be possible, remember?"

"Yes, but that was before all these problems."

"Lila, if everything works out with the Finmore thing, I'm pretty sure I'll be able to get my transfer in early January."

"I hope you are right."

The four policemen parked their car on Itsaraphap Road. They walked into the soi looking for two hundred and forty-five and found themselves in front of a pretty white one-storey house with a small terrace. Behind the white wooden gate was a manicured lawn with many flowerbeds. It was a pleasant place to live, in the city, and away from the heavy traffic of Bangkok. The police assesses the price of a house like this and figured that the occupant had some means. Yet they came to arrest him on a criminal court charge. *No wonder*, they thought.

They pressed the doorbell and waited. A young man appeared in the doorway.

"Good evening."

"Police, open up."

"Yes, I'm coming."

"Are you Payom Narkhirunkanok?"

"Yes, what is it?"

"We have a warrant for your arrest."

"What?"

Immediately two policemen grabbed Payom, put his hands behind his back and handcuffed him.

"Let's go."

"What have I done? What are you accusing me of?"

"You will be given this information at the police station. Walk!"

He found himself in the back of the police car, trapped between two officers. He asked questions, but no one answered him. When they arrived at the police station, he was rudely removed from the car and taken into the reception area where he was forced to sit on a chair in the waiting room. After five minutes, he was taken to the office of Senior Colonel Apsara Amornchantanakorn. He sat down opposite her.

"I did not allow you to sit down."

"I'm sorry."

He got up and stood.

"Your first and last name?"

"Payom Narkhirunkanok."

"Where do you work?"

"Mitsubishi Bank."

"And what do you do there?"

"I am a doctor of computer science. I am a project manager."

"Right. You are accused by Golden Star Bank and its managing director Mike Robertson of forging Mike Robertson's electronic signature to validate multi-million-dollar bank transfers to tax havens on behalf of five Russian-owned companies, whose directors are suspected of serious wrongdoing under the Kingdom of Thailand's organised crime laws."

Payom remained handcuffed and was shaking.

"What do you have to say to that?"

"I don't know anything about it. I admit I helped a friend but that's all. I want to contact a lawyer."

"If you don't want to make your case worse, I strongly advise you to cooperate. You're talking about John Finmore, I assume?"

"Yes. He told me that he was the CEO of this bank and that he didn't know how to put a signature in certain documents. But I don't know anything else. I just helped him."

"OK. Did you get paid for that?"

"No, never. It was a friendly service."

"Have you ever heard of Union Thai Trade? Or National Building Corp? Or Grand Construction Thailand? Or Ural Thai Corp? Or Kliutchevskoy Summit Invest?"

"Yes, I know the names of these companies. They often appear in the interbank movements that we have here in our market."

"But you have transferred millions of dollars to these companies."

"Me? No, never."

"The signature you forged was used for huge transfers. Millions of dollars, gigantic millions of dollars."

"But I didn't know that. I never wired anything, I swear."

"I want to believe that it wasn't you who made those transfers. However, you certainly knew who benefitted from these operations."

"I swear to you that I did not."

"We have a recording that was given to us in which you say you collaborated with John Finmore."

"Me? In a recording? That's not possible."

"I'll refresh your memory, I'll play you the recording."

When he heard the recorded conversation, Payom was flabbergasted. He understood that he had been fooled.

"But who is Bob? A policeman?"

"No. Bob's real name is Mike Robertson. He's the bank's CEO. And Finmore was his deputy. Finmore has been cheating on you for years. And he dragged you into a criminal enterprise. Now nothing tells me, except you, that you didn't know about the transactions."

"That can't be true. John couldn't have done that to me."

"Yet you work in a bank. How could you not have suspected what Finmore was doing? It's kind of strange, don't you think?"

"I didn't know anything about it, and I never thought John was doing anything illegal."

"In any case, you haven't given me any proof that you didn't know anything."

"But I do!"

"I am arresting you and placing you under a committal order. You will be kept in detention until the day of your trial. I am holding you on charges of forgery, complicity in money laundering and mafia association. You risk thirty years in prison."

"But that's not possible! I am innocent! I was deceived!"

"You will be sent to Klong Prem Central Prison. You can contact a lawyer now if you want. Officer, take him away."

"Yes, I want to call a lawyer."

"We have a phone box in the police station. Use it."

Payom went to the booth, escorted by a policeman and called one of his friends. After a few rings, the caller picked up. He described the situation, and the lawyer replied that he would come and see him the next day in the prison visiting room.

Payom was loaded into a cell van and driven to the Chatuchak district where the prison was located. After about thirty minutes, the van drove down a wide grassy driveway to the entrance of the prison complex, which housed some 20,000 prisoners. Payom got out of the vehicle and was escorted to the reception area. There he must undress completely, undergo a palpation, and put on the prison uniform. He was then taken to his cell. As he walked along one of the corridors, he was surprised to see prisoners wearing chains on their feet. The warden told him that prisoners on death row were always chained. He looked at him and with a smile told him that maybe after his trial he would join them.

Finally, he arrived at the gate of his cell. It must be about ten by five metres, he said, with about sixty men crammed in. The guard opened the door and pushed Payom in, who shoved those in front. He was punched in the shoulder and insulted. He soon realised that there was not enough room to lie down and that the men took in turns to sleep on the floor. There were also only ten blankets for the prisoners to share. Although he was dressed in the rags of his uniform that he was forced to put on, he was clean and his effeminate attitude attracted the eyes of some prisoners.

One of them came towards him, elbowing his way through. He invited him to follow him to the back of the cell so that he could rest. Payom, who was feeling nervously exhausted, did not resist and followed him, longing only to lie down and sleep. When he reached the back of the cell, one of the prisoners who had been sitting down saw him coming and got up to give him his place. He sat down, and two others got up in turn, beckoning him to lie down. He thanked and finally lay down.

No sooner did he begin to relax than the two who made room for him pounce on him, turn his face down and immobilise him. At that moment, the man who had invited him to follow him rips off his clothes, pulled down his trousers and sodomised him. Payom screamed. And five men would go over him as soon as the first one had satisfied his urges. Without any protection.

When the rapes stopped, Payom remained prostrate, completely terrified that he would have to stay here for perhaps months before being judged. And, after the trial, God knew how long he would have to endure this life. Perhaps until death. He got up and approached the only cabinet in the cell. He sat down and had a hard time defecating in public.

It was not long before he understood that there was no toilet paper and that the water was off. He was told that there was only water for two hours a day, from nineteen to twenty-one hundred hours. He could no longer sit down, his seat having been taken by those who raped him. He could not even lean against a wall; all the places were taken by the strongest. Some men coughed; some spat. So he stayed up until the early morning with the majority of the occupants.

Wednesday, 8 December 2010

Mike Robertson was at his desk. He decided to call San Francisco to see if the tide was turning in his favour, following the sending of his report.

"Hello, Gordon, how are you?"

"Hi, Mike. I'm fine."

"Did you get my report?"

"Yeah, I got it."

"What did you think?"

"It's a good first step."

"It's proof of Finmore's guilt. It totally exonerates me."

"Not really, you're the CEO, don't forget that. Then there's the State Department investigation and a hefty fine to pay anyway."

"What do you mean? Have you filed a report?"

"Not yet, but I certainly will."

"Gordon, you know very well that this story can be hidden, there's little risk of it coming out."

"But if it does get out and we haven't reported it, the fine will be even higher. I can't imagine the Big Chief not doing anything."

"Are you sure he'll inform Control?"

"I'm sure he will."

"And he'll report me to the authorities?"

"Yes, Mike, I'm afraid so."

"Gordon, head office compliance hasn't woken up to this story. Internal control should have called me to ask me to explain these transfers. But no one came forward. This is a mistake. And it will be easy to prove their failings. Especially over a period of three years.

"Can you imagine such radio silence? One wonders if there were no accomplices in this service on these cases… It will be easy to create doubt among the investigators. And the FBI will raid, with all that will go with it: crazy press, television channels, etc. An excellent advertisement for the banking group. I might as well tell you, Gordon, that I'm not going to take the rap alone if this is what happens. I'll make enough noise, trust me.

"And what's more, there's nothing to say that the threats I received didn't come from certain services that certain informed people in the Group would have paid for. I can also suggest this, and I assure you that it will cause a stir. The bank's image will suffer for a long time. Not to mention the time it will take to complete an investigation like this. So think carefully, Gordon. Don't forget that you'll be in the hot seat too. You are the manager of all the foreign branches. You'll be held responsible and you'll be exposed. And after a scandal like this, your name will be permanently associated with it. Good luck finding a job!"

"You bastard."

"Do you think I'd stand by and let you slaughter me? You don't know me very well. I'll give you the best advice ever: go to the Big Chief and talk to him like I just talked to you. There is no shortage of arguments. He is intelligent and will easily understand where his interest lies. And you see Gordon, I'm doing you a favour. Because once again, I'm telling you, you'll be one of the fuses. So listen to the voice of wisdom and avoid insulting me. You'd better thank me."

"We're not friends, Mike. We never were. Least of all today."

"Don't do anything stupid, Gordon. You're getting into some pretty rough stuff that could cost you dearly. You better make me an ally instead of an enemy."

"I'll see what I can do. Anyway, you're a beautiful bastard."

"OK, Gordon. Let me hear from you as soon as possible, I can't wait to hear what the boss's decision is going to be."

After that call, Mike met Steve Marsham.

"Come in, Steve, and have a seat."

"Have you heard anything?"

"I just got off the phone with Gordon Hoffman. We had a serious exchange in which he finally agreed that it is their responsibility."

"You mean that you would be exonerated from all responsibility?"

"Yes, from all responsibility."

"That's good news for you."

"Yes, and it's not out of the question that I might get an interesting transfer within the group."

"Still at the international level?"

"No, at headquarters."

"Definitely? Congratulations, Mike."

"It's not a done deal yet, but the chances are good."

"And when would that be?"

"Hopefully the end of the month or January."

"Oh, yeah? That's quick."

"Yes, I'm quite happy with the way it's going. I think it's possible that we'll have an on-site inspection later this month, given the situation. Is everything in order with the services?"

"Yes, they can come, there will be no problem."

"That's fine."

Marsham left the director's office to return to his department. Mike picked up the phone.

"The Shangri-La? Hello, I would like to book a room. I'll arrive tonight and leave tomorrow. In the name of Mike Robertson."

"Yes. OK, great. Thank you, Mister Mike. See you tonight."

He dialled a new number.

"Hello, Apsara? Hello, this is Mike."

"Hi, Mike."

"I'll see you at the end of the afternoon. Is that still OK?"

"Yes, it is. Do you have a place for me to go?"

"The Shangri-La bar. Do you know where that is?"

"Yes, I do. I'll meet you there at 7:00 pm, OK?"

"All right, then. See you then."

At the North Korean embassy, Brigadier General Yong-Joon Cheong of the Special Forces of the People's Army of Korea and a dozen other officers held a meeting. Secretary Ha-Neul Park wrote down the general's speech in full.

"Comrades, we are here to update you on the search for the Seukwang programme chip. We know that the Russian embassy to whom we entrusted the chip has been unable to protect it and has had it stolen. Such incompetence is impressive, given that they were supposed to hand it over to the Kremlin. You can imagine the anger of their leaders. I contacted the ambassador recently and he confirmed that they were onto something.

"Can we believe them? I doubt it. I know that this programme was funded by Russia, but let us not forget that it was our researchers in our beloved country who found and developed this programme. So Russia is our partner, I agree. They asked me to send them a new chip. I approached the leadership of our National Defence Committee, and this request was presented to our Supreme Leader.

"The answer was a resounding no. It is obviously not possible to entrust a new copy of the programme to people who do not have proper security. They even offered to hand over the programme to their ambassador in Pyongyang but this was refused in the same way and for the same reasons. It's bad enough that a programme is out there and everyone is looking for it. I have asked our relations in Podnimatsya Stal to actively search for it, but so far they have had no results.

"One American, however, has been identified. He is the manager of the American Golden Star Bank in Bangkok. I am very surprised that no one has really taken an interest in him. Neither the Russian embassy nor Podnimatsya Stal. I find it very strange. It is not impossible that he is a CIA agent or an honourable correspondent. I have heard that he has visited the American embassy several times.

"So that's something to look into. I also know that his wife is Russian and that they have a son who has dual American and Russian citizenship. I also know that he is seeing the number two man in the Russian embassy, the man with whom we have an official relationship, FSB Colonel Andrei Safronov. And finally, I also know that the companies of the members of Podnimatsya Stal have their accounts in the Golden Star Bank. I conclude that Robertson is the key. Is he doing counter-espionage for Russia? Does he receive subsidies from Ponimatsya Stal? All questions that we do not have answers to today. It is therefore important to have additional information on this mysterious character. In this way, I hope that we will be able to find the chip. Your mission is to find these answers and verify whether or not he is in possession of the chip and, of course, to bring it back. Do it!"

Mike arrived by taxi at the Shangri-La Hotel. He passed through the security gate, passed through the reception area and reached the large lounge overlooking the Chao Praya River. He was a little early and noticed that Apsara was not there yet. He returned to the reception desk to ask for the key to the room he had booked. He presented his passport to the receptionist.

She asked about his luggage. A little embarrassed, he replied that he had no luggage. The hostess, with a reassuring smile, invited him to follow her to show him his room and told him that he had been upgraded as a sign of welcome since it was his first time at the hotel. On the eighth floor, he entered the room, which was large and spacious, with a view of the river where the boats that organised dinner cruises for tourists passed by, or the Chao Praya Express bus boats that also travelled up the canals, known here as khlongs, where they took tourists who had come to visit the Venice of the East.

Mike thanked the hostess and went back down to the lounge. He saw a beautiful woman approaching him and recognises Apsara. She was no longer in the uniform of a senior police officer but was wearing a long red dress, her hair falling to her shoulders and replaced by the regulation bun.

"Good evening, Apsara. You look beautiful."

"Good evening Mike. Thank you, Mike."

"Did you just get here?"

"Yes, I came in my car. The traffic is heavy at this time of day. But I live not far from here, in a soi off Silom Road."

"Oh, very well. Let's go and sit down if you like."

"Yes, let's."

"I am very happy to see you again. I've been thinking about you a lot."

"Have you had time to think about me with your work? I imagine you must be very busy."

"Yes, I am. But it would be difficult to erase you from my memory."

"Thank you, that's very flattering to me."

"No, that's all right."

"I had the man you filed the complaint against arrested."

"You did? And what did he say in his defence?"

"He was very surprised. He claims that he helped your deputy in friendship and that he was unaware of the consequences of his actions."

"Does he know that it was me who filed the complaint?"

"Yes, because I played him the recording you made at his expense."

"What was his reaction?"

"I would say disappointed."

"I understand, one would be. But, for me, it was the only solution I had to confuse him."

"I'm not criticising you for having done it. On the contrary, it's very good."

"And he's in prison?"

"Yes, one of the prisons in Bangkok. He's going to stay there until his trial. It can take between three and twenty months. The prisons are full and many are waiting to be tried. The delays are long because of the overcrowding we have in Thailand."

"I imagine that the conditions must be harsh."

"Yes, they are. It is better to avoid prison here."

"So let's move on. Tell me about yourself. How long have you been in the police?"

"Since I was twenty-two. I'm forty-two, so that's twenty years. I'm an old lady, you see."

"You're joking, you're a beautiful woman."

"You're exaggerating Mike."

"No, I'm not. And you're brilliant, you've got an important job and high rank I noticed."

A waitress knelt down in front of their table and asked them what they wanted to drink.

"Would you like a glass of champagne, Apsara?"

"Oh, what are we celebrating?"

"Our meeting of course. OK, bring us two glasses of champagne, please. Yes, so tell me…"

"Yes. I've worked hard to get here, you know. Women here are not considered equal to men, and you always have to be on top to get ahead. And that requires a lot of effort, a personal investment of every moment."

"Yes, I believe you. The position of women in their professional careers is the same everywhere. In our country too, they have to be much better than men to get high positions. In fact, they always have to prove that they are the best, always do more."

"Yes, it is, and I can tell you that in Thailand it is especially true."

"And you are from Bangkok?"

"I've been living here for twenty-six years since I went to university at Thammasat, the Bangkok Law School and then to the Police Academy."

"It's like I said, you're bright and intelligent."

"Thank you."

"Otherwise, I am from Buriram. I come from a farming family. My father has a farm of about hundred hectares where he grows rice and also raises cows for milk. You could say they are middle class. I was able to study because my father loved me very much. It is very rare for peasant daughters to study. They usually marry very young, have children very quickly, and stay at home to do the housework. I have a rather independent character, and frankly, I couldn't see myself living like that. I always wanted to study. Otherwise, I have six brothers and I'm the only girl."

"That's fine. What do your brothers do?"

"My elder brother works with my father. He will take over the farm. One of my brothers is a lawyer here in Bangkok, another has a shop where he sells and installs air conditioners in Buriram, another is an accountant in an agricultural cooperative in the same region, another has a restaurant in Chiang Mai, and the last one has a masonry business in Sukhothai. And I am the youngest in the family. So you know my family. What about you?"

"As you probably know, I am married and have a child."

"I did not know that."

"And what does your wife do? Is she in Bangkok with you?"

"Yes, but she's growing unhappy here and wants to move to the States."

"Oh, I see. It's true that it's not very easy here for Western women."

"Yes, that's true enough."

At this point, the waitress serves the two glasses of champagne.

"So here's to you, Mike. And thank you for this invitation, which gives me great pleasure."

"To you, Apsara. It's a pleasure for me too, you can't imagine how much. I wanted to ask you, are you married? Do you have any children?"

"No, as I said, I am quite independent. And I don't have any children. I was raped when I was fifteen, I got pregnant and I had an abortion under difficult circumstances, and since then I can't have children."

"I am really sorry. It's a terrible thing. And do you have a fiancé or boyfriend?"

"Not at the moment."

And Mike took her hand. She didn't take it away.

"I am extremely fond of you, Apsara. I find you almost irresistible."

And he came up to her to place a kiss on her lips.

"Oh, Mike… no… that is not possible in public… we don't kiss here, it is not done. We are in Thailand, don't forget that."

"So let's have a drink and come with me. I have a room in this hotel."

"You booked a room?"

"Yes, I was so looking forward to this meeting… Do you agree? Do you share my feelings?"

"I like you, I do. I'll follow you."

They emptied their glasses. Mike asked for the bill and paid. They took the lift hand in hand to the room.

Once through the door, Mike took her in his arms and kissed her passionately. Their tongues mingled, and they were stuck together. He tried to slip his hand under her dress, but she stopped him.

"Mike, I'm going to go into the bathroom and undress. And take a shower. And then you're gonna do the same thing. OK?"

"Yeah, I'll do that."

"You've never had a Thai girlfriend?"

"No, I haven't."

"Now you have one…"

"That's wonderful. I'm so glad."

"Wait, you don't know anything yet."

"I'm not worried."

She went into the bathroom and locked herself in. She stayed there for about ten minutes and came out wearing a bathrobe she found in the wardrobe. He approached her and took another kiss, which she returned.

"Mike, it's your turn. I'll wait for you."

"Yes, I'm hurrying."

"Take your time, I'm not running away…"

"I hope not," he replies, laughing.

He went to the bathroom. After a few minutes, he returned completely naked. She was lying on the bed, still wearing the bathrobe. He approached the bed, kissed her and gently removed her dressing gown. Her breasts had a dreamy curve; a small black triangle at the level of her pubis attracted his mouth. He gently spread her thighs and introduced his tongue into her vagina, searching it conscientiously. His tongue then sought out her clitoris, and he began to suck on it. She sighed, and her body jerked. She took his head and pressed it against her thigh. He suckled her faster and faster, feeling the vibrations of her body. She took him by the hair and pulled him onto her. He penetrated her and inserted his tongue into her mouth. She squeezed him tighter and tighter and moaned. Then she pushed him away gently. She cuddled against him and moved down to his penis. She was on top of him. She took it in her mouth and sucked gently, her tongue moving back and forth along the glans. He had taken her buttocks and inserted his tongue into her anus. Sensing that he was about to cum, she stopped her movements and turned around. She impaled herself on him and started very gentle movements and eventually sped up. She suddenly let out a scream of pleasure as he exploded inside her. She collapsed on top of him, and they stayed like this for half an hour without speaking or moving. Finally, she stood up slowly, feeling her lover's sex come out.

"Are you happy, my darling?"

"Yes, my love, very happy."

"You mustn't worry about your wife."

"Why do you say that?"

"You know, the position of the second wife suits me perfectly."

"Second wife?"

"That's what we call a mistress in our country. It's much nicer, isn't it?"

"Yes, it is."

"So don't worry. And if our love story becomes a great love story, we can have a Buddhist religious wedding. It will be a marriage for us. You can stay married to your wife. There is no problem."

"I was not familiar with these customs, having never been around Thai families."

"Is this OK with you?"

"Are you sure you don't have a problem with me living with my wife?"

"No, it is not a problem. The second wife is an ancestral tradition in Thailand. And it is often a better position than the first wife. The second wife has everything that makes a woman happy: a man who is always in love with her, moments that are always extraordinary."

"Yes, it's true, when you look at it that way, you're right."

"So I'm your second wife from tonight."

"And I'm delighted."

After going to the bathroom again, the two lovers went down to the lobby. Mike returned the key.

"Where do you live, darling?"

"In the Onut district."

"Oh, that's a long way from here."

"I'll take a taxi. I'll be at least an hour. It's almost eleven o'clock, I won't be home until ten."

"I hope you won't have any problems?"

"No, I told the first wife that I had a meeting that would finish late."

"Oh, I see you're adapting quickly to the semantics."

"I'm a good student, aren't I?"

"You sure are. I didn't ask you, do you speak any Thai?"

"No, I don't. I only have English connections."

"Easy way out. Now you English speakers are exceptionally lucky that the whole world speaks English."

"Yes, I admit it."

"Well, darling, I'm going to go. I'll see you tomorrow?"

"Yes, around what time?"

"Shall I drop by your office? You don't mind? I'll introduce myself as the police officer who's following your case… Say around eleven?"

"OK, that's a good idea. We can have lunch together if you're free."

"Yes, we can do that."

"And do more…"

"We'll see."

"Well, I'm going to call a taxi. Aren't we going to kiss then?"

"You're a quick learner, that's good. Good night, darling, see you tomorrow."

He watched her leave and asked the bellman to bring her car around. He admired her. She was now with him. He felt a great sense of pride. He was besotted. His taxi arrived. He got in and gave the driver the address.

Thursday, 9 December 2010

At the U.S. Embassy, Richard Howard asked Tony Rogers to join him to discuss the results and decisions of the CIA and the US Government following the analysis of the documents transferred from their visit to the Russian oligarchs.

"Very good Tony, our guys at Langley did a hell of a job."

"I can't wait to see what they come up with."

"First up is Peru. The Shining Path grouping is called PROSEGUIR. It is listed in our country as a terrorist movement. But it is the leaders of this group that the oligarchs have established relations with. They buy the cocaine from them, which is sent through various channels to Europe and North America. So secondly, the group calling itself PODNIMATSYA STAL now has a label of association with a terrorist gang and drug trafficking.

"A wanted notice for the five oligarchs has been issued by the FBI and a request to Interpol. Secondly, the assets of the oligarchs. In view of their criminal activities, the countries hosting them are asked to seize all their assets. A request has already been sent to Interpol Thailand. We will see how they react. I think it shouldn't be long.

"In addition, our State Department has issued a red notice for each protagonist, so that they can be arrested and extradited to the United States to be tried for cocaine trafficking. Finally, the third point: Belize. This country has also been a member of Interpol since 1987. The problem is that the police resources are quite weak and that endemic corruption often paralyses the actions needed to be taken. We have requested the seizure of their bank accounts. We hope to have positive results because we are putting pressure on them."

"This is perfect. With this, we can ask for the support of the Thai police to search the other sites."

"Yes, as soon as we have confirmation that the Thai justice system orders the seizure of their assets. I have asked our services to keep me informed of what is going to happen."

"I hope we don't have to wait a long time."

"Yes, I hope so."

Olga Safronov served her husband coffee for breakfast. She had found him anxious for the past few days. She knew that the life of an FSB officer was not exactly synonymous with calm and serenity. That was why she had always been able to stand by her husband, discreetly, encouragingly and with unfailing support. Andrei particularly appreciated her qualities, which made her the ideal wife for him. If he had been able to climb the ranks of the military hierarchy, it was because she had always followed him without ever questioning or challenging anything. She was devoted to him without limits and would always approve of his choices. For Olga, there was no option: the only way was her husband.

"Andrei, you know I haven't heard from Lila since they came to dinner."

"I have, Mike called me."

"He called you at the embassy?"

"Actually, on my mobile phone. But I was at the embassy, yes."

"He's in trouble for calling you I think?"

"Yes, it's because of what he told us."

"And not to pry, but he's not in too much trouble?"

"I hope not. When he called me, he was fine. I haven't heard from him since."

"I'm glad they're OK. They were hoping to leave soon. Do you think they're still here?"

"I don't know."

"I'll try to call Lila later."

"Then you'll know where they are."

Andrei gathered his things, kissed his wife and son, and left for the Russian embassy. Olga went to prepare Yvan for school. The maid, Nawarat, cleared the table. When she was alone, she called Lila.

"Hello, Lila?"

"Hello, Olga, it's good to hear from you."

"How are you?"

"Let's say I'm fine. We are still waiting to leave."

"You haven't heard anything about it?"

"Mike is optimistic. He's had some encouraging news from San Francisco."

"Ah, good."

"Yes, but he doesn't think we'll be able to get back before the end of the month, or even January."

"That's three to six weeks at the most. It's not that long now."

"No, but you know I'm tired of being here."

"I can see why you're impatient."

"That's an understatement."

"And when are you going to Saint Petersburg?"

"I haven't made any plans yet. You know that every year we spend January 6 and 7 there with my family for our Orthodox Christmas. But now I really don't know. If we're still here, it seems difficult, since Mike will probably be on the verge of being transferred, and if we're gone, we'll be in the middle of relocating, and I doubt we'll want to fly again for such a long trip. Not to mention that Mike will have taken up his new post and I can't see him going on leave."

"Yes, of course."

"We'll certainly go for Easter, from the eleventh to the twenty-fourth of April. It will be easier. It would be nice if we could meet up there and celebrate together."

"Yes, that would be great."

"Ask Andrei if it's possible."

"Yes, that's an excellent idea. I'll ask him when he gets back tonight, it wouldn't be the first time we've been to St Petersburg for Easter. I think it's possible."

"I'd be so happy. I'd relax, I promise."

"Yes, so would I. Come on, I'll try to organise it and convince my dear husband."

"Well, good luck with the convincing!"

"I'll do my best, I promise."

"How much longer do you think you'll be in Thailand?"

"Did you know that they are thinking of Andrei for the rank of general?"

"You told me about it…"

"Yes, well, his transfer to Moscow is linked to that nomination. That's all I know. You know Andrei doesn't talk much when it comes to his work."

"Yes, he is. So you don't know much, it's all a bit vague."

"That's right. That's what happens to the wives of Russian diplomats."

"My poor Olga."

"It's all right, I'm not to be pitied. There are more difficult lives than mine."

"Yes, there are. I tend to complain a bit, but in the end, you're right, we're not the most unhappy. But, despite all, I'm worried about is the problems we've been facing lately."

"Yes, what Mike mentioned when you were with us?"

"Yes. And other things in his professional capacity. But I don't want to go into that. I'm getting tired of it in the end."

"Come on, Lila, get a grip. In a couple of months at the most, it will all be memories."

"God bless you, Olga."

"Well, I have to leave you, I have to take care of the house for a while."

"Yes, me too. See you soon, Olga."

At the Golden Star Bank, a young woman in a light blue dress approached the reception desk in the centre of the huge entrance. She introduced herself and handed her card to the secretary.

"Hello, Senior Colonel Apsara Amornchantanakorn of the police. I would like to see Mr Mike Robertson."

The secretary called Mary, Mike's assistant.

"We'll come and get you, Senior Colonel."

"Thank you."

Meanwhile, Mary went to see Mike and informed him that a police officer wanted to meet him. Her face was full of concern.

"The police again? One of those who came last time?"

"No Mike, this time it seems to be a woman."

"Well, bring her in."

Mary went down to reception. She was very surprised to find the police officer was a radiantly beautiful woman. She guided her to her boss' office.

"This is the Police Officer Mike…"

"Are you Mr Mike Robertson? Very well, I have a number of things to discuss with you."

"OK. You can leave us Mary."

Mary closed the door and returned to her office. As soon as they were alone, the two lovers fell into each other's arms and embraced. Their mouths met, and they kissed for a long time. Mike's hand crept under her dress and up to her crotch.

"Don't you have any panties?"

"Yes, in my handbag."

She undid his trousers and pulled down his underwear. He tipped her onto his desk and penetrated her. She started to moan.

"Shh, don't say anything, you can hear everything here."

"Fuck me."

"Yes, yes, I like to fuck you."

"Go ahead and fuck me, fuck me again."

"Yes…"

He came very quickly, so strong was the sexual tension between them. She was carried away by the desire she had for him and came too. He collapsed on top of her and kissed her.

"I'm beginning to like police visits."

She laughed.

"Next time I'll arrest you and put you in the holding cell."

"Can we have sex in it?"

"With two guards watching us, no thanks."

"I think I love you, my second wife."

"I think I love you too."

"Are we going to lunch?"

"Yes. Where are you taking me?"

"The Westin down the street?"

"I'll follow you."

They left the office together, with Mary looking on in amazement.

"Here, you're not trying to kiss me here?"

"We are in Thailand, it is not done, Senior Colonel!"

"You are definitely an excellent student."

"With a teacher like you, lessons are learned quickly."

At the Westin, they sat down in the large dining room and chose the buffet option. They talked about everything and anything and considered the present and the future and too their future holidays together.

Friday, 10 December 2010

Mike Robertson arrived at the bank early so he could reach Gordon Hoffman who had left a message for him to call back.

"Hello, Gordon!"

"Good morning."

"So tell me, what's the news? Did you get to meet the Big Chief?"

"Yes, I did."

"So what did he decide?"

"I explained the situation to him, especially the risk that the press can represent. He agreed and after weighing the pros and cons he decided to stay put. You're lucky, Mike."

"It's the smartest choice anyway. And did you tell him about my transfer to the States?"

"No. It was a big pill to swallow."

"OK, I admit it. Do you think a decision can be made quickly?"

"I honestly don't know. At no point, did it come up? It's a lot of things, you know."

"He was sensitive to my report though?"

"Yes, but I can tell you that he was not satisfied overall."

"I'll send you a written request for my transfer this morning. Will you present it to him so that you can get a quick answer?"

"OK, I'll send it to him."

"Thank you. Goodbye, Gordon."

At the U.S. Embassy, an official note from the State Department informed that it was requesting the seizure of the accounts of the oligarchs' companies for financing a terrorist group, drug trafficking and money laundering. The note was also sent to the Thai Embassy in Washington for transmission to the relevant Thai ministries. Tony Rogers made a formal request to Mike Robertson to freeze the accounts.

The Aeroflot Airbus from Moscow had just landed on one of the runways at Suvarnabhumi Airport, whose name referred to the mythical Golden Land mentioned in ancient texts of Buddhism. It stopped at its parking place, and immediately the passengers got up without waiting for the announcement of authorisation from the stewardess. They grabbed their bags from the luggage compartments, elbowing their neighbours, pushing each other and shouting at each other. The stewardesses were used to it and let it happen. It was the Russian folklore of economy class.

At the back of the plane, twenty-four passengers stood out because of their nightclub bouncer's bodies, with an average height of one metre ninety and about a hundred kilos. They too had stood up, and those whose seats were next to the ordinary passengers pushed them off without the latter daring the slightest protest. The disembarkation began. The passengers followed the information given to them by smiling agents posted along the passenger boarding bridge and at the entrance to the hall where they could take a series of conveyor belts following the "immigration" signs and admired the numerous sculptures and traditional pavilions reconstructed with reference to Buddhism, such as the Yakshas warriors who warded off demons, to reach the one hundred and thirty arrival control points.

After waiting for about half an hour in one of the queues, passengers reached the baggage hall, which they collected from one of the many carousels. They then proceeded to the customs posts, which let them through without asking. They finally arrived at the arrivals terminal where friends or relatives were waiting for them and if not, they had to take a conveyor belt that led them to the lower floor where taxis were available. Finally, even further down, they could use the Airport-Link, which was a train that would take them to the centre of Bangkok.

It was this last option that Aleksandr Khoudovekov's twenty-four henchmen choose, as a minibus would pick them up at the Makkasan station. After a journey of about thirty minutes, they arrived at the station and met the driver who was watching them with a sign in his hand, which read UNION THAI TRADE. Spotted, the men followed him to the vehicle parked on Kamphaeng Road. They finally arrived and got out of the minibus, greeted by Khoudovekov and Bohdan. Bohdan accompanied them to their rooms, two large rooms each containing twelve beds. A large shower room was adjacent with fifteen showers and thirty sinks. The men settled in and got their bearings.

The Ministry of the Interior in Bangkok had received information about the oligarchs and their illegal activities. This news was disturbing to them because the companies run by these men were flourishing and making money in the kingdom. On the other hand, they benefitted from a good network of contacts. The file went up to the minister himself. An internal report gave all the economic information. However, the United States was considered an ally, and its political weight was important. Since 2004, there had been a free trade agreement that allowed fruitful exchanges and American investments of around ten billion dollars annually. The case of the oligarchs had been heard: the minister had ordered the freezing of accounts and had set off tax inspections in each company. For the time being, he postponed a decision on the personal fate of the oligarchs and put the Interpol red notice aside.

Mike and Apsara met at the Shangri-La in the room he rented when they first met. They made passionate love for over an hour. Afterwards, they went down to the hotel lounge to have a drink and relax.

"I have to talk to you about something important, Apsara."

"I'm listening my darling…"

"I've applied for a transfer to the head office in San Francisco. I assure you, I won't be leaving immediately. I don't think it'll be for another year from what I know."

"Oh. I know you won't be here forever."

"I want my wife and son to leave, if only for their safety. We have a house near San Francisco, a little town called Sausalito. They'll be fine there, and my wife is all about living in that house anyway. It is a solution encouraged by my management."

"It would be a wise resolution under the circumstances. You never know what can happen, and the family is always the point of weakness."

"Yes, I really think so."

"What about us?"

"What about us? We can live together, don't you think?"

"Yes, I'll come and live with you. But always as a second wife, I want to. I want you to continue to take care of your family, it's very important to me. I don't want to hurt Buddha's feelings."

"Buddha?"

"Yes. Are you surprised?"

"I didn't know you were a practitioner."

"In Thailand, we are almost all of us. Our king is the equal of a God. And the Ramakian is the equivalent of your Bible. For us, it is very important to do good."

"It's a beautiful philosophy."

"It is a religion, Mike. It's a religion of a whole people."

"I know, I know."

"Do you have a religion, Mike?"

"Yeah, I'm a Baptist."

"It's derived from Protestantism, I believe?"

"Yes, that's right. It's a movement born in 1609 and 1612 in the Netherlands and then in England. We are Protestants and Evangelicals. I would define us as Christians who respect the Holy Scriptures, the Bible."

"And you are a believer, a practising one?"

"I am a believer, but I am not a practising one. When I was young, my parents and I went to church every Sunday, we lived in Phoenix, Arizona and I sang in the choir."

"Did you sing?"

"Yes, I was twelve years old and it continued until I was eighteen. After that, I wanted to quit choir. But I went to church once in a while. I still go now."

"That's good. I think it's important to be religious."

"Yes, I do too."

"And what's your wife's name?"

"The first wife?"

"Yes, the first wife."

"Lila."

"Like the flowers? That's romantic. What part of America is she from?"

"She's Russian, from St Petersburg."

"Oh, Russian? And her religion is like you?"

"No, she's Orthodox."

"Is that a Christian religion too?"

"Yes. She is Russian Orthodox, a Christian religion made for Russia. Like you are Buddhist according to the Ramakian, a Buddhist religion made for Thailand."

"You can say it like that, it's true. And you told me that you have a son, what is his name?"

"Marat. It's a Russian name of French origin."

"And why did you choose a name of French origin?"

"Actually, my wife chose it. There's nothing French about the choice. It's the name itself that has this origin. It was the name of a French revolutionary, that's why it became popular in Russia, I should say in the Soviet Union, as it was popularised at that time."

"When you leave here Mike, will you forget me?"

"Apsara I love you, I have no intention of leaving you."

"But if you go to work in America, we won't see each other anymore."

"I don't know yet how I will organise myself, it's still a bit far away. I want our story not to end."

"We will see. We have to enjoy our time together as if we were living our last day."

"Is that what we're doing, I think?"

"Yes, and I want it to stay that way, my darling."

Their discussion continued for another hour. They parted promising to meet again the next day.

Monday, 13 December 2010

An official from the Ministry of Justice arrived at the reception of the Golden Star Bank. He wanted to hand over an order to freeze five bank accounts held in the bank's books. Seeing the names on the document, the receptionist called Mary, Mike's secretary. She went downstairs and received the official who made the same statement and handed over the order signed by the minister. She thanked him and went to tell Mike. Mike was drinking coffee in his office.

"Come in Mary, what good news do you have for me?"

"I'm not sure it's good news, Mike. Here, read it yourself."

"Let's see…"

He read the order confirming the request he received the day before from the U.S. Embassy.

"Well, we have no choice. We will proceed immediately to block these accounts. Please prepare the document for me to sign in such cases."

"We will send it by mail? Don't you want us to call them? They are important clients."

"Do you have the emails of these companies?"

"Yes, we do."

"Well, then email them the document they'll receive in the post. It's the best thing to do in a procedure like this."

"Right, Mike. I'll bring the form for you to sign and I'll send them all the documentation by email and post."

At Grand Construction Thailand's headquarters, Igor Gounine was the first to receive the news that his bank account had been blocked. He immediately called the bank and asked to speak to the manager. The call was transferred to Mary who asked Mike if he would talk to her. He asked her to transfer the call to him. The man had a strong Russian accent.

"Mike Robertson."

"Igor Gounine. What right do you have to block my account?"

"It's a decision by the Thai authorities, sir. There is nothing our bank can do."

"But how do I pay my staff and my overheads?"

"We cannot be involved in this type of problem. It is none of our business as we are only complying with a requirement of the Thai administration."

"I don't see it that way. That money is mine. You will hear from me."

He hung up abruptly. This phone call didn't mean anything good to Mike. He called the head of security and told him not to let in the five oligarchs whose identities he gave him.

The five Russian oligarchs met at the Union Thai Trade. They all received the email informing them of the account blocks. Siantchouk spoke up.

"We are facing a full-scale attack from the Americans. Because I'm telling you, it's the American state that's behind this setup. And those stupid Thais are following in their footsteps. I got this information from one of the directors of the Ministry of Finance. We have our accounts in Belize but don't be too happy, they may well intervene there too, especially as it seems we have an Interpol wanted sheet on all of us. We have to act quickly and strongly. Aleksandr, you have the biggest company. How much do you have in that fucking bank?"

"Four hundred million dollars."

"And the rest of you?"

"A hundred million," said Gounin.

"Me too," said Yerkulayev.

"And you, Dmitri?"

"About two hundred million."

"And I three hundred million. A total of more than a billion dollars. And do you know what will happen next? Seizure, pure and simple. Not to mention our businesses and buildings. The loss will be colossal, we will not recover if we sit back and do nothing."

"What do you propose, Artiome?"

"Aleksandr, my friends. This is what we're going to do. We're going to break into that bank and take the staff hostage until they transfer all the assets to an account in North Korea. We won't actually steal anything, we'll just get what's ours."

"We don't have any accounts in North Korea…"

"We have had one for an hour. I contacted General Cheong. He has opened an account in the name of Podnimatsya Stal at the Daesong Bank, which will take all our funds without a hitch. This is the bank of Division 39, the secret government organisation with which we collaborate, and of the regime's apparatchiks. When I say all of it, it's also everything we have in Belize. I have already given instructions for the transfer of what I have there. I strongly encourage you to do the same in the next minute. The quicker we react, the less risk we take. A funny side note, you know what? Daesong Bank had a branch in Austria that was closed in 2004 called Golden Star Bank. Isn't that a sign for us?"

"Artiome, that account you opened, it's under your signature only."

"Yes, Aleksandr. Are you saying I can't be trusted? You'd rather leave your funds in Belize, working with Interpol? It's up to you."

"No, I trust you."

"Is there anyone who wants to opt out of our group? Anyone? Then I'll continue. The first thing you have to do is transfer all your Belizean assets. I'll give you the account details. Do it immediately."

Siantchouk gave them a paper with the account number. They logged on with their laptops and ordered the transfers. An hour later, two billion dollars appeared in the account opened in the Daesong Bank.

"Perfect, this is the first part of our operation. Aleksandr, are your spetsnaz there?"

"Yes, they have arrived."

"We're going to use them to back our investment, from the bank."

"Do they have a capable leader with them?"

"Yes, Bodhan."

"Bodhan, that's very good, we all know he's very capable. Well, call him and have him join us with the team. We will brief them on the plan of attack. It's ten o'clock, we'll plan the attack today at three o'clock."

At precisely 3:00 pm, twenty-five heavily armed men got out of a minibus right in front of the entrance to the Golden Star Bank. One last man, the driver, stayed in the vehicle and drove off to park a little further on, in a less busy side street. The last one, having passed the door, closed it and blocked it so as to prevent entry. The four security guards threatened by the Russians were put out of action immediately, neatly knocked out with rifle butts. The receptionist was stunned and looked at them without any reaction.

One of the men advanced towards her. He pulled her out of her chair, put a tape gag over her mouth, tied her wrists behind her back and forced her to lie on her stomach. One of the men stayed on the ground floor to stand guard; the others moved upstairs. The entire staff got the same treatment. No one wanted to be a hero, so everything went smoothly and quietly. They made their way up the twelve floors of the bank building, leaving one man on each floor to keep watch.

When the last twelve men reached the top floor, there were eight employees left to bind and gag. All of them were subjected to the same regime without fail. They finally arrived at the executive office. Mary screamed when she sees them, which alerted Mike who came out of his office. Mary was also bound and gagged. Mike could not make a move, having a Kalashnikov pressed against his stomach. The operation went very fast, in less than half an hour the mercenaries reached the heart of the bank without firing a shot.

"Who are you? What do you want?"

For any answer, the one who seemed to be their leader took out a mobile phone from his pocket and types a number. He spoke to the caller in Russian. Mike understood that the man's name was Bohdan. The man handed him his mobile phone.

"Speak!"

"Hello? Who is this?"

"Hello, Mr Mike Robertson. My name is Artiome Siantchouk. I'm here with my friends, who I'm sure you've heard of. Aleksandr, Dmitri, Igor and Serguei. We are all very good customers of your bank. And you, have blocked our accounts. That's not very nice, Mr Mike.

"You are not very grateful to people like us who have always brought you a lot of money. But these are strange times. That's just the way it is. We can't help it, and as you said to our friend Sergei when he called you this morning, we do, excuse me, you do what you are told. In short, you have no responsibility.

"I understand that, Mr Mike Robertson. So you see, the people in front of you, it's the same. They have no responsibility for what may happen. They are like you, they will carry out the orders given to them. You see how life is. Well, you have to be philosophical, don't you?"

"What do you want?"

"It's very simple, Mr Mike: get our money back. That's all there is to it. We're not here to rob a bank. We're honest people. We won't take a cent from you that doesn't belong to us. We want you to transfer our entire assets, which amount to exactly one billion one hundred million two hundred and thirty-two thousand eight hundred and forty-two dollars and twelve cents, to a bank account in North Korea. You see, we have no insurmountable demands. It is a clear and fair operation.”

“I cannot make a transfer of such a large sum today, it is not possible. I have to refer to the headquarters in the United States.”

“Mr Mike, I don’t think you understand very well. I want the account that Bohdan gave you to be credited with our assets within two hours. Otherwise, no one working in this bank, and I mean no one, will come out of this adventure alive. Have I made myself clear? And I never joke about money.”

“But what do you want me to do? It’s too late to call the head office in San Francisco.”

“You have my terms, I won’t repeat myself. If I don’t hear from you within the hour, we’ll kill the first hostage. Now put Bohdan on the phone.”

“Bohdan, you call me in one hour to check in.”

“Yes, sir.”

Mike called Gordon Hoffman on his mobile to inform him. Bohdan demanded to hear the conversation.

“Mike, have you seen what time it is?”

“I know Gordon, but we have a serious problem. The five Russians have taken over the bank with mercenaries and have taken us all hostage. They are threatening to kill us if we don’t transfer all of their assets frozen in an account in North Korea. I remind you that there are one hundred and forty of us here. If we don’t do it, it will be carnage because they are not joking. You know what the Russian mafias are capable of.”

“You’ve done nothing but shit in this job. But why the fuck didn’t you fire those accounts when you were appointed there? Shit!”

“I have to make this transfer, Gordon, or we’re all going down. I need you to give me the key.”

“How much is this shit?”

“Over a billion dollars.”

“Goddamn it!”

“I’m waiting for your call.”

“I’ll have you know I live in Bayview and the head office is in Richmond. So I’m gonna need some time to get there, OK?”

“Just get there as soon as you can.”

“I will.”

Meanwhile, at the front desk, the hostess, still trapped in her bonds and gag, had contorted herself to surreptitiously approach the security switch on a baseboard that sounded the alarm at the nearest police station. She managed to press it with the tip of her foot. A red light next to it started to flash. The mercenary on duty at the door saw nothing. Twenty minutes later, five police cars and two vans were positioned in front of the bank, setting up a security perimeter to protect pedestrians. It was all hands on deck inside. Bohdan called out to Mike.

"You son of a bitch, you called the cops!"

"No, you stayed with me the whole time. It's probably some customers who found the door locked and who knows if you left any armed men down there, they'll have seen them and informed the police."

Indeed, Bohdan realised that Mike had not left him since the phone call from Siantchouk. So it could not be him who alerted the police. He called every man on the floor with his walkie-talkie, and they all confirmed that the prisoners had not moved. Mike's explanation was plausible. He called Siantchouk to inform him. He gave him his conclusions.

"What do we do now?"

"Put Robertson on."

"Here, he wants to talk to you."

"Hello?"

"Robertson you're not very clever calling the police."

"But it wasn't me, I swear…"

"Listen to me carefully. Things have changed. I want you to make the transfer within fifteen minutes. Otherwise, we'll kill one person every ten minutes, do you understand?"

"You listen to me. I got my supervisor in San Francisco. Your henchman can testify to that, he heard the whole conversation. I need at least an hour to complete the transfer. I would point out that it is half past four in the morning in California. I got him out of bed and he has an hour to get to headquarters. Now I'm telling you straight out: if you kill even one person I won't make the transfer. And you'll probably slaughter us all but you'll never get a penny. So a word of advice: be patient. An hour isn't much."

"I agree. But don't get me wrong Robertson. If it goes wrong there won't be any survivors. One hour. No more."

Outside, the TV stations had arrived and were filming the bank. A crowd of onlookers had gathered behind the security barriers and were waiting to see the outcome of what was being described as a hostage situation. Senior Colonel Amornchantanakorn had arrived on the scene. Although she was not in charge of the case, she approached the police officers who let her pass to see the captain who seemed to be in charge of the operation.

When he saw her, he greeted her in the usual way. She asked him a few questions about what he knew. She was surprised that such a large number of hostages had been taken. For her, it could only be people who knew the place perfectly well. She opened up to the captain, who agreed to these remarks. Stepping aside, she tried to call Mike on his mobile. He picked up.

"Apsara?"

"Are you in the bank?"

"Yes, I'm fine."

The sound cut out. It was Bohdan who snatched the mobile phone from his hand and hung up.

"No phone calls! If they call you, you don't answer! Who was it?"

"A customer of the bank."

"With a Thai number?"

"We all have Thai numbers. This mobile has a Thai number. What's the problem? This is Thailand, right?"

"OK, OK. Don't try to be clever. Anyway, I don't want you to answer it anymore, OK?"

"Yes."

Apsara did not call back, she had understood the situation and did not want to put Mike in danger. She talked to the captain again to find out his intentions. He told her that for the moment he would do nothing and wait to make contact with the criminals to find out their demands. He had no idea how many hostages or how many hostage-takers there were.

She found out when the police were notified and concluded that almost all the staff must have been present when the attack started. To take the whole building hostage was probably an organised group that had been planning for some time. She estimated the group to be at least twenty men and told the police officer. After some thought, he agreed. He told her that he would call the number of the bank. She offered to assist him, which he accepted. The phone rang. No one answered.

"Captain, that's the number for the reception, no one will answer. We should call a colleague's number."

"Yes, but we don't have them."

"We can ask them at TOT. Ask them to transfer all the numbers to us."

"Yes, Colonel, I'll do it immediately."

Fifteen minutes later, the captain received all the numbers assigned to the employees of the different departments of the bank. A total of one hundred and sixty different numbers. He decided to call each number and let it ring for two minutes. On the thirtieth call, i.e., a little over an hour later, a caller answered.

"Hello?"

"This is Captain Tongproh. I want to speak to your boss."

"It's me," said Bohdan.

"What do you want?"

"For the moment we don't want anything. In a little less than an hour we will be going out with the bank manager and other bank executives. You have to let us out if you don't want a bloodbath."

"Who are you?"

"It doesn't matter who we are. If I see a cop trying to get in, I'll kill a hostage."

"How many hostages are you holding?"

"A lot of hostages. More than a hundred, anyway."

Bohdan hung up. The captain understood that he could not do anything without endangering the safety of the hostages. He had to go and answered the press briefing and left Apsara. The answers he gave to the journalists were transmitted on television channels. He remained vague as he had very little information. However, he said that he had contact with the leader of the hostage-takers and noticed that he had a strong Russian accent. Apart from that, he had little information and ended the conference.

At the Russian embassy, Andrei Safronov was following the hostage situation on a television set. He thought that Mike was one of the hostages. When he heard that the policeman was talking about a man with a Russian accent, he immediately made the connection with the five oligarchs. What if they were the hostage-takers? The modus operandi reminded him of the way the Russian military operates.

And there were many former Russian soldiers who hired out their services today. And taking a hundred people hostage was a well-thought-out, large-scale operation. But why would the oligarchs attack the bank that housed their own accounts? It was not possible. It was not their style at all. They were businessmen, not safecrackers. To take such risks when they were already very rich would be pure madness. No, it was something else. But what was it? Professional bank robbers? After all, maybe. He called Chelagin.

"Yes, Colonel, you asked for me?"

"Are our oligarchs still under close surveillance?"

"As you ordered, Colonel."

"What are they doing now?"

"They're meeting at Khudovekov's."

"Have you noticed anything unusual in the last few days?"

"About twenty men arrived at Khudovekov's house yesterday in a minibus belonging to him. He was seen leaving again today, apparently transporting the same men at around 2:00 pm."

"Well, that's interesting. How would you describe these men?"

"Probably henchmen. Spetsnaz style."

"Got it. You're going to take three men with you and head over there. If there are any guards, kill them. But I want the oligarchs alive. When you have made yourself master of the place, call me."

"Yes, sir."

Mike's mobile phone rang. He went to answer it when Bohdan interfered.

"Forbidden to answer, I said!"

"But it's my line manager for the transfer of funds!"

"Well, I want to hear what is being said. Answer it."

"Hello?"

"Yes, Mike, it's me. This is the code for the wire transfer: RSC96742056TYBSP."

"Got it."

"Good luck, Mike."

"Thank you."

He turned to Bohdan.

"I have to go to the computer room. I need the help of one of my staff."

"Who?"

"This one."

He pointed to Arjun Gotra.

"You have to untie him. He needs his hands."

"OK."

Mike and Arjun left for the room and were escorted by Bohdan and a mercenary. Arjun sat down at the computer keyboard. He entered his ID and typed in the code that Mike handed him. Mike showed him the amount of the transfer. Arjun looked at him in disbelief. Mike signalled him to enter the information. He entered his signature code, and Arjun completed the transaction. The transfer was completed.

"That's it."

Bohdan picked up his mobile and called Khudovekov.

"Yes, Bohdan?"

"It's done."

"Just a moment, we're checking. Artiome, are you watching?"

Siantchuk entered his code to access the bank account.

"No, there's nothing."

"Bohdan, we have nothing. You're being taken for a ride! Kill a hostage!"

"OK."

He walked towards the group of eight and stopped in front of Mary, pointing his gun at her head. Mike intervened.

"You're crazy! Stop it! We've transferred everything to you! Wait two more minutes!"

"An order is an order!"

And he shot Mary in the head, and she collapsed and died instantly.

"No! You bastard!"

But one of the mercenaries hit Mike with his rifle butt, and he went down. At that moment, Arjun grabbed a letter opener and ran at the mercenary, stabbing him in the neck. Bohdan turned and shot. He was shot through the heart and fell on top of the mercenary who was dying on the ground. Bohdan's mobile phone rang. It was Khudovekov confirming that the transfer had been credited to their account and that the operation was over.

"What do we do?"

"You take hostages, get back in the minibus, and leave for Don Muang airport. You'll see a Thai man with a sign that says STAL. He will take you to the private aviation boarding point where you can board the plane to Vladivostok."

"Very good."

In the boardroom of Union Thai Trade, the moment was euphoric. The oligarchs congratulated themselves on the success of their organisation.

"My friends, we have got our property back!"

"Bravo Artiome! Hurray!"

"Thank you, Aleksandr. Now we have to get out of the way of this whole circus. We will leave tomorrow for North Korea where we are expected. We have a flight via Beijing. And. in the meantime, let's drink this glass of vodka to our bright and rich future!"

Everyone congratulated each other, shouting "Hurray" and gulping down their vodkas. At that moment, shots rang out in the building. They looked at each other, astonished. Khudovekov took a pistol out of his pocket and walked out of the doorway. He saw a man coming up the stairs. He was armed. The man addressed him in Russian.

"Throw the gun away!"

Khudovekov fired, and the man tumbled down the stairs, hit in the abdomen. Lieutenant-Colonel Chelaguin appeared and shot back, killing the oligarch. Followed by two armed men, he arrived in the room where the other four accomplices were waiting.

"Don't move! All kneel down! Stand there, all of you facing me!"

The four men complied, having no choice but to obey. Chelagin took out a mobile phone and typed in a number. Safronov answered.

"Do you have them?"

"Yes, Colonel."

"Put it on speaker, I'll talk to them."

"Yes, Colonel."

"Good morning, gentlemen. I am Colonel Andrei Safronov of the FSB. I have a few questions for you. First of all, to be absolutely sure, Klotz was working for you?"

No one answered.

"Are you mute? We'll see about that. Give me your names:

    Siantchouk

    Gounin

    Ahkremenko

    Yerkulayev."

A silence followed.

"And the last one?"

"He's dead, Colonel. He killed Boris and I shot him. Self-defence."

"I see. OK, then. Are you gentlemen going to answer my question?"

"We're Russian citizens. You can't treat us like this. You should protect us. What the hell is this? You are overstepping your rights!"

"Excuse me, I'm sorry. Who are you?"

"I am Sergei Yerkulayev, President of Ural Thai Corp. You owe me a minimum of respect and consideration. I served in the army and then the FSB just like you. I was a colonel. We have the same rank.

"And we can get along very easily. We are rich, very rich. And we are going to be able to develop some very juicy business. Yes, Colonel Safronov, you can be one of us. There is a lot of money to be made.

"Much more than you can imagine in your wildest dreams. So let's stop this little game and meet. We both know what a colonel's pay is. No need to do anything crazy. Join us."

"I'm not for sale, unfortunately for you. And there's something you need to get into your filthy mafia heads: I'm not patient. And I still don't have an answer to my first question. Lieutenant Colonel, kill this arrogant character. Do it!"

A shot rang out, and Yerkulayev, who was on his knees, fell face down.

"Well, gentlemen, who want to answer my question?"

"Yes, Klotz was working for us!"

"Well, there you go. Who answered me?"

"Dmitri Ahkremenko."

"Congratulations Dmitri! Now another question. Are you the one who attacked the Golden Star Bank?"

"Yes."

"Good, Dmitri. But why did you rob the bank? Were you planning a robbery? I can't believe…"

"The bank had frozen our accounts."

"They had? Why did they do that?"

"It was a request from the Thai Ministry of Finance."

"What was the reason?"

"It was a request from the Americans."

"You really need to get the words out of your mouth. And why?"

"For money laundering."

"Here we go. And you want to leave the bank with your savings?"

"Yes, I do."

"You asked for a transfer to an account, I assume? From which country? Answer, I don't have much patience."

"North Korea."

"It's a kind of tax haven, I understand. And you were planning to flee there, I believe?"

"Yes, I was."

"And your team at the bank? Are they going there too?"

"No. They are going to Russia."

"By which flight?"

"A private plane."

"Good. We know enough. Lieutenant Colonel, take them out."

"Yes, sir!"

The first two shots rang out. Suddenly, a voice rose. It was Siantchouk's.

"Stop it! Stop it, stop it! I can give you a billion dollars! I can give you a billion dollars right now! We can work it out! Safronov, can you hear me? A billion for you!"

"I'm incorruptible, haven't you understood yet? Kill him!"

Another shot broke Siantchouk's voice.

In front of the bank, the policemen were showing signs of irritation. They had heard the shots inside and thought that the hostages had already been killed. A police general had come to take command of the operation and had asked Apsara to stay out of it. He intended to lead alone. He had retrieved a map of the bank and located a back entrance to the building. He ordered a forty-man patrol to enter the bank through this door.

But, just then, the main door opened, and Mike, along with fifteen other hostages, emerged flanked by the entire mercenary troop. Bohdan used his hands as a megaphone and addressed the police.

"We have hostages! If the slightest shot goes off, we will kill them all! We are going to leave and we don't want to be followed. If we spot a car following us, or a police helicopter, we kill them!"

The general took out his revolver and shot Bohdan. The mercenaries sprayed the police with their Kalashnikovs. They immediately retaliated with their HK G36s. After ten minutes of heavy fire on both sides, it was a massacre. About fifty policemen were killed, including the general, and all the mercenaries were shot. Not a single hostage survived. Apsara who witnessed the massacre wiped away tears. She was desperate.

On television, a speaker from Thailand's BEC Channel 3, gave this information: "A major hostage crisis took place this afternoon at the Golden Star Bank in Bangkok. Russian mercenaries, acting for oligarchs who own five companies in Thailand but are wanted for money laundering and drug trafficking in the United States, took the bank's one hundred and forty employees hostage. The objective of this mafia gang was to transfer funds to a tax haven. When they tried to make a forced exit, using fifteen hostages as human shields, they immediately fired at the police, killing General Kunchai who demanded their surrender. The police force retaliated killing all the attackers. Fifty-two police officers were killed. Thanks to their courage, the police managed to rescue one hundred and twenty-five hostages who were bound and gagged in the bank. The Prime Minister praised the sacrifice of our police and will present General Kunchai with the Order of Military Merit posthumously. The oligarchs were found shot dead in the boardroom of Union Thai Trade. It is most likely a settling of scores between rival mafia gangs."

Lila was walking through the big Central World shopping centre. She was with Thanit who was escorting her. About an hour later, she decided to go to her friend Olga's house. The car arrived in front of the building where the Safronov couple were living. She was happy to see her friend again but immediately noticed that she had a broken face.

"Hi, Olga, what's wrong with you? Has your new maid let you down again?"

"My God, you don't know anything. The television just announced some terrible news. Oh, my poor Lila! There was a hostage situation this afternoon at the Golden Star Bank. They killed Mike and fifteen other hostages."

Suddenly, everything became blurred, and Lila fainted. Olga called the maid who brought her a bowl of water and a flannel. Olga took it and patted Lila's cheeks and put fresh water on her forehead. Lila came too.

"Olga, this is a nightmare. Tell me it's a nightmare. It isn't."

"My poor Lila… My poor Lila…"

The two women hugged each other and cried.

"My God, this is so horrible. What will become of us, Marat and me? Why God? Why us?"

"You know you can count on us, Lila. We won't leave you."

"It's terrible. Poor Mike! How unfair, how awful!"

The front door opened. It was Andrei Safronov coming back from the embassy. He found Lila crying with his wife.

"Oh, Lila, Lila! I am so deeply sorry. Lila!"

She burst into tears in Andrei's arms. He tried as best he could to console her, knowing that nothing would probably ever console her.

"Do you want to stay with us tonight, Lila? I'll send for Marat, and you can sleep here. Will you do that?"

"Yes. But I'll ask Thanit to go and get him. He's used to Thanit, you know."

"All right, all right. I'll send the maid to ask him."

Nawarat went to find Thanit and gave him the order from her boss. She also informed him of the dramatic events of the afternoon and of Mike's death. He was speechless when he heard this sad news. He deduced that Lila and Marat were going to need him because from now on he was the only one they had left to protect them.

Olga had turned on the television, and they were all watching the pictures of the hostage situation on the various channels. A picture of Mike was shown, the announcer presenting him as the general manager of the bank who was murdered by the mobsters.

"As long as we have people like this in Russia, we will have problems. We have to hunt them down and eliminate them. There is no other way."

"You're right, Andrei. If I could, I'd kill them myself."

"These were all killed, Lila. Even the masterminds. They were found with a bullet in their head. I heard it on TV, at the embassy."

"My poor Mike. My poor darling."

"Lila, I know this may sound like a small thing to say, but you can always count on us. You know that."

Lila started to cry again. She needed to cry. She had so many regrets. All that they had to do together. All that life.

Andrei had gone to see his son in his room as he did every time he came home from work. He asked him about his day, about what he did at school. He liked to know if he had had any sports lessons. He encouraged his son to try harder to run faster, jump higher and be stronger than the others. Ivan was a slightly sickly boy who was not really attracted to physical exercise.

He preferred to draw and was interested in music, especially the piano. When his mother started playing the piano, he ran over and listened to her. He wanted to try playing but refused to take lessons. He didn't need lessons in drawing. He was naturally gifted and reproduced perfectly everything that came into his sight and charm.

And his other passion at the moment was playing marbles. As he was not very tidy and had a habit of leaving everything lying around, it was the maid who tidied up when he was at school. And when he came home, he was, of course, upset because he had to look for where she had put his things. He usually took everything out, causing a mess that irritated his father.

And so it was today. Andrei stepped back to pick up a tennis ball that was lying around and made his son put it away when he felt something crack under his foot. He looked at what he had stepped on: small shards of glass, and in the middle, he saw a tiny black square. He bent down and picked it up.

"Dad, you crushed my ball! It was unique! It was the one I won the other day off Marat!"

"Oh, from Marat you say?"

"Well, yes, and now I don't know where I'll find one like it."

"Don't worry, you'll find one when you play with your friends."

Andrei went out of the room and isolated himself for a few moments in the room that served as his library. He looked carefully at the object. It was a computer chip for sure, and it looked exactly like the one in the Seumkwang programme. But the chip they were robbed of was not in marble. He returned to his son's room and arrived just in time to stop Nawarat from picking up the debris.

He picked up the biggest piece and discovered that the ball had a screw thread that allowed it to open in two and thus hide something inside. The American spy had therefore hidden the chip in a large ball. If it was indeed the same chip, it remained to be seen. He returned to the library after confirming with the maid that she could do her cleaning job. He slipped the chip into a small decorated wooden matchbox and put it in a drawer.

He would collect it tomorrow when he went to the embassy and had it checked. He thought that in this little box, he held his appointment to the rank of general. He smiled. He heard a noise at the entrance. It was Marat arriving, accompanied by Thanit. He went to kiss his mother and asked if his father was already there, which brought tears to Lila's eyes.

"Mum, why are you crying?"

"My darling, come to me."

"What is it, mum?"

"Oh, my darling. Your daddy… We won't see him again… ever."

"Why, mum?"

"He's gone to heaven my darling. He's in heaven with the good Lord."

"Does that mean daddy's dead?"

"Yes, my love. Yes."

"Why, mummy?"

"He was killed by bad people, darling."

"That's not fair. I'll kill the bad guys."

And he started to cry. A little boy was heartbreak that moved everyone around him, including Andrei. Ivan, who learned the news at the same time as his mother by seeing the television report, understood his friend's sadness and came to place a kiss on his cheek. He gently invited him to follow him to his room to play.

Tuesday, 14 December 2010

In the Safronovs' flat, everyone was in the dining room for breakfast. The children were up and dressed. Lila had decided that Marat would go to school despite the events, believing it to be the best therapy. Better to have a busy mind than in sadness. And Ivan was waiting for the bus to take him to NIST International School in the Wattana district.

Lila drank tea but eats little. Olga stayed close to her and tried to support her as best she could. Andrei told her not to worry too much; they would always be there for her. He asked her about her immediate plans. She wanted to go back to America and returned to her home in Sausalito. Marat would go to a school in the city. She thought of Willow Creek Academy, which Mike had told her about and which had a good reputation.

She didn't know when she would be able to return to St Petersburg. She thought it would be complicated and didn't foresee a stay with her family until 2012. Olga told her that it was a pity, but that she understood where the priorities were at such times. Lila stood up and looked out the window at the Bangkok she loved and now hated. She looked away and saw a book on the console behind the table. Pushkin's Eugene Onegin. She grabbed it and opened it at random. She came across these few lines, which she read:

You have fled from days of joy,
O golden days of my youth!
Alas! what will tomorrow bring?
It is bathed in thick mist,
I try in vain to glimpse it,
But whatever my fate may be,
They pass me by without harming me,
Watching, sleeping, all is laid out…
Blessed be the day, its cares!

Blessed be the night too!

Tomorrow, when the dawn will have him,

When the fatal hour sounds,

Shall I go down alone into the night,

To my sepulchral abode?

The swift waves of Lethe

Will carry away my memory!

But O you, virgin of beauty,

Will you come to my grave?

On my urn, dear mourner,

Shed a tear and think:

He loved me and dedicated to me

The dawn of his stormy life?

My wife, my beloved,

Come, come to me, my desired one!

Putting the book back down, she could not hold back her tears.

"Oh, Mike, my poor Mike, my poor love."

Olga took her in his arms.

At the North Korean embassy, General Cheung followed the news and learned of the death of the five oligarchs. This was good news, as the account he opened in the name of Podnimatsya Stal only worked with his signature. He was supposed to give the five mafiosi signing authority when they travelled to his country, but now that they are dead, he was the only one who could dispose of the funds. This bank was special, as it was the Supreme Leader's bank. And Cheung knew perfectly well that the movement of funds had already been brought to his attention. He decided to call the secretariat of Prime Minister Choe Yong-rim.

"Brigadier General Cheung."

"I am listening, Comrade Brigadier General…"

"Please convey the following information to the comrade Prime Minister: We have received fund transfers totalling three billion four hundred million two hundred and twenty-three thousand US dollars. The people who ordered the transfers are unfortunately deceased. The bank account is in the name of Podnimatsya Stal. I am the account holder. I wish to officially offer the total sum to our Great Man Descended from Heaven."

"Very well, Comrade Brigadier General. It will be done within the hour."

"Thank you."

Barely an hour later, Cheung received a message from the Prime Minister's residence giving him an account number where to transfer the funds. The message included congratulations from the Supreme Leader and a promotion to Major General with immediate effect. His new uniform would arrive in a diplomatic pouch. He was very satisfied but did not forget that he still had to find the chip of the Russian-North Korean programme. He called his staff and called a meeting out of the blue. He ordered secretary Ha-Neul Park to take note.

"Comrades, I would like to inform you of my appointment to the rank of Major General by our Dear Father."

The ten officers stood up as one and congratulated him at attention.

"We have not made much progress on the search for the Seumkwang. Agent Mike Robertson was killed yesterday by spetsnaz who had come specially from Russia and were in the employ of five Russian oligarchs who turned out to be mafiosi. They too are dead, murdered by who knows? So the tracks are narrowing. But I think I've got it. This Robertson has a Russian wife. That's where we need to look. Execution!"

Andrei Safronov called Anton Kuznetsov, the embassy's computer engineer.

"Are you all right, Chugunkin?"

"You're addicted to Bulghakov, Colonel! You do this to me every time."

"Your name is Kuznetsov, the blacksmith. And Chugun is cast iron. Well, I know, a blacksmith and cast iron, that's not really it. And yes, I like Bulghakov, and especially his book '*Dog's Heart*'."

"You're in a good mood this morning, Colonel."

"Yes, and I hope it lasts. Please check it out."

"Well, I'll be damned. But… is it the famous chip?"

"It could be. You tell me. Come on, I'll go with you to your office."

Kuznetsov inserted the chip into his computer and typed in the entry code for the Russian-Korean programme. Immediately, SEUMKWANG appeared on the screen in Korean and then in Russian.

"Hurrah!"

"Fantastic! Bravo Anton!"

"I had nothing to do with it! It was you who brought her back, Colonel. May I ask where she was?"

"It's too long a story. No time. All right, I'll take it back and put it someplace safe. No one's going to steal it this time."

Safronov would put the chip in a safe. He immediately informed his superiors in Moscow. He also contacted the Korean embassy.

"Major General Cheung speaking!"

"Safronov. Have you gained rank?"

"Yes, Colonel. To what do I owe your call?"

"To inform you that we have recovered the chip."

"Really? And who had it then?"

"Mike Robertson, who was killed yesterday."

"I knew he was a CIA agent. I wasn't wrong."

"So anyway we have it. I'll have it sent to Moscow this week. Our forensic services will liaise with yours in your country under our agreements."

"Very good, sir."

"Goodbye… Major General."

"Goodbye Colonel."

A secretary brought him a message. It arrived from Moscow, from the Lubyanka, the FSB headquarters. Andrei read it quickly. He was asked to be in Moscow on 16 December with the chip. He passed the message on to his secretary to book a flight that evening. He decided to go home and took the chip.

"Andrei, what is going on?"

"Nothing, Olga. I have to be in Moscow the day after tomorrow. I'm taking the Aeroflot night flight."

"You mean tonight?"

"Yes, I do."

"Are you all right, Andrei?"

"Yes, don't worry. I think it has to do with my future appointment."

"General, then?"

"Yes, Major General."

"Congratulations, General!"

"Wait, it's not certain yet."

"I'm sure you'll be appointed."

"Until then, I'm still a colonel. By the way, did Lila leave?"

"Yes, she wanted to go home. She has to go to the funeral."

"Do you know the date?"

"Tomorrow."

"I won't be there. I wouldn't recommend going. There's been too much trouble around Mike lately. I think some CIA people are going to be there."

"It's embarrassing, Andrei. Poor Lila…"

"Olga, listen to me. Don't go."

"I won't, OK. I'll pack your suitcase. It'll be cold in Moscow. Will you take your coat and your chapka? How long will you be gone?"

"I think two days in Moscow. I'll be back on the evening of the 17th if I can get a seat on the morning flight."

"And the coat and the chapka, you haven't answered me?"

"Yes, I'll take them with me, in my cabin bag. In the suitcase put the jumpers and the thick socks and my corduroy trousers. Also my winter uniform. I'll change on the plane before we land."

"Which hotel are you staying at?"

"The Savoy, not far from the Lubyanka."

"The Savoy? You're giving up small, cheap hotels?"

"You see, if I come back general…"

"Ah, you see you're sure!"

"Almost…"

At eight o'clock, Andrei Safronov boarded the flight that would take him to Moscow. He sat down in his Aeroflot business-class seat. The stewardess offered him a glass of champagne, which he accepted. At 8:45 pm, the plane took off towards the cold Russian winter.

Lila spent her day organising her husband's funeral. It was a difficult time, and she had to pay for each service. She returned home tired and asked Nok to prepare a meal for her and Marat. They went to bed around nine o'clock. Around midnight, Lila heard a noise on the ground floor.

It seemed to her that the lock was being picked. She took the pistol that Andrei Safronov had given to her husband. With her heart pounding, she slipped towards the staircase from where she had a view of the main door of the house. She realised that someone was indeed trying to open it. She quietly descended the stairs and went to the room where Thanit was sleeping.

She knocked gently on the door. He opened it for her. She explained in a few words what was going on. Thanit, shirtless and in shorts, went to the door. He had taken Mike's baseball bat that he slept with every night. He asked Lila to go back upstairs to be safe.

She climbed the stairs and hid in the doorway of her room, waiting to see what happens. Eventually, the door opened, and three hooded men were about to enter when Thanit smashed the skull of the first one with the bat in one swift motion. The other two men didn't have time to react as the bat came down on them killing them instantly. Thanit bent down and removed their bonnets. They were Asians.

He looked through their clothes for any documents that might point to their identities but found nothing. He went outside and into the street. He spotted a Nissan Sylphy with Bangkok plates that he had never seen in the neighbourhood and deduced that it was the attackers' car. It was not locked. He got in and started a systematic search.

There was nothing in the car, not even the registration papers. As far as he was concerned, they were not Thai but foreigners. He realised that they were most likely Mike's killers or if not, they certainly had something to do with the crime. He returned to the villa.

"Madam, there is no one left. There is no threat."

"Thanit, what are we going to do?"

"We have to tell the police right away. If you want I'll take care of it."

"Yes, I'd like that."

"Madam, we are in danger. These men are probably not Thai. They are foreigners. And I think they have something to do with the murder of your husband."

"Yes, that's very likely, Thanit. But what can I do? Mike is not even buried yet."

"Ma'am, you have to leave Thailand. If you stay here you are in great danger, and so is your son. These are professional killers, they show no mercy. You must return to the United States as soon as possible."

"You are right Thanit. After Mike's funeral, I'll leave."

"That is a wise decision, Madam."

A police car arrived and noted the deaths of the three men and Thanit's self-defence. They said that the investigation would continue and that they would be kept informed if there was any news. Three ambulances followed, loading the corpses.

Wednesday, 15 December 2010

Mike's funeral was held at the Church of Christ, a Protestant religious association, in the Phetchaburi district. There were almost all the staff of the bank, about a hundred people, some Thais, including policemen. Lila had left Marat in the care of Nok, the maid. She noticed a woman in a police suit who must be a high-ranking officer, wiping tears from her cheek. She asked Thanit if he knew her.

He said he didn't, but noted that the woman had the rank of senior colonel, the highest rank of a senior officer, just before general. They both found it strange that she seemed sad. Lila said she wanted to talk to her, but Thanit advised her to see her after the ceremony, which she agreed to do. After the service, the coffin was taken by the hearse to the Protestant cemetery on Charoen Krung Road.

A minibus took the relatives, some bank executives, Thanit and Lila. After the final blessing, Lila and Thanit returned to the minibus, but not without looking for the police officer. They saw her leaving to get into a vehicle and call out to her. She turned around and saw Lila and Thanit. She stopped in front of her car and waited for them.

"Hi, I'm Lila Robertson. I'm Lila Robertson, Mike's wife. Did you know my husband well?"

"Yes, I did. Yes, I knew him well."

"May I ask how?"

"I'm investigating his complaint against Payom Narkhirunkanok."

"Who is he?"

"The person who forged his signature at the bank."

"Yes, I see. I was surprised to see you crying earlier."

"I knew your husband well. I'm so sorry. I loved him. And he loved me."

The sky was falling for Lila. She discovered a side of her husband that was completely unknown to her.

"I don't understand it. It can't be true."

"It's not a crime to fall in love. I'm so sorry."

"Oh, my God. Oh, my God. It can't be. That's awful."

"I understand how you feel. I can tell you that Mike would never have left you. He truly loved you. And I never encouraged him to leave you. That's how we loved each other. With respect to his family."

"My God. What respect are you talking about? A lie… a betrayal… Love has nothing to do with it."

"I am sorry, Madam. I can say no more. I have told you everything. I apologise but I must go. Be strong. Know that the drama that affects you, we have it in common. Goodbye. Goodbye."

"Wait, what's your name?"

"Apsara."

With that, she got into her car and drove away.

"It's horrible, Thanit, to make such a discovery at a time like this. I don't know what I feel. Sadness or anger, in fact, both. What a disappointment, but also what a shame. I cry for some reason. It's just too much."

"I'm so sorry for all this, Madame."

"I know, Thanit. Thank you for your support."

"I won't abandon you. You know you can count on me. I will do everything to protect you and Marat. There's one thing I wanted to ask you. Do you have Mr Mike's gun with you?"

"No, I left it at the villa."

"My advice to you, Madam, is never to part with it. Wherever you go, keep it with you. It's safer."

"Yes, you're right. I'm a fool."

"No, you just have so many things to think about that it's normal. Are we going home now?"

"Yes, Thanit. Let's go."

They got back in the minibus that drove them to the church where they had left their car. Once in the car park, Lila got into the back of the Mercedes as usual. Thanit got behind the wheel and started driving down Charoen Krung Road. After a few minutes, he turned onto South Sathorn Road, driving in the left-hand lane. At that moment, a motorbike appeared from the right rear with two men, one of whom was armed with a gun. He shot at the car, and the right and left rear windows shattered and grazed Lila's face.

"Get down, get on the ground, quickly!"

"Lila rushes to the floor of the car, screaming."

Thanit fell back onto the motorbike, which narrowly avoided him, climbing onto the pavement and coming back onto the road, chasing him again. A bullet was fired at the rear window, which shattered but did not hit the car's occupants. Thanit accelerated and ran the red light, miraculously avoiding four cars crossing the road towards Lumpini Road. The motorbike did the same and chased them. The motorbike ran up beside them and reached the rear windows again.

At this point, Thanit slammed on the brakes and accelerated towards the motorbike. Both men lost their balance under the impact, and one was crushed by the car. The other was thrown to his right and went under the wheels of a truck. The Mercedes was badly damaged, but they still drove. Thanit decided to continue without stopping. They arrived at the villa in Onut. Lila got out of the car trembling.

"Nok, are you there?"

The maid appeared on the terrace with Marat.

"Yes, Madam, we are here."

"Go inside the house, I don't want you to go outside anymore, it's too dangerous."

"Yes, Madam."

Lila came in after them. Marat ran to his mother who hugged him. She couldn't hold back the tears.

"Mum, you mustn't cry. I am with you and I will protect you from all these bad people. I will kill them all with my sword."

"My love. My little darling. Thank God I have you."

Meanwhile, Thanit saw the damage to the Mercedes. The back end was badly dented, but the engine didn't seem to have been touched. The front end still looked good. The car had generally held up well.

Lila turned on her computer and logged on to the American Airlines website. She booked two one-way business class seats for the next day's flight. Then she packed her clothes and Marat's into two suitcases. She informed Nok and Thanit of their departure. She paid the two employees a full month's salary, thanking them for their dedication and kindness. She asked Thanit to take them to the airport by 8:00 am, as their flight is at 1:00 pm. She didn't want to stay in this house anymore; she couldn't stand it. The sooner she was registered the better. She was suffocating in this heat. She was suffocating in this fear; she was suffocating in anger; she was suffocating in despair. It was too much. She felt she was losing her footing. So many unanswered questions and so much persecution of her and her son. She picked up her mobile and called the American embassy.

"This is Lila Robertson. I want to speak to Tony Rogers."

She waits a few seconds and hears Rogers' voice.

"Hello, Lila, I am so sorry for your loss. Mike was a good man. I'm deeply sorry about what happened."

"Mr Rogers, the house was attacked last night, as you probably know, and people on motorbikes tried to murder us when we returned from my husband's funeral."

"My God, that's not possible. Did you get away?"

"My driver and I escaped with our lives."

"What about the people who were after your lives?"

"I think they're in a bad way after their bike swerved."

"The important thing is that you got away safely."

"Mr Rogers, I'm requesting protection until tomorrow morning. My son and I are going back to the States tomorrow. We can't stay here any longer. We are targets."

"I understand. I'm gonna send you two of our guys. Their names are Frank Sheldon and Sam Chenney. They'll be at your house in two hours."

"Thank you very much."

"You don't have to thank me. It's only natural. I wish you a safe journey tomorrow."

She informed Thanit who reassured her. By being three guards tonight at the villa, especially with well-trained CIA agents, she and Marat would be safe.

Sheldon and Chenney arrived at the villa. They were greeted by Thanit. They saw the damage to the Mercedes and told him they were lucky to get out. They wondered who could be stalking them like this. They didn't know what to think. Thanit showed them through the house and introduced them to Marat who comes to meet them.

"Hi, champ, I hear you're a big brave guy?"

"Yes, I'm going to kill the bad guys. What's your name? Are you a policeman?"

"I'm Frank. And this is Sam. We're like policemen. Anyway, we chase bad guys."

"Do you have a gun and does your friend?"

"Yeah, we do. Does your mum have a gun?"

"Yes, she does."

"Hi, I'm Lila Robertson."

"Hi, Frank Sheldon, and this is Sam Chenney. We heard about your husband. We're very sorry."

"Yes, it's very sad."

"Your son told us you're armed? It's a wise precaution. Don't let go of your gun for any reason. Always remain vigilant. We will be here until you leave tomorrow morning, and we will escort you to Suvarnabhumi Airport."

"Thank you."

"We will take turns standing guard in the lounge."

"I am ready to assist you if necessary. I will also sleep in the lounge."

"Thank you, Thanit. If there is a problem, you can be useful."

"Well, I'll ask Nok to prepare the meal. I am not very hungry myself. I'm exhausted."

"Go and rest, Madam. We are watching. You are safe with us."

"Yes, I'm going to bed, I need to recover from these emotions. I need to clear my head. Nok, will you take care of Marat?"

"Yes, ma'am, you can count on me. Sleep well. I will put him to bed after dinner."

The evening passed quietly. After dinner, the three men retired to the living room after a tour of the villa. Nok put Marat to bed, Lila not having woken up. The night was calm.

Thursday, 16 December 2010

The sun rose in the early morning. Nothing had happened. Thanit loaded the luggage. Lila went down the stairs with Marat and headed to the dining room for breakfast. The CIA agents sat down at the table and helped themselves to coffee.

"Good morning ma'am, did you sleep well?"

"Yes, thank you, Agent Sheldon. And you, your night on call went smoothly."

"Yes, thank you."

An hour later, Lila and Marat said goodbye to Nok and got into the Mercedes. They left the villa, closely followed by the CIA agents' car. The journey to the airport went smoothly. The Mercedes parked in front of one of the entrances. Thanit got out and opened Lila's door. Then he took the suitcases out of the trunk.

Their damaged car did not go unnoticed and attracted all eyes. Thanit went to get a cart and put the two suitcases in it. Lila thanked Thanit and wished him a quieter life than he had with her. He laughed and told her that it had been a rewarding experience to serve her and her husband and that his family would always be in his heart.

Lila was moved and took his hands. Tears flowed from her eyes, and she told him that she had never met anyone so good, kind and honest. She gave him a kiss on the cheek. He knelt down to kiss Marat.

"You are a man now Marat. You'll look after your mother."

"Yes, I will protect her. I will learn to fight like you."

"You are right. That's very good. I'm sure you'll be very good."

"Well, let's go, Marat. Goodbye, Thanit."

"Goodbye Madame. I wish you all the best."

"Thank you very much."

She greeted the two agents, thanking them also for escorting her.

Lila entered the airport and headed for the American Airlines desk. She gave her passport and her son's to the stewardess, who inspected and printed their tickets. She checked their luggage and gave Lila their travel documents. Lila took Marat by the hand and went to the gate reserved for business and first-class passengers.

She passed her handbag and jacket through security and went to the police station where she handed over the passports and travel documents. The police officer did a routine check on his computer and looked at Lila several times. He got up from his seat and went to a small office behind his counter. He returned accompanied by a superior.

"Hello, ma'am, are you Lila Robertson?"

"Yes, I'm Lila Robertson."

"You can't come on board, ma'am."

"What do you mean you can't board?"

"You can't leave the country."

"But why not?"

"We have a police report on you."

"But that's not possible. What am I accused of?"

"It is noted that you must remain at the disposal of the police. I can't tell you anything else, I have no other information. But I can confirm that you can't go through. You have to go back to the hall, you can't stay here. I'm sorry."

"But my luggage? It's been checked in."

"We'll have them searched immediately. It's only a matter of twenty minutes or so, and you can pick it up at the desk of the airline you bought your flight with."

Devastated, Lila went back into the lobby with Marat. She returned to the American Airlines desk and froze in front of the stewardess who had issued her tickets. The stewardess informed her that she had been made aware of what was going on. She apologised on behalf of the company although she was not responsible for what was happening.

She asked Lila to wait until her bags were brought back. Lila called Thanit and told him what she considered to be a real disaster. He told her that he was turning back and coming to get them.

After half an hour, a baggage handler arrived with Lila's things. He fetched a trolley and put her bags on it. She took a conveyor belt down to the lower floor, the arrivals floor. She stepped out onto the pavement and saw the Mercedes pull up in the visitors' lane. Thanit got out and ran to get the luggage while she and Marat got into the car.

"It's terrible, Madame Lila."

"Yes, it's terrible. I don't know what to do."

"We're going to the villa, do you agree?"

"For the moment there's no other solution."

Andrei Safronov left the hotel in his colonel's uniform where he had spent the night. It was a dry cold day. The thermometer on the hotel wall read minus seven degrees. The sun was shining on the snow covering the gutters along the pavements. It was 8:00 in the morning. Traffic was already heavy.

He walked down Rozhdestvenka Street and then turned left onto Teatralny Proyezd to Lubyanka Square, where the huge neo-Baroque building housing the country's secret services and political police stood. He walked around the building and entered Bolshaya Lubyanka Street. There he passed the door of the FSB headquarters after showing his card and asked to be received by General Droski. The corporal at the reception desk called the general's secretariat and announced him.

Safronov then went to the lifts and climbed to the third floor. A captain who introduced himself as the general's orderly invited him to follow him. He was ushered into a large meeting room whose wood-panelled walls were decorated with portraits of the former directors of the secret services, the Vetcheka, better known as the Cheka, the GRU, the NKVD, the MGB, the MVD, the KGB and the FSB. A large solid oak table had twenty-five black leather armchairs arranged around it. Andrei placed his briefcase, chapka and coat on one of the seats.

He looked at the portraits to keep the weight at bay: Felix Dzerzhinsky, Vyacheslav Menzhinsky, Genrikh Yagoda, Nikolai Yezhov, Lavrenti Beria, Viktor Abakumov, Semyon Ignatiev, Vsevolod Merkulov, Ivan Serov, Aleksandr Chelepin, Vladimir Semichastny, Yuri Andropov, Vitaly Fedorchuk, Viktor Chebrikov, Leonid Shebarchin, Viktor Barannikov, Nikolai Golushko, Sergei Stepashin, Mikhail Barsukov, Nikolai Kovalev, Vladimir Putin, Nikolai Patrushev, Alexander Bortnikov. He noted that Chebarchine, Bakatine and Kroutchkov, actors of the 1991 events, were missing. He thought that among all these portraits, a certain number had violent deaths, particularly during the Stalinist era.

He understood that this room was reserved for important events. The door opened, and General Drosky appeared surrounded by four major generals and two lieutenant generals.

"Welcome to the Lubyanka, Andrei Sergeyevich! May I introduce to you Generals Yakov Viktorovich Brobroff, Konstantin Pavlovich Chubin, Nikita Illich Friazine, Evgeny Fyodorovich Ghliebnikov, Stepan Petrovich Gruchetski and Genady Denissovich Lipovsky?"

"How do you do?"

"Well, well, well! Do you have the chip?"

"Yes, General, here it is."

Andrei pulled from his pocket the decorated wooden matchbox that he had taken from his bookcase to hold his precious, tiny cargo. He opened the box, took out the chip and handed it to Droski.

"Perfect. You checked it, of course?"

"Of course, General."

"Yevgeny Fyodorovich take it to the control room and come back to confirm that everything is in order."

"Yes, General."

"Did you have a good trip, Andrei Sergeyevich?"

"Yes, thank you, General."

"Are you at the hotel?"

"Yes, I have no family in Moscow."

"Where are you staying?"

"At the Savoy."

"Very nice. Very nice address and not far from here."

"Yes, it's convenient, I came on foot."

"Ah, here's Yevgeny Fyodorovich back. What's up?"

"Everything is in order."

"That's great! Well, I can't hide the fact that I'm very satisfied with your services, Andrei Sergeyevich. So our board of directors has decided to nominate you for the rank of major general."

"This is a great honour, General."

"Russia has always rewarded its loyal and efficient servants. And you are one of them. I congratulate you, Major General Andrei Sergeyevich Safronov."

"Thank you, General. You know that I am completely devoted to the Motherland."

"I know that, Andrei Sergeyevich. That is why we have arranged for you to be transferred here to the department for the protection of the constitutional system and the fight against terrorism. You will work in the anti-terrorist department and assist Lieutenant General Genyad Denissovich Lipovsky. We want you to take up your post on the second of January. Make arrangements accordingly. We'll help you find a flat. We have a dedicated department for that."

"Thank you, General."

"I think that Genindi Denissovich will take you with him to talk to you about your future mission here and introduce you to the department."

"Very well, General."

"We will all meet at noon to have lunch together. I have reserved a table at the St Regis restaurant. It's very close, on Nikolskaya Street. We'll be on the eighth floor in the rooftop. And we will celebrate your success."

"Thank you, General, it's a great honour."

Andrei was leaving with Lipovsky to visit the department he was now responsible for.

"Are we on familiar terms, Andrei?"

"Yes, all right, Lenindi."

"I congratulate you on getting the chip back. I can tell you that no one here believed in it anymore."

"It's a happy ending."

"Well, I'll tell you about our role. Since the adoption of the new anti-terrorism laws, it is possible for us to set up military anti-terrorist operations anywhere on the orders of the president. We are gradually regaining our place in the world, thanks to the actions of our president. Russia is becoming strong and respected again. The FSB is accompanying the president's actions all over the world. You already know that."

"Yes, I do."

"Here we collect information that all our diplomatic missions pass on to us concerning, for example, popular movements, or even possible preparations for attacks that we may know about through infiltration. Or any association, small group or active minority, whether in Russia or in other countries. Our objective is to know everything before the others in order to be able to give instructions to our armed forces or police for interventions."

After lunch, washed down with vodka, Andrei returned to his hotel. He called Olga and told her about the upheaval in their lives. They had little time left to organise themselves. Olga had not expected to leave Bangkok so soon. She did not mind the prospect of living in Moscow, but she was worried about finding a flat in such a short time. Andrei reassured her that there was an FSB department that offered them to staff. This information did not reassure her. She didn't want to end up in one of the new buildings that had sprung up on the outskirts of the capital. She would like him to find something on the Arbat or Tverskaya or Kitai-Gorod. Andrei told her that these were expensive areas and that even if his salary was increased, it would be difficult for him to pay the rent, which he considered exorbitant. She retorted that they had savings and that they could sell their dacha in St Petersburg, which was well situated in a sought-after neighbourhood, not far from the Follenweider pavilion. She insisted and told him that Moscow was good, but not just anywhere. Andrei agreed, but he couldn't do anything at the moment, as he was flying back to Bangkok at 8:00 in the morning. She told him that she would ask her cousin Elina in St Petersburg to put their dacha up for sale and go to Moscow to look at flats in the areas indicated. Andrei grumbled to her to do as she pleased although he said that there was little chance of finding anything affordable in what he called tourist areas and that two weeks was an impossible time to sell a dacha and buy a flat.

Friday, 17 December 2010

Lila decided to go to the U.S. embassy to try to get an explanation for the refoulement she had been subjected to and to try to get the support of the diplomatic mission to find a solution to the problem. Thanit drove her. When she arrived, she asked to be seen by Tony Rogers. After an hour's wait, Rogers came to meet her up.

"Hello, Lila. I'm sorry, I was in a meeting."

"Hello, Mister Rogers. That's all right."

"Follow me, let's go to my office."

She followed him and realised that he didn't have the same office as last time when she came with Mike for the polygraph session.

"Have you changed offices?"

"Yes, the colleague who was here went back to the US, and this is bigger and more comfortable, so I took advantage of it. You know what they say: 'If you go hunting, you lose your job'. What brings you here?"

"Yesterday, I was supposed to fly to San Francisco. I was denied boarding."

"You were? Did they give you a reason?"

"Yes, I was told that I was the subject of a police report. That I was to remain at their disposal."

"That's strange. Have you had any contact with the police?"

"Do you remember the three men Thanit killed?"

"The ones who tried to break into your house, yes… But the police concluded that it was self-defence, right?"

"Yes, they did."

"So it's not that."

"Could you contact the Thai police?"

"Yes, that's what I was thinking of doing. We'll ask them what's going on."

"Do you think you'll get a quick answer?"

"They usually respond pretty quickly. I mean, within a week."

"A week? That's a long time."

"I understand you want to get out of here quickly after what happened."

"You don't have to say that."

"You can count on me, I'm doing my best. I'll call you as soon as I have any news."

"Thank you."

"You're welcome, Lila. Bye-bye."

Tony Rogers sent a complaint to the Home Office about Lila Robertson, an American citizen under the protection of the U.S. consular authorities. He was indignant that she was not able to board her flight home and asked for any valid explanations to be provided.

Cheong reassembled his staff at the North Korean diplomatic mission. Secretary Ha-Neul Park was present, but he forbade her to take notes.

"Comrades, the Seumkwang was found by the Russians. Colonel Safronov informed me of this. I have confirmation that CIA agent Mike Robertson had it. As you know, during the attack on the Golden Star Bank, he was killed. However, he was friends with Safronov, and his wife is Russian. The fact that the Russians got their hands on the chip before we did is an affront. All affronts must be paid. I want you to eliminate the wife and son. Do It!"

The Aeroflot plane landed in Bangkok. Andrei Safronov got off and headed for immigration. He took the corridor reserved for diplomats and presented his passport to the policeman on duty. He passed through and collected his suitcase from the carousel corresponding to his flight. Leaving the airport, he climbed into the embassy car that was waiting for him.

"Good evening Colonel, did you have a good trip?"

"Major General Roustem."

"I didn't know, excuse me. Congratulations, sir."

"Thank you, sir. Come on, let's go. To the house."

"Right, General."

The Russian embassy's Nissan Teana pulled up in front of the building, and Andrei grabbed his luggage and took his leave of the driver. He greeted the concierge and got into the lift. He entered his house. His son Ivan ran and threw himself into his arms. Olga looked at them expectantly.

"How is my General Major?"

"He's doing very well!"

"I hope you realise that I am a marshal in this house?"

"I've known that for a long time!"

"That's fine. I expected no less!"

She approaches him and kisses him tenderly.

"I called Elina. She has a friend in Moscow who is a real estate agent. She put her on the case. And we already have offers that she sent me by email."

"And the prices?"

"Not as expensive as you think. I have selected two flats: the first one is in the Arbat area. It's small but very cute. A three-room apartment of thirty-five square metres for nineteen million roubles. But the best is in the Tverskaya area. It's in an old building from the Stalin era. A renovated flat for twenty-two million roubles. It's sixty square metres and has four bedrooms."

"Yes, these are affordable prices."

"If you agree, I'll put an option on the one in Tverskaya. We have ten million roubles in savings and we can take out a loan for the rest. We don't even need to sell our dacha in St Petersburg."

"Well, that's fine. But are you sure about what we're buying?"

"I'll call Elina and tell her to go to Moscow tomorrow. We already talked about it together last night, and she agreed. With the Sapsan, the new high-speed train, she will be able to go there and back in a day."

"The Sapsan. It's been in service for a year now. It's practical, it took I think three hours and forty minutes to make the journey."

"Three hours forty-five exactly."

"You have a vocation as a stationmaster!"

"Laugh at me. Well, I'm calling Elina."

Monday, 20 December 2010

The weekend passed quietly. Lila's mobile rang. She picked up.

"Hello?"

"Hello, Lila. It's Tony Rogers."

"Hello, Mr Rogers."

"We got a reply this morning from the Thai Ministry of the Interior."

"What did they say?"

"You've been banned from leaving the country. This is because of the case Mike was involved in. You know, the John Finmore case."

"But Mike had nothing to do with that!"

"The police came to question him and told him that he could not leave the country until the investigation was over."

"But I personally did not see anyone. I do remember that. Mike told me about it, he said he saw two inspectors."

"The authorisation to travel will be issued when they have finished their investigation."

"Yes, but I never saw anyone. Why are they confusing the two?"

"You're his wife and they've lumped you in with Mike if I can put it that way. For them, it's the norm for foreigners."

"Now that Mike is dead, do you think there is any chance that they will close the case?"

"Normally yes. In my opinion, it's a question of time."

"But how much time?"

"How much time? I don't know. That's the administration, you know. They have a habit of not rushing things, that's the reputation they have. And we're not there yet, Lila. The investigation is still ongoing at this point."

"What can I do? I'm threatened here. And so is my son. I need protection."

"We have limited manpower here. We can't send agents to you every day and night."

"But you must protect your people."

"We will do what we can to protect you, but what I mean is that we don't have enough means to provide you with permanent protection."

"I need protection, especially in the evening."

"Look, I'll send a man over tonight. I'll see what I can do for the following nights."

"Thank you. Now, can't you intervene again to ask the Ministry of the Interior exactly where the investigation stands to get an approximate date of closure?"

"We can ask again. We will do so."

"Thank you for your help."

"The embassy services are doing everything they can to resolve the situation, rest assured. We will contact you as soon as we have any news."

"Thank you very much."

"Tonight, Agent Sam Chenney, who you already know, will be coming to your home."

"All right, then. Thank you. (chuckles) Oh, by the way, I have an idea."

"I'm listening…"

"Maybe if I go to the police, I mean the detectives that Mike had met with, I could explain the situation to them and make them understand that I'm not involved in this."

"I don't know if that will help."

"I've got nothing to lose anyway. I'll try. But I don't have the names of those policemen. Do you have them?"

"Yes, I got that information from the answer they gave me. Let me see… Let's see… Here. Have you got something to write with?"

"Yes, go ahead."

"Major Yoobamroong and Lieutenant Larpthawornkiet."

"Do you know where I can find them?"

"Yes. They are at the Bangkok Metropolitan Police Headquarters, 323 Sri Ayutthaya Road, Dusit District."

"Well, I'll contact them and meet them."

"Please try. I wish you good luck."

"Luck, that's what I need most right now, you know…"

"I know, Lila. I know you do. Good luck anyway."

Lila asked Thanit for a ride. They left the villa. The driver was careful not to be followed, which confused Lila. Thinking aloud, she said that she would be safer if she travelled with the underground. And she finally ordered to be dropped off at the next station.

"Thanit, what is the next skytrain station?"

"Phra Khanong."

"I'll get off at this station. You meet me at the police station."

"OK, Madame Lila. Be very careful. You'll have to pick me up at Phaya Thai station."

"Yes, ma'am."

The car stopped, and she got out. She climbed the stairs to the platform. The train arrived; the guard signalled to the passengers to move back beyond the security line on the ground. She got into a carriage. The air-conditioning was strong; the temperature must be seventeen degrees inside; the amplitude with the outside was important and favourable to flu and colds. She looked at the posted traffic map and counted ten stations to her destination.

It was ten o'clock and not too crowded. The rush hour had passed. The passengers were quiet and smiling, in the normal way, and she didn't see any angry faces around her, which reassured her. She told herself that this type of travel was the best, if only because of the constant traffic jams that offered killers the perfect opportunity to carry out their crimes. From now on, she thought, she would organise herself in this way.

She would always take the skytrain or the metro and asked Thanit to meet her at the destination she indicated. And, to return, she would follow the same plan. She would go to Onut station where the driver would be waiting for her. The train stopped at Phaya Thai. She got off the train, walked down the stairs to the lower level, and went to the glass office where the cashiers worked.

A young woman opened the door and told her that to get out she had to insert her card or token into the electronic reader in the mechanical corridor. She replied that she knew this but needed information to go to the police headquarters. The employee gave her the information. She thanked her and left on foot. She reached the police building after about fifteen minutes of fast walking.

The orderly on duty stopped her and told her that the police museum was a little further on. She asked to see Major Yoobamroong. The orderly was surprised but agreed to call the officer. He went back to her and asked why she wanted to see him. She gave him her name, arguing that this would be enough for the officer to agree to see her.

And, indeed, the orderly confirmed that someone would come to pick her up and take her to the inspector. An elderly woman in uniform arrived and invited her to follow her. They entered the building, and she beckoned her to sit down on one of the chairs provided for visitors.

As soon as she sat down, she saw a man in his forties arrive, with a paunchy build and a shuffling gait.

"Hello, I'm Major Buncha."

"Hi, Major Buncha. Actually, I'd like to meet Detective Yoobamroong. Do you know if he's here?"

He answered her with a laugh.

"Oh, that's me. I'm Major Buncha Yoobamroong. In Thailand, we all call each other by our first names. It's very rare to be called by your last name."

"Please excuse my blunder."

"No, that's all right. So you're Madame Lila?"

"Yes, I am. I'm Mike Robertson's wife."

"Oh, I heard about your husband. It's a tragedy. I'm sorry for your loss."

"Thank you."

"Come on, let's go to my office."

"All right, come on in."

"Here, come in and have a seat. Can I offer you some fresh water?"

"Yes, please. It's hot outside."

"Yes, it's winter, but some days are like that. Otherwise, it's much cooler, have you noticed?"

"Yes, you're right."

"So tell me what I can do for you, within the limits of my powers and within the law of course."

"Major Buncha, as you probably know, my husband could not leave Thailand because of an investigation you were doing on the murder of John Finmore."

"Yes, that is true. Unfortunately, your husband is now in the kingdom for eternity."

Lila was taken aback by the policeman's inappropriate comment and was speechless for ten seconds. But she thought she'd better not mention it if she wanted to win his good help.

"Unfortunately, yes. I recently learned that this restriction applies to me too, and apparently to my young son. But since my husband has died and neither my son nor I are in any way involved in this matter, can you confirm that this measure is no longer necessary?"

"Madame Lila, the investigation file is not closed. We still don't know who killed Mr John Finmore. And our laws do not allow us to lift this kind of measure while the investigation remains open."

"But imagine that your investigation stalls and you find nothing. Your case could stay open for years!"

"Yes, you are absolutely right. But don't worry. I will arrange for your visa to be extended for another year. You won't have any problems with the police. If you have your passport and that of your son with you, I'll take care of it right away."

"Major Buncha, I think there's a misunderstanding. I didn't come here to get an extension on my visa. I want to go back to the States. I have nothing to keep me here, you understand. I want you to lift the deportation order against me and my son."

"I will do one thing: I will lift the ban for your son because he is still very young. He will then be able to return to his country without any problems. But I can't do more than that."

"But that's no use! My son is ten years old, he can't stay alone."

"You don't have any family in the United States?"

"No, I don't."

"No relatives?"

"No, I don't have any relatives."

"There's nothing else I can do, I'm sorry."

"But if your investigation never ends, does that mean I'll be here forever?"

"No. If in four years' time, the case is still alive and there are no developments against you of course, then you can go back to your country."

"Four years? Four years to spend here? That's crazy."

"You don't like Thailand?"

"It's not about that. I'm a stranger here. I have no one."

"I will point out that you have no one in your country either."

"It is not the same, you know that."

"Madame Lila, I can't do any more, I've told you. Do you have your passports with you?"

"Yes, I have."

"Give them to me."

"Here you are."

"Well, let's see. Ah, but you were born in Russia. You have dual American and Russian citizenship?"

"Yes, I am."

"Do you have family in Russia?"

"Yes, I do."

"Your parents?"

"Yes."

"Well, you can send your son there. Provided he has dual nationality too."

"He has it."

"So what is the problem? In Thailand, in many families, grandparents bring up the children and it is very good."

"I want my son to stay with me."

"So it's a choice. But now don't say that, at least for your son, we are preventing him from moving around. Well, I'm going to have both your passports extended for another year from now on anyway. If you are still here in a year's time, you will have to come back here for a new extension, and so on every year."

"I hope I will be gone before then."

"I hope so for your sake. Wait for me here."

Yoobamroong returned after ten minutes with the passports.

"You are in order, Madame Lila. And I have lifted the ban on your son leaving the kingdom."

"Do you alone decide? Do you have that power?"

"Yes, within the limits of the law."

"Which means that it was not necessary to impose such a measure on my son?"

"No, it didn't."

"I'd like to know what could possibly be going through your head to have done this."

"Don't lose hope. The investigation is going on as usual. If there are any developments, I'll call you to let you know. Goodbye, Madame Lila."

"Goodbye."

Thanit waited on the pavement in front of the entrance to the police headquarters. He saw Lila coming and understood from her look that things must not have gone as she expected. She confirmed this and told him that there was every chance that she would have to stay in the country for another four years. She told him that she preferred to take the skytrain back to Onut and that he would wait for her at the exit of the station with the car. The return journey was smooth, and when she reached the exit, she noticed that the Mercedes was not yet there.

She thought about the chronic traffic density and called Thanit. He confirmed that he was going very slowly because of the traffic jams and that he would be able to reach Onut in about thirty minutes. To pass the time, she wandered into the covered market next to the station. She wandered from stall to stall for half an hour. Finally, she saw the car. They returned to the villa.

Frank Sheldon was with Thai police in the Union Thai Trade building. At the request of the American embassy, which had reported the unexplained disappearance of Peter Keldrik, and following the assassination of the oligarchs who were the subject of an international search launched by Interpol, new searches had been ordered by the courts. Frank asked for the garden to be turned over so that nothing was left to chance. Finally, a policeman from the team discovered Keldrik's corpse. Frank ran over and had a vision of horror when he saw the body, whose skin had been completely removed.

His feet were covered with a kind of membrane that an officer lifted. It was the skin of the victim, in one piece. A professional job. A few policemen stood aside and start vomiting. The supervising police officer ordered the body to be removed and sent to the forensic institute for an autopsy. The coroner confirmed that Keldrik was properly flayed, as his torturer was certainly experienced in this type of torture. Frank took photos at the site and in the morgue to show Tony Rogers. It was so gruesome that Rogers turned pale with horror.

"It's really inhumane what poor Peter went through. I can't imagine what he suffered. What a bunch of bastards. I'm glad they're all gone. I don't know who shot them, but I can tell you that's all they had to do. And still, they had a very sweet death compared to this."

"They deserved the same, Tony."

"I've seen horrors before in my career, but this is the worst. They are animals."

At about seven o'clock, Sam Chenney arrived at Lila's house. He took an M16A2 rifle and an M230 grenade launcher from the car, unloaded a box of M855 ammunition and stored it in the house.

"Hello, Sam."

"Hi, Lila, how are you? No problems today?"

"No, it seems to be calming down. I'm keeping my guard up."

"I have to!"

"Hi, Sam."

"Hey, Marat. So how are you?"

"I'm good. Is this all about killing the bad guys?"

"Yeah, it is. If they get close they won't stand a chance. I can tell you that."

"How many rounds can your rifle fire?"

"Thirty."

"That's a lot of rounds."

"Yes, that's what we need."

"What about this one?"

"That one is for throwing grenades. Whoever gets this will be picked up with a spoon."

"Will it be pulp them?"

"Yes, exactly."

"I'd like to learn to shoot. When I grow up I want to be like you, a soldier. And you know, Thanit is a karate champion. And since I don't go to school anymore, he shows me how to fight."

"That's good my boy. Thanit, are you really good at karate?"

"I can manage."

"What level do you have? What school did you attend?"

"I am a fifth dan Shotokan. I was a member of the Thai national team until two years ago. I was Thailand's all-round champion at the age of twenty-five."

"How old are you?"

"I am thirty years old."

"And you still practice in a dojo?"

"Yes, I am a teacher, and I still train. But with what's going on right now, I haven't been to the dojo for three weeks. I can't leave madam alone, it's too dangerous."

"That's fine, Thanit. What about Thai boxing?"

"I did that too when I was young, I practised from the age of ten to nineteen. I did it at the same time as karate, which I started at the age of five. I won a lot of boxing fights. But I decided to invest myself fully in karate, and I left boxing."

"Anyway, that makes you, I think, a formidable fighter."

"Yes, even if I never underestimate the opponent, I am not afraid of anyone. I teach my students that the secret of victory can be summed up in three words: precision, speed and determination."

"That's a good point. It is indeed what gives you the upper hand."

The evening passed quietly. At about 11:00 pm, the doorbell rang. Sam picked up the M16, and Thanit asked the visitor to introduce himself. It was a young woman with a little girl who wanted to meet the lady who lived in the house. Thanit approached the gate, Sam covering him.

He opened the door, and the young Thai woman, who was carrying a small dog in her arms, told him that she and her little daughter, who looked to be about four or five years old, wish to offer the dog. Thanit, suspicious, smiled but did not answer. He looked around to make sure that everything was quiet and that no one was lurking around the house. Sam came to the armed gate, which frightened the young woman.

She took the little girl by the hand and left. Thanit caught up with her, assuring her that she was safe, that they were taking precautions because they were attacked a few days ago by thugs. She agreed to come back, but not without suspicion. Thanit called Lila.

"Madame Lila, this young woman wants to see you."

"Hello. What do you want?"

"Do you have a little boy?"

"Yes. Why do you ask?"

"My granddaughter saw him and wants to give him this little dog."

"Oh, thank you, but I don't know if I should accept."

Marat, who had not yet gone to bed, saw his mother talking and ran to her.

"Look, mummy, a little dog!"

"The little girl took the dog from her mother's arms and offers it to Marat."

"For you."

"For me?"

"Yes, for you."

"Yes, for you. Thank you. Do you agree, Mum? Please say yes!"

"But what are we going to do with it if we go to America?"

"We'll take it with us, mum. Come on, say yes."

"All right, then."

"That's great! Thanks, mum!"

"Say thank you to the little girl, she's the one who gave you the dog."

"Thank you. What is your name?"

"Ying."

"And I am Marat. And the dog?"

"Teelek. He's eight months old, but he's a good boy, he'll get to know you soon."

"My name is Lila. And yours?"

"Janjira."

"Do you live in the neighbourhood?"

"I live with my sister, it's the house next door, a hundred metres away."

"Thank you very much. That's very kind."

"It's our pleasure. This is my sister's dog who has had puppies. It's a purebred dog. Lhasa-Apso."

"Thank you very much."

Lila thought that she didn't know how much longer they would have to stay and that the dog would be the company for her son. She watched him go to his room with the dog. She was happy to see him so happy. These were the first moments of happiness for Marat since Mike disappeared. A tear rolled down her cheek.

The night passed peacefully.

Tuesday, 21 December 2010

At four o'clock in the morning, eight men took up position in front of Lila's villa. They moved quietly, climbed over the entrance gate, and progressed to the terrace. Suddenly, they heard barking and stopped. At that moment, inside, Sam leapt from the sofa where he had been dozing and grabbed his M16. Thanit, who had been sleeping on the floor, got up. One of the eight men kicked the door hard, but it was stronger than he thought and did not open. Sam shot through the door, and the man collapsed. The other members of the commando team shot through the door in turn. Sam and Thanit had shifted to protect themselves. Thanit went up the stairs to the rooms. Lila had come out in a panic. Thanit reassured her and told her to take refuge in Marat's room. He advised her to keep her pistol loaded in case these men reached the rooms. Marat had woken up and called for his dog. Thanit told him that the dog was downstairs and that for the moment, it was not possible to go and get it. Marat called him by name several times, and Thanit was surprised to see him come running. The shooting continued unabated, and the door ended up looking like a sieve. One by one, the windows shattered. Sam took a shot and killed another assailant. Four of the assailants positioned themselves in front of the door and emptied their magazines at the same time. The door collapsed, leaving the commandos free to move in. Sam grabbed the M230 and fired at the four men. The grenade exploded killing them all. A member of the commandos who was behind the first wave emptied his clip on the entrance and hit Sam who collapsed. The last two assailants then entered the house and very quickly dived to the floor, covering each other as they went. They now climbed the stairs and reached the second floor, when Thanit, who was standing on a ceiling beam, jumped on the second man. He grabbed him from behind and pushed him violently onto his accomplice, which had the effect of throwing them both off balance. He pounced on the first and killed him with a punch to the base of the nose and immediately turned on the other who had taken his weapon. He didn't have time to use it, Thanit kicked him in the knee and broke his leg. The man screamed, and Thanit disarmed him.

"Who are you? Who are you working for?"

"The man looks at him and spits in his face."

Thanit thrust his fingers into the fractured area, and he screamed.

"Answer!"

Still, without an answer, Thanit tried again, but the result was the same. Lila came out of the room armed with her gun and discovered the extent of the damage on the ground floor. She stood next to Thanit threatening the man with the gun. Thanit turned towards her, and just then the man pulled a knife from his belt and was about to strike him when a shot rang out. Lila pulled the trigger and killed the assailant. Thanit thanked her; she had saved his life. Lila walked around the house with Thanit who had taken Sam's M16. They counted the eight dead commandos. They were all Asians, like last time, Thanit remarked. But he maintained that they were not Thai. He had no idea about their nationality. He searched them but found nothing, no papers, no documents. Neighbours came out and surrounded the house. They didn't understand these attacks. One of them called Thanit, while Lila went to call the American embassy.

"This can't go on!"

"I know it can't. We'll call the police."

"No, the police do nothing. It's a score-settling exercise by the mafia. They'll be back, you know. We can't accept this in our neighbourhood! You must be drug dealers!"

The other people presented take the side of supporting their neighbours and booed Thanit.

"You are Thai like us. You have no business with foreigners who traffic. You have to leave this house, and the woman has to leave. We don't want her here anymore."

"Calm down! She has nothing to do with it. She's a banker's wife. She doesn't do any business."

"Yes, I know the husband is a banker. He's dead. And you're her lover, right? That's why you're crashing at her place. Is it a good job at least? Does that bitch suck ok?"

Suddenly, Thanit swivelled and delivered a roundhouse kick that hit him in the neck. The man collapsed.

"Are there any other takers? No? No one? Then listen to me, all of you! This woman has absolutely nothing to do with any trafficking. We don't know who these people are yet. They are killers, that's all we can conclude from this. Today. I will call the police. I agree that this cannot continue. That's why I'm ringing the police, to ask them to protect the condominium. And therefore to protect you too. Now go home. The battle is over."

The onlookers went home without saying another word. The young woman from the previous day approached Thanit and asked him about Marat and Lila. He confirmed that they were safe and sound. If she wished, she could come later. She insisted on coming to help tidy up the house and did the cleaning. Thanit thanked her and said he would talk to Lila. She left him her mobile number. Thanit called the police.

Meanwhile, Lila had managed to reach Tony Rogers and told him that Sam was dead. He was appalled and announced he would visit straight away.

The local police were on the scene and took their initial briefing. They had called in the criminal police because of the number of dead people, the weapons found at the scene and the damage done. Tony Rogers also arrived. He saw that his agent is dead. He was furious.

"Hello, Lila."

"Hi, Tim."

"Anyone ever tells you you're a jinx?"

"It's not my fault this is happening. I don't even know why these people want to kill us. Who are they?"

"We'll find out soon enough. Look at their weapons: they're Type 68s. North Korean version of the Soviet AKM. Did they have anything on them? Did you search them thoroughly?"

"Yes, they had nothing."

"They're complete morons, they should have taken less identifiable weapons, at least more common ones if they didn't want to be recognised."

"You think they're North Korean?"

"There's a good chance."

A new police vehicle arrived. Major Buncha Boomyanroong was getting out.

"Hello, Madame Lila. It's definitely not easy having you as a visitor to our country."

"What do you want me to do about it, Major?"

"I'm Tony Rogers from the American embassy. I have an agent of mine who was killed in the shoot-out."

"What was he doing here?"

"He was assigned to protect the occupants of the house."

"Madame Lila, why didn't you inform the police that you were under threat?"

"Are you kidding me? Since my husband was murdered, I've had security problems in your country. The police already came the other day for an attack of this type. My driver managed to put them out of action without a shot being fired. So the police are well aware of my insecurity. And they never offered me anything."

"You should have told me."

"Major, need I remind you of your reluctance to help me?"

"You're pushing it a bit hard. I've done everything I can for you."

"And, of course, you don't know any of these men? Don't you know anything?"

"Yes, Major. Ninety-nine per cent of them are North Korean."

"How do you figure that, Mr Tony?"

"It's not complicated. Look at their weapons."

"Oh, yeah… their weapons… and… what are those exactly?"

"Are you kidding me? They're Type 68s."

"Ah… yes…"

"You need to point your investigation in that direction. North Korean nationals. There's a few of them here, I've seen restaurants run by them."

"Yes, but you know, these are people who have fled the regime in their country, the ones who have restaurants."

"It wouldn't be a mafia from this country that would operate these establishments?"

"No, we wouldn't allow that."

"You've got to be kidding me."

Tony collected Sam's guns and ammunition and loaded them into his car. Lila came over to him.

"Mr Rogers, what do you think you can do to keep me safe?"

"You see, Lila, with an agent killed, I don't have many people left. And between you and me, if you regularly have this kind of assault, I don't want to lose all my agents to protect you. Now you and your son have Russian citizenship. Ask them to protect you. After all, it is also their role, when we hear your president claiming on all the international media that Russia will protect its citizens all over the world. Go ahead, this is your chance to see if the Russians are putting their words into action."

"So I can't count on you anymore?"

"I'm afraid not. On the other hand, did you hear from the criminal police officer? It seems he's ready to protect you."

"Goodbye, Mr Rogers. I don't think we have anything more to say to each other."

Behind her, Buncha was waiting for her turn to speak to him. As Rogers left, he called her.

"Madam Lila, we need to have a talk."

"Yes, I'm listening. Can you get me some protection?"

"I'll take care of it. But I wanted to tell you that given what's happened here, you're an important witness."

"So I can't leave the country, right?"

"Yes, Madame Lila, that's exactly it."

"So if I understand correctly, I have two deportation orders now?"

"I'm sorry, but that's it. And your son witnessed all this violence, didn't he?"

"No, he stayed in his room with me actually."

"Normally he should stay here because he's old enough to testify. But I'm going to skip over that to be nice to you."

"I suppose I should say thank you?"

"I understand your annoyance, Madame Lila, but don't make my job any harder than it already is."

"I'm the one who should be complaining. They are determined to kill me, and on top of that, they forbid me to go back to my country. Don't you think so, Major?"

"I will always do everything in my power to help you, Madame Lila."

"So what do you propose to do for my protection? I need policemen here tonight, do you realise that?"

"It can't be done in a minute. I'll have to check with the head of the local police station in Onut. I'll contact them and go see the officer in charge of this area."

"Will you do it today?"

"Yes, of course."

"What do you think of Rogers' deductions?"

"The American who was here?"

"Yes."

"We can't jump to any conclusions. There's nothing to tell us that they're Korean. We don't know that. We'll see what the forensic institute tells us."

"But the weapons? These are weapons used by the North Koreans, according to Rogers. And I think he knows about weapons."

"Yeah, but you know, these are weapons that could have been purchased on the black market. The mob is used to that."

"So you don't actually believe they're North Korean?"

"I have no opinion at the moment. We have to investigate seriously instead of making assumptions like the Americans did."

"But it's a path that needs to be verified quickly, don't you think?"

"Everything will be checked, Madame Lila. We are professionals, have no doubt about it."

"Good. I'll expect to hear from you later today then?"

"Yes, I promise."

"And I'll have policemen outside my house tonight?"

"I can't guarantee that for tonight, but I'll do what I can. On my way out of here, I'll stop at the police station in Onut."

"Well, we'll see…"

Lila saw Janjira arrive. Janjira told her that she wanted to come and help her clean up the house and put it in order. Lila thanked her and accepted her help. They entered the house together. The ambulance drivers who had come with the police had already taken away the bodies. There were blood stains, broken glass and splinters of wood all over the ground floor of the villa. Lila introduced Janjira to Nok. They set to work without wasting time. Thanit assisted them to pick up the glass fragments that littered the floor. Marat stayed upstairs in his room. He had been able to retrieve his dog and was playing with a tennis ball. The little dog ran to catch it. He took it in his mouth and brought it back to his new young master.

Lila thought about it and came to the conclusion that she was not safe anywhere. Especially not in this house. The people who were after her know that she lived there. She didn't understand why they wanted to kill her, but she did understand one thing: It was a powerful organisation, to always be able to send new killers. With the support of Thanit and the American embassy agents, they had already killed thirteen men. Who were they? What did they want? What Rogers said intrigued him. He couldn't have been wrong about the origin of the weapons, he knew what he was talking about. So what did the North Koreans have to do with it?

And, if that was the case, these weapons were North Korean army weapons if Rogers recognised them at first glance. So North Korean soldiers… What were they doing in Thailand? Their presence was illegal in the country, that's for sure. If that was the case, then they must be under the control of the North Korean embassy.

They would then be members of that country's secret service. Would Mike have had contact with them? With the ambassador perhaps? And did things go so wrong that they wanted to kill her and her son? Probably something very serious, but what? She was at this point in her thoughts when Thanit approached her.

"Madame Lila, will we have anyone from the American embassy here tonight to protect us?"

"Unfortunately not, Thanit. They don't want to lose any more agents. They're afraid."

"Them, the Americans? Afraid? I can't believe that."

"We have to face the facts, Thanit."

"It's incredible that they're afraid. What a lack of courage."

"The Thai police inspector who came told me he would try to send us some policemen tonight."

"Thai police? I don't think so."

"We'll see. I'm going to call my friend Olga. I want to see if her husband can do anything for us. But there are more pressing matters. We have to find somewhere else to live. It's become too risky to live here. Thanit, do you know a place where we can take refuge?"

"Let me think and make some contacts. And I say Madame Lila."

"Thanit, just call me Lila."

"Yes, Madame Lila."

She laughed.

"Lila."

"Yes, I have to get used to it… Lila."

"That's better."

An hour later, Thanit came back to Lila. He informed her that one of his uncles had provided her with a house in the countryside, in the northeast of the country in the Isan region. The advantage was that it was located in a small village and no one would come looking for them there. Lila longed for peace. She immediately agreed to his proposal. Thanit raised another problem.

The Mercedes was too conspicuous; especially with the grille and bonnet down, they were easily spotted. The only way out was to buy a common car in the local landscape, such as a Toyota Altis. There were second-hand markets. You just had to go there and buy the car. The other problem was that Lila did not have a work permit in Thailand, so the law did not allow her to buy a car. So it would be in Thanit's name.

Lila didn't want to waste time; her mind was made up. Abandoning the idea of moving with the Mercedes, they took a taxi to Rama IV Road where they found a second-hand car dealership. They found a seven-year-old Toyota Corolla Altis with a hundred thousand kilometres for ten thousand baht. Lila paid cash in accordance with local customs. They left with the car and returned to the villa. As a precaution, Thanit parked the car in the car park behind the Onut skytrain station, and they took motorbike taxis to their condominium. They paid the bikers at the entrance of the condo and walked home. Janjira and Nok were still scrubbing when they reached the threshold of the villa. Marat called his mother to show her his progress in training the dog.

"Look, mum, he understands if I ask him to sit!"

"That's good, Marat. Later you will work in a circus and you will be a dog trainer."

"Does that exist?"

"I think so. Well, Nok and Janjira, you've done a good job."

"We are almost finished. But we have to replace the door and put in new windows."

"Yes, I'll see to that later. Nok, I'm going to take a few days off, I'm exhausted from all these events. I'm going to Phuket with Marat. Thanit is coming with me to protect us."

"That's good, Madame Lila, you need it. Go without worrying about the house. I will look after it and take care of it while you are away."

"Thank you, Nok."

"Mum, mum, should we take Teelek with us?"

"Yes, Marat."

"Great!"

Thanit looked at Lila with round eyes. He didn't understand why she would change her plans without informing him first. She realised that he didn't understand and went out onto the terrace, beckoning him to follow her.

"Thanit, we're going to your uncle's house."

"But then? What you told them?"

"It's to cover our tracks. Since I don't trust anyone, I'm going to tell everyone that I'm going to Phuket. So if anyone talks, we'll be safe."

"That's very clever."

"It has to be."

Lila called the U.S. Embassy and insisted that she be put through to Tony Rogers.

"Yes, Lila, what do you want now? I told you that my services would do nothing more."

"This is not to ask you anything but to inform you that I am going away for a few days. I am going to Phuket to rest."

"Well, have a good holiday!"

He hung up.

Then she called her friend Olga.

"Hello, Olga."

"Lila, how are you? I was just thinking about you."

"It's really not easy, you know. Besides, we were attacked last night by armed men, real commandos."

"My God."

"There was an American embassy agent for protection, but he was killed. He and Thanit managed to get through it anyway. They all died."

"It's terrible. But do we have any idea who it was?"

"One of the embassy officials who came this morning tells me that the weapons used came from North Korea. He is convinced that they are North Korean. From what I understand, he suspects a mafia group."

"But what do they want from you? It's completely crazy."

"I don't know. I'm beginning to think that Mike might have been involved with these people… I really don't know."

"Did you see the police?"

"Yeah, I saw them. The police came this morning to check on the damage and pick up the bodies. The house has no doors, there are no windows, you can imagine the damage that Kalashnikovs can do…"

"How can you stand all this, I couldn't. Oh, my poor Lila."

"The worst thing is that the American embassy doesn't want to hear from us anymore."

"Is that possible?"

"Yes, they do. I decided to go to Phuket for a few days, hoping to get some peace."

"You're right, staying in Bangkok is becoming untenable for you and Marat."

"I'm tired of it all. What about you? Any news?"

"Andrei has been promoted to General and transferred to Moscow."

"Good for him! You'll congratulate him for me. When are you leaving?"

"At the end of the year. He has to take up his post in January."

"You must have a lot to do, especially to find accommodation, in Moscow, it's not easy because of the prices."

"Yes, but do you remember my cousin Elina?"

"Yes, I do."

"She has a friend who works in real estate and she found us a flat on Tverskaya. It's in a building from the thirties, but completely renovated. We decided to buy it."

"You're lucky, Olga. Nothing but good news."

"I wish I could help you, my poor Lila."

"It's all right, Olga. Leaving Bangkok will be good enough for me."

"Well, in any case, don't hesitate to call me. We're still here until the end of the year."

"Yes, of course. I have to go now. I have to pack. See you soon, Olga. Say hello to Andrei for me."

"I will. Love to you."

Finally, Lila looked for Major Boomyanroong's business card and called him. She got him straight away and realised that it was his mobile that he was left for her.

"Major Boomyanroong?"

"Hello?"

"It's Lila Robertson."

"Oh, you're here to check on your protection? I saw the chief of the police station in Onut. He's got a problem, it's manpower. He doesn't have enough men and he can't spare one of his officers to stand guard outside your house. I'm really sorry. I'm still looking for another possibility."

"I can see that you are efficient, Major. It's like the investigation. Same results."

"No, the investigation is progressing."

"Have you got any news?"

"I can't say anything, it's professional secrecy, you know."

"Yes, it's very useful when you want to hide your incompetence."

"Madame Lila, I won't allow you. You are talking to a member of the Royal Police, don't forget that."

"No, I'm not forgetting that, sir. I wasn't calling you for that anyway. I'm going away for a few days and I wanted to inform you."

"Where are you going?"

"Phuket."

"Are you taking a holiday?"

"I need a rest from all the horror."

"I understand that. And which hotel will you be staying at?"

"I don't know yet."

"You haven't made a reservation? It's not very wise, it's the end of the year, and Christmas and New Year's Eve are coming up. It's a very touristy season in Phuket. It is not sure that you will be able to find a room when you arrive unexpectedly. I strongly advise you not to go like this. Make a reservation first."

"Otherwise, what? You're not going to allow me to board the plane? On what grounds? Ongoing investigation?"

"Madame Lila, I'm giving you this advice for your own good. It's not an order. And you think you'll come back on what date?"

"You really are a zealous policeman. I don't know exactly when I'll be back. As you so aptly suggested, it depends on hotel availability."

"But do you have an idea of a hotel?"

"I'll see. There is a choice. Sheraton, Hilton, Sofitel and so on. There's no shortage of them in Phuket."

"I see. Well, the best thing is for you to keep me informed. For the sake of my file, it's best if I know where you are and when you'll be returning to Bangkok. Call me when you have found your place of stay."

"Thank you for your concern. Goodbye, Major."

"Have a good holiday, Madame Lila."

"What a jerk that guy is. If he thinks I'm going to call him, he's up to his elbows in it," she thought.

With the luggage ready, Lila asked Marat to take the dog in his arms, as he had no leash to hold him. They left the house on foot, Thanit carrying the two suitcases that Nok had prepared. They again took three motorbike taxis, which transported them to the car park where they recovered their Toyota. Marat admitted his surprise when he saw this grey car whose interior was far from the ostentatious luxury of the Mercedes.

"Mum, why are we taking this car?"

"It's Thanit's car. The Mercedes had a big crash, and we have to get it fixed."

"Are we going to the seaside?"

"No, we're going to the countryside."

"But I thought we were going to Phuket?"

"No, we'll be much better in the country. There are fewer people and your dog can run around with you."

"Oh, yes, that's a good idea, mum."

"Thanit, where exactly are we going?"

"We are going to Buriram. That's about four hundred kilometres. It should take us five hours to get there. Then we'll go to a village called Ban Hua Wua. The house is outside the village, it is isolated. It is a farmer's house. There is a large field, which is good for Marat."

Thanit didn't drive very fast. The kilometres went by as they crossed the provinces: Pathumthani, Saraburi, Nakhon Ratchasima and finally Buriram, which bore the same name as the city that was its capital. They stopped to eat and resumed their peregrination. After Buriram, the car engaged small roads to finally arrive at the village of Ban Hua Wua. They passed the village and continued for two kilometres.

Thanit took a muddy road, which led to a typical Thai peasant house. It was a house on stilts, made of wood, of about a hundred square metres. A few large pots with free-growing plants were scattered here and there. Under the house, a small fence was open. Under the stilts was a dusty old table with rusty tools on it. Lots of weeds. Two large openings in the front with shutters but no windows.

"Is this the place?"

"Yes, Lila. We are here."

"It's a luxury house!"

"No, it's a simple village house."

"I was just kidding."

"There's electricity and running water, isn't there?"

"No, none of that. Nobody has lived here for a long time."

"But what are we going to do?"

"We will live according to tradition. Come, I'll show you. Don't be afraid, Lila."

They got out of the car. The dog, happy to be free again, ran through the grass. Marat ran after him.

"Mum, it's great here!"

First, they went around the house. There were three more openings on the side but still without windows. Behind the house was a kind of savannah with grass at least one metre high. A buffalo was grazing towards what appeared to be a ditch.

"Come and see."

"Thanit, isn't it dangerous to go near this buffalo?"

"No, come with me."

They walked towards the buffalo which was looking at them. Lila was not reassured and preferred to stand behind Thanit. When they reached the buffalo, he slapped it on the side, and it slowly pushed itself away. They then discovered a small pool of water into which a spring flowed.

"This is 'bonam saksit'."

"Is that the name of the water?"

"No, it means miraculous spring. Here when we find a spring we say that, and we call the monks to bless it and put it under their protection."

"OK. This water is good, we can use it."

"This water is good, we can drink it."

"Is it?"

"Yes, look."

And Thanit slipped his hand under the water that came out of the earth and brought it to his mouth.

"It is fresh and good. Go ahead if you are thirsty."

Marat, who had just arrived with the dog, bent down and dipped his lips directly into the clear water, imitating the dog's greedy lick.

"Marat, no, don't drink that."

"It's safe, Lila. It's very pure."

"Are you really sure?"

"Yes, I'm perfectly sure. I grew up here and I've always drunk this water. And you see, I'm still alive."

"Well, if you say so."

"Drink it, mum, it's good!"

And Lila bent down and took a little water in her hand and put it in her mouth.

"I hope I don't get sick!"

"No, I assure you, you won't. Let's go into the house if you don't mind."

"Let's go into the house. Are you coming, Marat?"

They went up a staircase on the other side of the house, which led to a small recess where the entrance was located. Lila discovered a single large room. A table had been pushed against one wall.

"There are no bedrooms?"

"No, this is a peasant's house. Everyone lives in the same room, and everything happens in the only room in the house."

"But where are we going to sleep? There is no furniture…"

"We'll sleep on a blanket on the floor."

"And the kitchen?"

"The kitchen is outside, by the fire. There's the pot again. I'll clean it and we'll prepare the meals in it."

"We'll have to clean it with products. You can't cook in something like that!"

"There are products. I asked my uncle to bring some. And look, he even brought a pot from home. This one is not old and it's clean."

"Have you seen the dust on the floor?"

"Yes, I know. I'll sweep it up and it will be fine."

"Thanit, I'm exhausted when I see the work that needs to be done to make it more or less liveable. And the water?"

"We get it from the source. I'll go and get some."

"And the toilet?"

"Outside."

"What do you mean outside?"

"In the tall grass over there."

"That sounds promising…"

Saturday, 25 December 2010

Life is getting organised in the country house. The house was now clean, and Lila had taken Thai cooking lessons with Thanit's aunt who came to visit them to prepare lunch and dinner the day after their arrival. Marat was happy in this setting and had become acquainted with the buffalo, which was peaceful and friendly.

Lila was afraid at first when he went running in the field, but she was getting used to it and was watching him a little less. It was Christmas Day, and although she had nothing to offer, she felt that her new quiet life was a gift from heaven, both for her son and for herself. For the past four nights, there had been no noise, no violence, no danger.

Thanit's aunt and uncle were coming to share Christmas dinner with them and bring friends. And, at nine o'clock in the morning, she saw the aunt arrive accompanied by five women carrying food in basins. Thanit explained to her that they would prepare the festive meal. There would be about fifteen of them for the feast, so a lot of things were needed and, of course, many cooks.

All the guests had arrived. About fifteen adults and ten children. Marat was delighted. The whole day was spent in games. For him, it was the best Christmas present. The meal went on until the evening. All the Thai gastronomy was reviewed: traditional pad thai, pad thai with vegetables, tom kha kai, laap kai, snakehead fish, nua nam tok, pla ra, khao niao, grilled grasshoppers, som tam, mou yang. This was an opportunity to discover little-known culinary delights for Lila and Marat, made by expert hands. The men drank local sang som whisky and chang beer.

The whole group spoke in Thai, and Lila didn't understand a word but felt at ease with these simple and welcoming people. Marat seemed to be able to communicate easily with the children. He had learned a basic Thai vocabulary at school, and this seemed to be enough for him to express himself and understand what he was told. Lila was very proud of him and hoped that in a few weeks, he would be able to return to school. This thought alone made her a little sombre because going back to school was a good thing, but where? With the ban on leaving the country, she would have no choice but to return to Bangkok to put Marat back into the American school. An idea slowly germinated in her mind. They came all the way here by car. They could cross a border like Vietnam or Cambodia and then fly to America. She decided to tell Thanit about it the next day.

Sunday, 26 December 2010

The house was quiet, Marat had gone to bed late and slept soundly, his dog lying next to him, his little head on his legs. Lila had got up and gone to the garden to breathe in the morning. Thanit was with her. On a branch of a frangipani tree, she noticed a long, green shape moving about.

"Look Thanit, a green snake in the tree over there, just before the white flower…"

"Yes, it's a ngou kwio, a green snake. Its venom is almost as poisonous as that of the cobra."

"It is very big, look…"

"Yes, it can measure up to two metres."

"Is it dangerous to let Marat play here?"

"No, not really. This snake is very shy. If it sees humans it runs away. The attacks are only for self-defence."

"Even so, I am wary. I hate reptiles."

"Not many people like snakes."

"Thanit, I was thinking about something last night. We're not very far from the Cambodian border here?"

"No, we're not. The nearest big Cambodian town is Siem Reap."

"How far is that?"

"From here, about eighty kilometres to the border I think, and about two hundred kilometres more to Siem Reap and then another three hundred kilometres to Phnom Penh if you want to go that far."

"Are the borders difficult to cross?"

"Relations between Thailand and Cambodia are not great. The controls are quite rigorous."

"I see. But I think we can try. If we get through it's good. If not, too bad, we'll come back here. I'll get the stuff together, wake up Marat and we'll leave within the hour."

“That fast?”

“Yes, since we are not far from the border. How long will it take to reach it?”

“Two hours.”

“That’s fine.”

She quickly packed her bags and lifted Marat, who was grumbling. By eight o’clock, they were in the car, which started off for Cambodia. Thanit followed small roads to a border crossing not far from the Cambodian town of Thma Puok. The car stopped at the Thai customs barrier. The official looked inside the vehicle and asked everyone to get out.

He took the passports and left for the adjoining post, where he stayed for about ten minutes. Lila saw him pick up his phone and talk for five minutes, which to her did not bode well. Finally, the customs officer returned. He said that Thanit could go through, but neither Marat nor she can. He didn’t want to give an explanation, being particularly stubborn.

They had no choice but to turn back. Lila begged Thanit to try another passage at another place. He told her that this involved the risk of being spotted, but as she insisted, he finally agreed. He decided to go further south, ninety kilometres, to the Cambodian border town of Poipet. An hour and a half later, they stopped in front of the border post.

A customs officer arrived and asked to see their passports. Thanit handed them over. He looked at them, and when he got to Lila and Marat’s passports, he bent down to distinguish them and asked them to wait. He went to the station and picked up the phone. Lila sighed and said to herself that it would happen again. After five minutes, the man returned and asked Lila to get out of the car. She complied. Thanit got out to translate.

“You’ve already tried to cross the border.”

“Yes, I have.”

“You know you’re not allowed to leave Thailand?”

“Yes, I know that.”

“So you are in violation of the law.”

“What does that mean?”

“A fine of twenty thousand baht.”

“I don’t have that kind of money with me. I only have two thousand baht.”

She handed the two notes to the customs officer who put them in his pocket and went back to his booth after telling her to leave.

They had no alternative but to return to Ban Hua Wua. Lila was a little disappointed but remained positive.

"I wouldn't be satisfied if we hadn't tried. It didn't work, but that's OK. I'll think of another option."

After three hours of driving, they reached their village and their house.

Monday, 27 December 2010

Lila wanted to go out into town and asked Thanit to take them to Buriram. They took the old Toyota and arrived in the city centre in just under an hour. The streets were busy and crowded with vans loading and unloading goods. Parking was not easy, and the whole place looked a bit messy. Thanit managed to park in front of a bazaar that must sell a bit of everything apart from food.

Stalls on the pavement displayed a series of bowls with roosters painted on them. It was a fairly crude and common dish in Thailand. Lila took a quick look around and continued on her way to the fruit and vegetable traders. She chose a number of different things and went to pay. She stepped back to make room for the shopkeeper and bumped into a Thai woman behind her.

She turned to apologise and suddenly recognised the female officer who had confessed to her that she was her husband's mistress at his funeral. She gave her an angry look and returned to the merchant who was weighing his vegetables. The officer, without any embarrassment, addressed her:

"Are you still in Thailand?"

"I don't see how that's any of your business. It's none of your business. And I don't want anything to do with you."

"Excuse me, I was just surprised to see you here. I thought you'd be back in America by now."

"But then again, your stupid laws and your stupid colleagues would have to allow me to go!"

"What do you mean by that?"

"I mean I'm not allowed to leave this damn country! Do I have to draw a picture?"

"What do you mean? Are you directly involved in a criminal case?"

"Of course not!"

"Then there's no legal reason to keep you here."

"No legal reason? Did you say no legal reason?"

"I guarantee you, I know what I'm talking about."

"Then how come I'm being reported everywhere? I tried to get back to the States, but I got turned away at the gate. Just yesterday we wanted to drive to Cambodia and the customs officer refused me passage."

"It was someone from the police who entered a "no departure" flag into the central computer."

"But, in your opinion, he didn't have to do that?"

"No, he didn't."

"But what can I do? The police officer I met said that there was nothing else he could do, that he would be breaking the law."

"He lied to you. But I can help you."

"You can?"

"Yes, I can. I have nothing against you. You're the one who has something against me."

"Yes, that's right. You took my husband from me."

"I didn't take him from you. He didn't leave you and he never would have, I wouldn't have allowed it."

"You are strange and incomprehensible."

"We don't think like you in this country."

"I've noticed that."

"Do you want my help then?"

"I've got no choice."

"Well, what's the name of that policeman who tells you stories?"

"Buncha Yoobamroong."

"You have a good memory. It's not often that a Westerner retains a Thai name."

"You know, I've had the opportunity to speak with him many times."

"And do you know where he works, I mean his office address?"

"Yes, he's in the police headquarters in Bangkok."

"Great, I'll take care of it. How can I reach you?"

"I have a mobile phone, but we're in the countryside and there's hardly any reception."

"You are?"

"Yes, I'm here with my son and my driver."

Meanwhile, Thanit came into the shop and went up to the two women.

"Hello, there."

"Oh, I see. We give lessons to others but we act the same way."

"It's not what you think. Don't think so. Thanit is my driver."

"I see."

"Where are you staying?"

"In a house in the country. Thanit, what's the name of the village we're near?"

"Ban Hua Wua."

"I know where it is. I will come and see you the day after tomorrow."

"What do you say?"

"Do you think you can solve my problem in such a short time?"

"Yes, I do indeed, Lila."

"You know my name?"

"Mike talked about you. He loved you."

"What's your name?"

"Apsara. So I'll see you in two days."

"OK. I'll be waiting for you. I'll be waiting for you. Goodbye."

"Goodbye, Lila."

On the way home, Lila remained doubtful about the real powers of this woman who had been her husband's lover. Why would she help him? In general, mistresses are the sworn enemies of their wives. They did everything to make their husbands at least turn away from their legitimate wives and at worst divorce them. She talked to Thanit to get his opinion on the matter.

"You know, Lila, Thai women are very different from Western women. Here the word mistress is not used. We say the second wife. It is a very honourable and rewarding position. Being the first wife, it is true, is still the first. But the status of a second wife is often very enviable. And the second wife rarely tries to become the first. She knows how to stay in her place because she benefits from it in many ways, both in terms of the affection of the man who has chosen her and in terms of material and financial benefits."

"I am beginning to understand. In fact, this woman does not harbour any hatred towards me."

"No, that's not at all in our culture. On the contrary, I think she genuinely wants to help you. For her, it is a posthumous proof of love for your husband."

"This is very strange for me. But now I understand a little better. It is really another world."

Tuesday, 28 December 2010

Apsara went to the Buriram police station. She presented her card and her rank of senior colonel and instantly received respect and obedience from the local police officers. She asked to be introduced to the Brigade Commander. She was ushered into the office of Major Jackri Chavalit.

"Senior Colonel Apsara Amornchantanakorn of the Bangkok Judicial Police Department."

"Pleased to meet you, Colonel. Is there anything I can do for you?"

"Yes, there is. I'm investigating a case of abuse of power and I need access to the mainframe database, and for that, I need access to your terminal."

"Of course, that is no problem. You can use my password and go to my office. How long do you think you'll be?"

"An hour at most."

"Please, have a seat. I have to go. I'll be back in half an hour."

"Thank you."

Apsara sat down at the computer, and after entering the Major's password, she went to the ROBERTSON file. She discovered the various reports relating to Mike. There was nothing about Lila. She went back to the menu and searched for LILA ROBERTSON. She discovered her file filed at L. She opened it and realised that there was a simple note ordering her and her son Marat to remain in the kingdom. The justification for this note was terse: an order from Major Buncha Yoobamroong.

She called the Bangkok police headquarters and asked to speak to Buncha.

"Hello?"

"Major Buncha?"

"It's me."

"Senior Colonel Apsara Amornchantanakorn of the Bangkok police headquarters."

"Yes, Senior Colonel, to what do I owe the honour?"

"Do you know Lila Robertson?"

"Yes, I do."

"Did you put a ban on her leaving the kingdom?"

"Erm… yes… There are suspicions about her…"

"You have absolutely nothing on her. I'm ordering an investigation to check all your files."

"Oh… Senior Colonel… I will immediately withdraw this ban… Do we agree?"

"Yes, I do. I'm on the network and I see that the notification is still there."

"I'm cancelling it, I'm cancelling it. I'm cancelling it. It's done. Can you see that too, Senior Colonel?"

"This time I can. You'd do well to avoid this kind of zeal, Major."

"I'll make a note of that. Excuse me again, Senior Colonel."

"It's not me you have to apologise to, but your victim."

"I am humbly sorry, Senior Colonel."

"Goodbye, Major."

"My respects, Senior Colonel."

Apsara returned to the terminal and logged in under her own name to access her data. She wrote the following note to the commanding general of the Bangkok police force.

Senior Colonel Apsara Amornchantanakorn
Directorate of Judicial Police

To
General Commander of the Bangkok Police Force
Subject: *Abuse of power, corruption, harassment of witnesses, spreading a degrading image of the police and the kingdom to foreigners, leading to the equivalent of a crime of lèse-majesté.*
General,
I have noted various actions of Major Buncha Yoobamroong, whose full report on the case of Mike Robertson, his wife Lila and his son Marat is attached.

I leave it to you to arbitrate this matter and am at your command.

Yours faithfully.

Wednesday, 29 December 2010

A car entered the yard of the house. Marat approached and saw the door open, and a beautiful brunette woman emerged.

"Hello. I think you are Marat."

"Yes, and this is my dog, Teelek."

"Hi, Teelek!"

"Have you come to see mummy? She's in the house."

"Will you guide me?"

"Yes, come."

Lila was sweeping the floor of the house when Marat appeared and gave Apsara his hand. This sight disturbed Lila, but she tried not to show it.

"Hello, Lila. I see that you are in a real traditional Isan house."

"Are you making fun of me?"

"No, I'm not. It's true that there are no comforts, but I really like these old houses that represent our history. It is always interesting, the past allows us to understand the evolution of our society."

"Yes, that's true."

"Lila, you are no longer banned from leaving the kingdom."

"Are you serious?"

"I've never been more serious."

"So I'm free?"

"As free as a bird."

"Could I go to the States tomorrow if I wanted to?"

"Yes, absolutely."

"Oh, that's wonderful! Thank you, thank you! Oh, thank you!"

And Lila hugged Apsara and placed a kiss on her cheek.

"Thank you again, Apsara. And I apologise for being unpleasant to you the other day. We don't have the same culture and some things are difficult for me to accept and understand. But I know that you are a good person and that you are fair and generous. Thank you again on behalf of myself and Marat."

"Don't thank me, Lila. I did it for you and your son with great pleasure. And you know, I can't stand those crooked officials who, because they have an ounce of power, allow themselves to break the laws in order to establish a perfidious and manipulative hold over foreigners who are obviously ignorant of our laws."

"It's true that this policeman, this Buncha, was particularly unpleasant, especially in the way he looked at me. A pig."

"That's probably the explanation for all this. He expected something from you."

"How awful."

"And now, what's your agenda?"

"I want to go back to Bangkok and leave. I don't want to hang around there with all the problems and attacks we've had. We are not safe there."

"Attacks?"

"Yes, several times. We've had to deal with hit squads."

"When do you want to go back to Bangkok?"

"Tomorrow morning."

"If you want, I can put an armed squad of ten men in front of your house."

"Really? And Buncha told me it was impossible."

"He probably would have wanted to negotiate that protection. Can you imagine how…"

"My God, when I think of it!"

"Listen Apsara, we'll return to Bangkok tomorrow morning. I'll go to the airport to check on flights, and hopefully, and now I can believe we will coming back because of you, Marat and I can find two seats to San Francisco. But, if that's not possible, then I'll call you so you can set up our protection."

"I will. Call me no matter how your day turns out."

"Yes, of course."

Apsara took her leave. The two women embraced and kissed.

Thursday, 30 December 2010

In San Francisco, the Golden Star Bank was besieged by journalists. The attack on their Bangkok branch and especially the killing of seventeen American executives had not gone unnoticed. Moreover, the bank transfers made by Mike Robertson aroused the interest of the banking supervisory commission, which asked for explanations. The matter reached the ears of the media, and the bank made the headlines.

At a strategy meeting, it was decided that Mike Robertson would take the blame. A memo to the press stated that for three years, with the complicity of his number two, John Finmore, they organised a super leaching operation for the benefit of a group of Russian mafiosi. Although nothing had really been proven to date, it was clear that the two accomplices must have been paid handsomely in some tax haven.

This was, of course, impossible to trace, as the funds transferred to Belize had disappeared and that country refused to disclose anything. For the shareholders, it was therefore a whitewash. The board estimated that the two criminals received a total of one hundred million dollars each. Given the size of these sums, the bank decided to file a complaint against their beneficiaries and requested the seizure of their assets in the United States.

Gordon Hofmann was given the task of investigating the case for the trial and notifying the widows of his former employees. He sent letters to their addresses but received no information in return.

The trial was conducted smoothly, and since the evidence of the transfers and the signatures authorising them were not in dispute, the beneficiaries were ordered to reimburse the bank jointly with the sum of two hundred million dollars. The machine quickly got underway and proceeded to seize the assets. In the meantime, the U.S. State Department imposed a mega fine of seven hundred million dollars on Golden Star Bank.

Lila, whose Thai mobile phone number appeared on some of the documents, received a phone call from a bailiff who wanted to inform her about what was happening to her detriment, being surprised that she had no reaction to the proceedings. She was stunned when she learns what was going on and finally understood that the steamroller of American justice would leave her with only her eyes to cry.

She was desperate because a return to the United States was now impossible, as she had nowhere else to go. The only alternative left to her was to return to Russia. She had never thought of returning to her native country, and she was thinking about how to do it. She had $10,000 left in the Golden Star Bank. She decided to go there to try to withdraw the whole amount, hoping that the seizure has not been communicated to the Asian branch.

Lila walked through the door of the bank. She asked to withdraw her account balance. The teller stared at her.

"You are Mike's wife, aren't you?"

"Yes, I am."

"We're all very sorry about what happened."

"I thank you for your sympathy."

"Do you want to settle your account?"

"No, just make a withdrawal."

"From what you have?"

"Yes, I do."

"Good. Then sign the withdrawal slip. Shall I put the money in an envelope for you?"

"Yes, please."

"Here you are. Have a nice day, Mrs Robertson."

"Thank you."

Lila was aware that for a second time, luck was on her side. The Bangkok branch had probably not received any instructions from headquarters. She hurried back to the car where Thanit was waiting.

Given the situation, she called Apsara and told her that she had no plane until the next day. But she wanted to get her affairs in order, including the return of the keys to the villa to the owner, so she told her that she intended to fly out in two days, which required two days of close protection of the house. Apsara confirmed that a group of about ten policemen would be on duty in front of her house from 8:00 pm.

When they arrived at the condominium they found Nok who was happy to see them all again. The house was clean. The traces of the last fights were still clearly visible. There were still no front doors or windows. Bullet holes were visible on the walls. Lila knew that the house is rented by the bank.

For the time being, the bank had not come forward to notify her of the termination of the lease, but she was sure that this would happen soon. And the same went for the Mercedes, which was in a very bad way. She stifled a laugh with her hand, thinking that she would leave and they would discover the damage while she was away. After all, they would get what they deserved after seizing her house.

She called her friend Olga, but nobody picked up. It was true that they might have already left for Moscow. She remembered Olga's cousin Elina and looked for her number. She found it and called her.

"Hello?"

"Elina? Hello, it's Lila."

"Lila? This is a surprise! How have you been?"

"I'm still in Thailand, you know. I wanted to know if Olga is already in Moscow?"

"Yes, they arrived the day before yesterday, it's very recent."

"I'd like to call Olga but I don't have her phone. Do you have it by any chance?"

"Of course, I do. I'll give you Andrei's mobile because she hasn't got a new phone yet."

"All right, thank you."

She dialled the number Elina gave her.

"Hello?"

"Andrei, good evening! It's Lila!"

"Oh, Lila? Good evening, how are you?"

"Problems as usual. Is Olga there?"

"Yes, I'll put her on."

She told in detail everything she'd been through in the past week. What affected her most is losing her house in Sausalito. With no other options left, she wanted to return to Russia, even though she was not very happy about it. She had no specific plans, thinking of looking for a job in the tourism sector as she spoke English perfectly, but wanted to settle in St Petersburg where she had her parents. Her immediate problem was housing for her and Marat.

Her parents lived in a two-room flat in a Krushchevka, in sixteen-storey brick or concrete panel buildings built throughout the Soviet Union in the 1960s, and it was not possible for her to move in with them. But, since Olga had a well-equipped dacha that was empty most of the time, she asked if it would be possible for her to occupy it while she found a job and a small flat. Olga seemed to hesitate but finally agreed. She told her that they should meet when she arrived in Moscow to give her the keys. Lila thanked her and confirmed that she would call her back very soon to give her the time and day of her arrival.

After hanging up with her friend, Olga opened up to her husband about her wishes. She told him about her conversation and in particular that Lila had lost all her possessions in California. Her disappointment was understandable, but the aversion she seemed to have to return to her country irritated Andrei. He told his wife that if she did not like her country, she should go to the Americans who had treated her so well. For him, this attitude was scandalous and unacceptable. So, when Olga told him that she had agreed to lend her their dacha in St Petersburg he got angry.

He told her that giving her the dacha was madness, that she could stay there for as long as she liked without paying anything, that it was not even certain that she would be able to find a job and that if she did, she was guaranteed trouble. Olga was confused but she could not take back her word. Andrei told her that they would only have problems and that when it was too late and she realised her mistake, it would indeed be too late. He went to bed without a glance at his wife, who started to cry.

Pyongyang, Ministry of Foreign Affairs

The Minister's Chief of Staff, Yi Chul-Moo, wrote a note to the minister and the Supreme Leader.

Comrade Minister,

We have learned from a secure source that Major General Cheong Yong-Joon of the Special Forces, who is posted at the diplomatic mission in Bangkok as a correspondent of the secret service, has taken it into his head to pursue a woman and her 10-year-old son with his personal vengeance. They are Lila Antonova Robertson and Marat Paul Robertson, citizens of Russia and the U.S.

Cheong hired special forces to assassinate the two fugitives. The reason given at an officers' meeting held in Bangkok on 17 December 2010 was that the Russian embassy in Bangkok had informed him that the Seumkwang had been recovered and that he considered this a personal offence. And, as a result, both Robertsons had to be eliminated.

In the note we obtained, it turns out that the woman's husband, Mike Robertson, was a high-level banking officer with probable CIA links. I stress that we have never had any confirmation that he was CIA.

The consequences of Cheong's actions are as follows:

- *13 special forces agents killed*
- *11 guns seized by Thai police investigators*
- *2,000 rounds of ammunition lost*
- *A 600cc Honda motorbike worth US$10,000 completely destroyed*
- *An investigation by the Thai criminal police into these cases, which may be traced back to our embassy*

A request for information from the American embassy on the destabilisation actions undertaken by North Korea in Thailand

A request from the Russian embassy for information on the relationship between North Korea and a mafia group called Podnimatsya Stal.

We have evidence that Cheong opened a bank account in North Korea in the books of Daesong Bank in the name of this mafia association of which he was the sole beneficiary and for which he alone has the signature. In this account, he received funds from Belize and Thailand totalling US$3.4 billion 223,000 dollars.

This sum was offered by Cheong to our Supreme Leader. It should be noted that since the funds were money laundered, and the members of the mafia association were Russian citizens who were the subject of an Interpol red notice and a US wanted persons notice for drug trafficking, it is clear that Cheong is involved in dark dealings and is deliberately trying to pollute the Supreme Leader's aura by offering him corrupt money.

The conclusion of this note is that Cheong has become a danger to the image of our glorious country and the aura of our Supreme Leader. It is imperative that his criminal actions come to an end.

Long live our Sun of the Communist Future!
Yi Chul-Moo

The minister reading this letter grimaces. In the afternoon, while inspecting a military parade, following the Supreme Leader like a good dog followed its master, he slipped him a note with a copy of the letter.

Lila and Thanit watched as police cars lined up along the villa gate. There were five vehicles, and ten officers armed with Colt M4A1 rifles. One of them, who appeared to be their leader, gave Thanit a friendly wave as he walked up to meet them. He told him that they had nothing to fear, that they would stay until nine o'clock the next day and that they would return for a final night's guard duty the following day. Thanit thanked him and returned home to inform Lila.

Friday, 31 December 2010

Major General Cheong arrived at Pyongyang Airport. He had been summoned by the Prime Minister himself who wanted to talk to him about certain matters. He had no doubt that it was about his new transfer to a position that he imagined to be prestigious. Perhaps aide-de-camp to the Supreme Leader. He thought it was deserved, given the huge sum he offered him. He kept nothing for himself, not a single dollar.

Such dedication, such honesty could only be royally rewarded. Being still single despite his advanced age of forty-nine, he thought that it was now time to stop frequenting prostitutes and that he would be powerful enough to find a good match in the families gravitating around the Father of the People. He would benefit from the prebend of the regime's apparatchiks, a nice limousine, a nice house and a holiday on Nampo beach on the Yellow Sea. And most certainly he would be invited tonight to the table of the Great Man Descended from Heaven for the New Year's Eve party, which would bring together all the great ones of the Hermit Kingdom… Suddenly, a soldier pulled him out of his dreams.

"General Cheong?"

"Yes…"

"In the name of our Supreme Leader, we arrest you. Seize him!"

"What's up? I have an appointment with the Prime Minister! Let go of me!"

"You fool, move!"

Two hours later, Cheong was questioned under torture and confessed that he was the head of the Podnimatsya Stal mafia network and that he had been passing classified information to the American embassy, of which he was an undercover agent. If he had been asked if he was the Pope, he would have admitted it. He was convicted of high treason and shot on the spot.

At the Ministry of Foreign Affairs, Cabinet Director Yi Chul-Moo wrote a note to the Personnel Department:

Klong Prem Central Prison, Bangkok, same day

A prison guard opened the cell door and called Payom. He shouted his name several times over the noise of the inmates. With difficulty, he pushed the prisoners aside and made his way through. Some hit him; others put their hands on his buttocks. He was almost naked, with a dirty, half-ripped pair of pants that he held in one hand so as not to lose them. The guard called out to him.

"What have you done with your uniform?"

"I don't have one anymore."

"We'll give you another one, but you'll have to pay for it. That's two thousand baht out of your savings. But, first, you go to the shower, you stink."

Payom followed the guard to the shower corridor. He entered a cabin without a door, and the guard pulled the lever, which caused a shower of cold water to rain down on Payom, who shrieked. He took the cube of soap thrown to him by the guard and slid it over his body. He wanted to cleanse himself of the stench of the cell, to purify him from the successive rapes he had been subjected to for two months. The guard finally got impatient.

"Get out now. You're not in a hotel here!"

Payom complied and grabbed the clean, new-looking uniform the guard handed him. He put it on and felt a sense of well-being that he hadn't known for what seems like forever.

"Today, you're going to court to stand trial. Put this on your feet!"

The guard threw chains at him.

"I am not sentenced to death."

"The chains are compulsory to go to court. They'll come off when you get back here. Unless, of course, they sentence you to death."

Payom shackled his feet, and the guard closed them. He escorted him to the door where he stepped out onto the forecourt of the prison entrance. He breathed in the air and the scent of the flowers. He had the impression that this was the first time in his life that he had discovered the emanations of plant fragrances. He would like to stay there, breathing, smelling and enjoying the scent.

But a guard took him by the arm and forced him into the cell van. No sooner was he seated than the van starts, heading for the Bangkok South Criminal Court. The journey was short, about thirty minutes to Charoen Krung Road. The guard helped him out of the vehicle and escorted him into the building. Many prisoners were waiting like him to be tried.

He sat on a bench. His lawyer came to see him and told him that everything would be fine. After an hour's wait, a policeman came and took him to one of the courtrooms. The judge looked at him and called the case to the roll. He gave a brief account of the facts of the case and gave the floor to the lawyer.

The lawyer tried to emphasise the innocence of his client, who had been fooled by a stranger out of stupidity without profiting in the least. The judge immediately pronounced the sentence: two months in prison, and given the time spent in pre-trial detention, he ordered the defendant's release. Payom thought he had misunderstood. He glanced at his lawyer, who nodded with a winning smile. He was amazed, as he had expected to receive a thirty-year sentence.

The policeman released him from his chains. He walked out of the court a free man. He asked his lawyer if he could go back to the prison to get his clothes. The lawyer advised against it. It might take a week for the judgment to be sent to the prison administration.

"Do you want to stay there for another week, Payom?"

"No, thanks, I don't. I never want to see that awful place again. But I want to buy a pair of trousers and a shirt. I don't want to keep these clothes on any longer. Can you advance me some money? I'll pay you back within the day."

"Yes, of course. I will accompany you, it will be more comfortable for you."

They took a taxi and stopped in front of the MBK shopping centre on Phayathai Road. It took Payom three minutes to put on a bright yellow shirt and beige trousers. The lawyer advanced him to two thousand baht. He felt like a new man, enjoying his freedom like never before. He finally went home, paid the lawyer back and thanked him for finding the right words to convince the judge so quickly.

Payom took a taxi back to the Bangkok Hospital complex on Phetchaburi Road. He entered the large reception area and asked a nurse if he could see a doctor. He immediately got an appointment and was asked to wait a few minutes. He was introduced to a practitioner who asked him what was wrong. He explained that he had many pustules on his body. The therapist asked to see them.

Payom opened his shirt and unbuttoned his trousers to reveal his body covered with various pimples.

"How long have you had this?"

"About two months."

"You should have come sooner before you got to this stage. What exactly happened?"

Payom explained that he was imprisoned for two months without any possibility of treatment. The doctor immediately understood the problem. He gave him treatment but advised him to take a blood sample for various tests. Payom agreed to this. So he waited for the blood test. The nurse informed him that he would have the results in an hour if he didn't mind waiting. He confirmed his agreement and settled into a chair. An hour later, a nurse came to collect him and invited him to follow her to see a doctor. The practitioner was a stern-looking older woman.

"Sit down, Mr Payom. I don't have good news. You have AIDS. You will have to be tested again in a fortnight."

"That is bad news."

"If you have multiple unprotected sex, you shouldn't be surprised. I suppose you're gay?"

"No, I'm not."

"So you frequent prostitutes?"

"No, not anymore."

"Well, that's your problem if you don't want to say anything. It's your life after all."

"I just got out of prison. I was raped."

"You were? So you have to keep your life straight to stay out of prison, the worst place there is. Well, I'm not giving you anything yet. We'll see you in a fortnight for a new blood test and confirmation of the diagnosis."

"I sleep very badly, I have nightmares. Could I have some strong sleeping pills?"

"Yes, I'll give you that."

"Thank you."

Payom stopped at the hospital pharmacy to get his sleeping pills. He went to the pharmacy for his sleeping pills, where on a stage a four-piece ensemble was playing Mozart's Quartet for Piano No. 1 and Strings in G minor K. 478. He sat down, took the numbered card handed to him by a receptionist and waited for his turn.

He heard his name on a loudspeaker and walked towards the box office number that had just appeared on a monitor in front of him. He paid and left, asking the bellman who organised the return of visitors for a taxi. AIDS. He thought about it. But, still, the news had taken him into another world. He was stunned. He needed to calm down, to come to his senses.

Back home, he walked around each room as if he were rediscovering his own world. He caressed the exotic wooden doors. He looked at the books in his library without touching any of them. He went out into his garden to breathe the fragrant air of the flowerbeds invaded by weeds. He spent about twenty minutes pulling out the invasive weeds and then returned to the house. He went up to his room with a glass of water and lay down on his bed. He opened the capsule containing twenty sleeping pills and swallowed them all one by one. He fell asleep very quickly, and his mind flew to his ancestors.

Saturday, 1 January 2011

In the villa, everyone wished each other a happy new year. Lila declared that she would not regret the one that had passed, which for her was the worst of her life. The champagne was long gone, but there were still a few bottles of wine, Sauvignon Blanc from New Zealand. Thanit opened four bottles. One for Lila, Nok and himself, and he brought the other three to the policemen who thanked him warmly.

Lila called her parents to wish them well and then dialled Andrei. He answered.

"Hello?"

"Happy New Year! It's Lila!"

"Happy New Year! I'll put you through to Olga."

"Lila? Happy New Year and good health!"

"Happy New Year too, Olga! Did you have a party last night? Andrei doesn't seem to have slept much…"

"Oh, er… yes… He had a headache last night. We didn't go out. We stayed in the flat."

"The poor guy. I hope he's better?"

"Yes, he's fine now. And you?"

"We stayed at home too, with a group of policemen on guard."

"Well…"

"Yes, I was able to get protection from the local police."

"That's good. By the way, I wanted to ask you… You're thinking of working in St Petersburg, aren't you?"

"Yes, of course, I am. It's necessary, I have a child to raise."

"You're right. Do you have any idea what you want to do?"

"I'd like to get a job as a tour guide, specialising in American groups. With my Californian accent, I should fit in just fine. And you remember that I got a master's degree in history at the University of St Petersburg? So I think I have the right profile."

"Yes, when you put it that way, you do."

"Thank you for worrying about me, but I'm not too worried. Tourism is important in this city. Anyway, it's very kind of you to lend me your dacha. Without you, I don't know what I would have done."

"Anyway, it won't be for long? As soon as you have a job you can take a flat?"

"Yes, of course, don't worry. It's a matter of three months at the most. I don't want to squat in your dacha!"

"I know you don't."

"Well, I'll call you tomorrow and give you my flight."

"OK, Lila. See you tomorrow."

Sunday, 2 January 2011

Thanit drove Lila to the airport. He pulled into the terminal car park and went to take a parking space. She got off and quickly walked away to the entrance and headed for the Aeroflot ticket office. The stewardess offered her a flight departing that evening at midnight and landing in Moscow the next morning at 10:00. She bought two economy-class tickets.

Bangkok Police Headquarters, Same Day

Major Buncha Yoobamroong was on duty. The day after the party was generally quite calm, apart from the drunken driving that the Thai were quite used to, and the accidents that ensued. It was just a routine day. He looked at the pictures of Lila that he had taken with his mobile phone. One was of her face, another of her breasts, another of her thighs. There were not many people in the building, and he enjoyed the quiet of his office. He lay down, putting his feet up on the desk and falling back in his chair. His hand unbuttoned his fly, and he grasped his hardened member, excited by the photos he kept ogling. He started to move back and forth when suddenly the door opened. Completely surprised, he violently pushed the chair backwards with his foot, which threw him off balance and he ended up on the floor, provoking the hilarity of three policemen who were looking at him.

"What do you want?"

"Sorry to interrupt your work! And zip up your fly if you don't want the bird to fly away!"

"But… Do you know who you're talking to? I won't allow you…"

"In the name of the King, we arrest you! Stand up!"

"What is it?"

"We have an order to bring you in. Here it is. Guys, cuff him! And pick up his mobile phone! Evidence… And we can testify to the activity you engage in during working hours."

"But what am I charged with?"

"Crimes of lèse-majesté."

"But… No… This is not possible… This is a mistake… I respect the King and his family… No…"

Yoobamroong was taken by the three officers in a car to a special courtroom given the seriousness of the charges against him. A court-appointed lawyer stood and did not say a word, as the offence was indefensible. The judge read the accusation, mentioned the evidence in the case file and, at the request of the three police officers, agreed to listen to their testimony and to look at the documents seized at the place of arrest, that is, the photos of the laptop. He asked him to explain himself.

Buncha swore that he knew nothing, that he had done nothing, that he respected the King and that he worshipped him like a god, that he was a god. But nothing happened. The judge pronounced the sentence in the nick of time: fifty years in prison. The sky had just fallen on Major Yoobamroong's head, and he was sent to Klong Prem Central Prison.

Onut's Villa, Same Day

Lila dialled Andrei's number.

"Yes?"

"Andrei, how are you? Do you mind?"

"Hi, Lila. Tell me…"

"I'll arrive in Moscow tomorrow on an Aeroflot flight at 10:00 in the morning."

"All right, I'll send a car for you. Are you coming with Marat?"

"Of course, I am!"

"The driver will have a little sign with both your names on it. He'll take you to my office and then we'll go to my house."

"Thank you, Andrei, that's very kind."

"You're welcome, Lila. Have a good trip and see you tomorrow."

"Give Olga a kiss for me. See you tomorrow."

That evening, Lila said goodbye to Nok. Marat had to be reasoned with to make him understand that the dog could not go with them to Russia. And it was with great reluctance that he ended up accepting to give him to the maid.

"You'll be a good boy, Teelek. You will not forget me."

Last trip to Suvarnabhumi Airport. Lila felt melancholy, a sense of sadness at leaving Thanit who was so loyal, and happiness at leaving this country where she had lost everything. They had arrived. Lila approached Thanit. She took his hand.

"Thank you, Thanit. I will never forget you."

She placed a kiss on his cheek. She turned away to wipe away a tear. She took Marat by the hand and headed for the gate. She went through all the controls and joined the Aeroflot flight.

Monday, 3 January 2011

The plane landed on one of the runways at Sheremetyevo 2 airport in Moscow. The temperature announced by the captain was minus twelve degrees. Lila took out jumpers for herself and Marat from a bag. She put a scarf around her son's neck, a cap on his head and helped him put on a coat. The door of the aircraft swung open, and a gust of cold air entered the plane.

The passengers got out and hurried to the terminal. Lila and Marat followed. They reached the checkpoints. They queued for about ten minutes, presented their passports to the police officer and then reached the baggage claim area. On the information screen, they found their flight number and the associated conveyor belt number. They then waited in front of the carousel until the first bags appeared.

Marat stood in front of everyone else and watched for his mother's bags. After fifteen minutes of waiting, he saw their luggage and called Lila. Having collected their belongings, they followed the flow of travellers and reached the last doors that open onto the arrivals terminal where a crowd of people were waiting for their families or friends. Lila looked around and spotted a soldier holding a small sign with their names on it. She approached him.

"I am Lila, hello."

"Hello, I am Oleg, your driver. Welcome to Moscow. Aren't you cold?"

"A bit, we're not used to it anymore."

"I'll take your word for it. Follow me, we're going to the car."

The soldier took the two suitcases and guided them to the car parked in front of the airport. A sign on the dashboard reads: FSB. A pass to park anywhere. They got into the black Volga model 31029 from the nineties. They drove the thirty kilometres or so in an hour. The car entered a car park reserved for the administration, and the driver took them to Andrei's office. At his door, they could read a sign saying GENERAL MAJOR ANDREI SAFRONOV. The soldier knocked on the door, and Andrei was heard shouting, "Come in."

Lila and Marat went through the door followed by the soldier who put the suitcases in a corner.

"Lila, Marat, hello! Did you have a good trip?"

"Hi, Andrei! Yes, it was a bit long but it's OK."

"It's good to be home again, isn't it?"

"I can't say I feel at home in the Lubyanka!"

"Marat, go with Oleg, he'll make you some hot chocolate."

The child followed the soldier, who took him gently by the hand.

"Lila, I wish we could get to the bottom of this."

"Yes, I'm listening?"

"I know who chased you and tried to kill you in Bangkok."

"You do?"

"Yes. It was North Korean intelligence commandos. They wanted to assassinate you because they originally thought that Mike was a CIA agent and that he had a top-secret program in the form of a computer chip that another CIA agent had given him before he died."

"This is absolute madness! Mike was never in the CIA."

"Yes, I know that now. My department had this chip stolen. And we were actively looking for it too."

"But why would they come after us when Mike was dead?"

"Because they thought you had it now."

"That's crazy."

"Then I found the chip. And get this, it was hidden in a marble that Ivan had won playing with Marat. I accidentally crushed that marble and that's when I discovered the chip. When you think about it, this story is incredible. So many deaths for something that had been in my house for weeks!"

"It's unimaginable."

"Of course, I warned my North Korean counterpart to stop the search on his side."

"But tell me, do you have relations with these people?"

"Our two countries have good relations, and with the help of their engineers, we have developed an exceptional uranium enrichment programme that allows us to go three times faster than the current methods. We will also be able to help our Iranian friends with their nuclear projects."

"Russia always makes the wrong choices when it comes to its friends: evil. As George Bush said, you are indulging those who are part of the axis of evil. I find that really shameful."

"It is your speech that is shameful! Are you Russian or American? I think you are 99.99% American. There's nothing Russian left in you. You are contemptuous and you don't love your country which does so much for its people."

"Let me laugh, Andrei. Tell that to anyone you like, but not to me. We know what our country does for its people: not much."

"I won't allow you to judge your country. You betray it every day with your subversive thoughts. You are not worthy of living here. Or it's something else, you have a mental illness. Imagination and reality are mixed up in you. We call it schizophrenia. You are dangerous to yourself and to those around you, especially your son."

"What's wrong with you, Andrei? Have you gone mad?"

"You are the one who is crazy. You're seriously ill and you don't realise it. You need treatment. And the problem is, if I let you go, I know you won't get better."

"What are you talking about, Andrei?"

"We're going to have to take certain measures in your interest, Lila. First of all, we'll take care of Marat."

"Take care of Marat?"

"Yes, we'll put him in a military unit of the Younarmia, the youth army. This will give him the education he deserves, which you are unable to give him. This will make it easier for him to enter the military classes at university later on. We will then guide him towards a good career in the FSB, his bilingualism being an exceptional asset."

"Does Olga know about all this?"

"I am a professional and I work in the FSB. So I never discuss my work with her."

"You're out of your mind. I'm leaving, I've heard enough! Where's Marat?"

"Sit tight. You'll never see Marat again. He's already on his way to his new life!"

"Marat! Marat! Marat answer me!"

Lila ran through the huge corridors, opening all the doors and calling desperately for her son.

"Stop that madwoman and bring her back to me!"

Three women in uniform ran up and overpowered Lila. They took her back to Safronov's office and forced her to sit down.

"You can criticise us, but we Russians take care of our people. We are going to treat you because, unfortunately, you are sick. You can't tell the difference anymore. Look at your erratic behaviour! It's about time we took care of you. It's for your own good, my poor Lila. We only want you to be well."

Lila cried in despair.

"Give me back my son, I beg you! Give him back to me for pity's sake… Andrei, I beg you… I'll do anything you want, but give him back to me!"

"Lila, your presence is harmful to Marat's health. It is better for him if you never see him again. If you love him, accept the situation, since his future is marked out in the glory of our fatherland."

Suddenly, Lila got up, threw all the papers off Safronov's desk to the ground, turned towards one of the women guarding her and punched her in the face. Blood spurted out. The other two women pounced on her and finally subdued her. Another woman entered the office with a syringe in her hand. She stuck the needle into Lila's arm and pressed hard on the plunger, drawing the liquid into her body. Lila screamed in pain and insulted everyone around her.

"You stupid girl, this is for your own good!"

"You bastards! You bastards! Scumbags!"

"We will heal you, Lila. It will take as long as it takes. But I can assure you that you will regain your sanity."

"Aaaaaaaah."

Lila fell into a coma, and two nurses arrived. They carried her on a stretcher and tied her up. An ambulance was waiting in the car park. The stretcher was loaded into the back of the vehicle, which left for an unknown destination.

Thursday, 22 March 2018

Chelyabinsk Psychiatric Hospital, Western Siberia

Lila Antonova Robertson sat on a chair in room 265. Her head shaved, her eyes blank, a little white drool at the corner of her lips, wearing a sort of grey nightdress, she was unrecognisable. She waddled slowly. She hummed a melancholic tune all the time, which had only one word in its lyrics: Marat.

The Same Day. Kazan Officers' Training College

The Russian colours were hoisted on a flagpole. A young officer stood at attention. Another officer called out:

"Marat Mikeilovich Safronov! Salute the colours of the Motherland!"

Marat saluted with an impeccable gesture.

Lieutenant General Andrei Sergeyevich Safronov gave him his midshipman's diploma.

THE END

Milton Keynes UK
Ingram Content Group UK Ltd.
UKHW022028081223
434043UK00008B/399